Also by Amy Sandas

Fallen Ladies

Luck Is No Lady

The Untouchable Earl

Lord of Lies

Runaway Brides

The Gunslinger's Vow

The Cowboy's Honor

Christmas in a Cowboy's Arms anthology

Longing for a Cowboy Christmas anthology

RUNAWAY BRIDES

THE OUTLAW'S HEART

AMY SANDAS

To my son, Ryle. Quietly brave. Strong and clever in ways still undiscovered. May your loyal and compassionate heart always love widely and your charming grin not get you into too much trouble.

Published by Sourcebooks Casablanca, an imprint of Sourcebooks
P.O. Box 4410, Naperville, Illinois 60567-4410
(630) 961-3900
sourcebooks.com

Printed and bound in Canada.
MBP 10 9 8 7 6 5 4 3 2 1

ONE

Perkins family mansion
Beacon Hill, Boston
May 1883

Evelyn regulated her breath to a slow and shallow rhythm. Anything more than that sent streaks of fire across the lashed skin of her back.

She lay on her stomach in the center of her bed. The sheets were drawn down below her hips, exposing her naked back to the kitchen maid who was the only servant in the household allowed to tend Evelyn in the days following one of her husband's rages. That Matthew Perkins chose the youngest and lowest member of his servant staff to see to his wife's needs was intentional. Just another way to prove what little consideration Evelyn warranted.

Lettie bathed Evelyn's back with a soft cloth soaked in cooling water and lavender. It was a ritual they'd developed in the months since Evelyn had married. Matthew was quite fond of what could be accomplished with the elegant strike of a whip. The scars left behind were to serve as a reminder of Evelyn's failures so that she might be inspired to improve in her efforts to please the man she called husband.

Of course, he made sure that the evidence could always be carefully hidden beneath the fine clothing he so generously afforded her. A secret shared only by the two of them…and the meek young maid who would not dare speak of such private matters.

As Lettie's ministrations neared the worst of the wounds, her touch became tentative, in sympathy perhaps for the pain her attention would undoubtedly cause.

Evelyn wished she could tell the maid not to worry. After each punishment, she'd become more and more numb. But they weren't allowed to speak to each other during these encounters, and Evelyn couldn't say if the numbness was in her nerves or in her mind.

It had also become easier and easier to hold back tears and keep her thoughts of shame and utter confusion concealed. She had gotten to a point where she could acknowledge the pain without really feeling it. It was as though a veil existed between her physical experience and her mental perception of it.

She was grateful for the separation. It allowed her to endure the discomfort of Lettie's careful attention while she thought of other things. And there was something in particular she needed to focus on.

Because something had been different this last time. Matthew had been different.

And it terrified her.

Though she never knew what might trigger an episode, she had at least come to expect a certain pattern when Matthew flew into a rage. He was nothing if not dedicated to his routines. Once he meted out whatever punishment he deemed appropriate, he would leave her. Without a word. One moment the whip would be slashing at her back, and in the next moment, a door would click shut and he'd be gone.

But last night had been different.

After concluding his punishment, he'd stood behind her as she lay across the bed, another of her fine lawn nightgowns torn to shreds. She had waited with involuntary tears burning in her eyes to hear his retreat.

Instead, his labored breath filled the silence of the room and then he spoke, clearly and concisely. "Your pride will be the death of you, my dear. If I must flay every bit of flesh from your bones, you will learn to be a proper wife. You will learn to beg for my mercy. And if you do not..." The promise in his voice—so cold, confident, and eerily calm—had sent a shock of ice through her body. "If you are incapable of learning the humility I require, I may decide I have no use for you."

Up until that very moment, she had somehow believed that if she could just figure out what she was doing wrong, he would stop finding reasons to punish her. But something in his vow enlightened her with a sudden, fierce flash of clarity.

He would never stop. Not until she was broken.

But Evelyn's pride—the thing inside her that refused to cower and cry out when the whip met her flesh, that kept her from revealing the truth of her marriage to friends or family—wouldn't allow it.

It was her *pride* that he wanted to beat out of her. And he would always find justification to do so. No matter what she did, he wouldn't stop. And someday, it would kill her.

That realization hit her with cold certainty.

Having washed away all the blood, Lettie set the cloth

aside and picked up a jar of salve. While the maid applied the cooling cream, Evelyn's thoughts wandered back to a time before her marriage. Had it really been less than a year since she been so confident and content? She'd once been supported by her family and loved by two dear friends. And now she felt so utterly alone.

Slowly and in subtle ways undetected at the time, Matthew had started drawing her away from those who cared most about her, even before their marriage.

Her cousin and one of her best friends, Alexandra Brighton, had settled out in the wild landscapes of Montana, and Courtney Adams, the third friend in their tight circle, had followed her westward just last summer. Because of the scandals they had each caused by not going through with their Boston marriages, Matthew had convinced Evelyn to leave them off the guest list for their wedding…for appearances' sake. It was terribly disappointing not to have her two closest friends present for her big day, but Boston society was an unforgiving one, and Matthew's position was important and required proper appearances to be upheld. Alexandra and Courtney had both understood.

But that was just the beginning of a separation Matthew continued to orchestrate, not just with her friends but with her family as well.

Though they had never been particularly close, at least Evelyn had always believed that her mother had her best interests at heart. And Matthew Perkins was everything her mother had wanted in a son-in-law. Wealthy beyond compare, respected and revered in the elite Boston society that her mother was desperate to be a part of.

Just as he had with everyone else, he effectively—almost

effortlessly—charmed her mother into believing he was truly a prince among men. So, when he suggested at one visit that with all of the constant socializing required of them, he never seemed to have enough time alone with his wife, Judith Reed was more than happy to limit her visits so they could enjoy their time as newlyweds.

To the entire world, Matthew was a bright and handsome gentleman of privilege and distinction. He had a way about him that inspired confidence and admiration.

Evelyn had been just as easily fooled as everyone else.

She'd believed herself half in love with him in the weeks leading up to their marriage and never would have expected him to be capable of making her life the hellish existence it had become.

And now she was trapped.

Sharp, stinging pain suddenly sparked on her back, dragging her focus to the present. It felt as though her nerves had been poked with a burning needle.

It happened again. And a few seconds later, again.

Opening her eyes, she looked over her shoulder at Lettie to see if the girl had noticed anything.

The maid sat stiffly beside her. Her head was bowed over Evelyn's back as she gently spread the salve over open wounds. A single tear rolled down Lettie's cheek, glistening for a moment before it fell, causing another point of stinging pain. It was no burning needle awakening Evelyn from the numbness, but the salt of the maid's tears.

Somehow, the maid's compassion reached further into Evelyn than anything had in a long time. She lifted her hand to rest it on the maid's slim wrist.

The girl stilled, raising her sad and frightened gaze.

"Ma'am?" she asked quietly, the sound a mere murmur in the weighted silence of the room. She began to shake her head back and forth. "I can't do it," she cried gently. "I can't watch you suffer anymore."

The words were barely more than a breath, but Evelyn glanced to the door in fear, worried Matthew might hear them and come charging in. But the door remained closed. As was his routine, Matthew had left hours ago, and the house was as silent as a tomb.

"I'm sorry, Lettie," she whispered sadly. Was she now to lose Lettie as well? The girl was the only source of kindness she had in this household.

There was a brief flash of indecision in the girl's brown eyes before she covered Evelyn's hand with her own and shifted to crouch beside the bed. Leaning close, she whispered directly into Evelyn's ear. "There's a man I know. He sometimes helps people…disappear." Lettie paused but didn't move away. Evelyn held her breath, fearing the maid's hesitation. "I can talk to him for you."

Evelyn closed her eyes. The hope that had flared at Lettie's words died a swift and painful death. "No. It's too dangerous. You should go," she whispered to the maid.

The maid remained quiet and unmoving. The compassion in her eyes made Evelyn's heart ache. Then she stood and gathered her supplies before she swept quickly from the room, leaving Evelyn alone.

For a long time after, as Evelyn lay on her bed in too much pain to move, she thought about what Lettie had suggested. One word slipped persistently in and out of her mind, tempting and tormenting her. The word itself was as elusive as its meaning, easing through her thoughts in quiet whispers and sighs.

Disappear.

Could she do it?

The idea awakened something inside she'd thought long gone. Hope.

If she tried and failed, the punishment would be severe.

But then, even death would be a kind of escape.

If she succeeded, however…

She could start fresh, far away, as someone else entirely.

The longer she lay there with the thought swirling through her mind, the stronger the hope inside her grew.

But leaving would mean never seeing her family or friends again.

She thought of her mother with a clench of regret. Mrs. Reed would likely believe whatever lie Matthew chose to tell of his wife's sudden absence. But perhaps someday… once Evelyn was assured there was no longer any threat…

No. Matthew would always be a threat. As long as her mother knew nothing of Evelyn's whereabouts, she could not be manipulated into revealing anything. Her mother's ignorance would also serve as protection against Matthew's wrath. It was unlikely he would ever reveal his true nature to Mrs. Reed, but if he thought the older woman was hiding Evelyn, he might become angry enough to do something drastic.

It was safer for everyone if Evelyn simply disappeared.

She could not—would not—live the rest of her life this way. Never knowing when Matthew might decide she had broken yet another unspoken rule.

She'd had enough of his constant manipulations—the way he made her question her own thoughts, the tiny insults and mocking looks that kept her in her place, the subtle and not-so-subtle threats, the control he exerted over every aspect of her life, showing her every day that she belonged to him.

But not for long.

Matthew was a man of consistent patterns and routines. She would take advantage of that to plot her escape. But the current window of opportunity would not be open for long. She had to act swiftly.

As soon as her husband left the house the next day and the servants he set to watch her were conveniently distracted with other tasks, Evelyn secreted a small bag containing a traveling dress and only the most essential personal belongings out in the garden where she hid it beneath a flowering bush near the gate that opened to the alley.

For a successful escape, she'd also need funds, but Matthew refused to allow her even the smallest amount of pin money. All her purchases were made on credit, and he received every receipt. Keeping her clothed in the most elegant gowns and richest accessories, with jewels and fans and the finest of everything, was just another way he declared her one of his possessions—an object to show off to his friends and social adversaries.

There was only one thing for which Matthew required cash.

The monthly casino night at his club.

For some reason, rather than playing on credit as most others did, Matthew preferred to show up with a flashy wad of bills tucked carelessly into his pocket.

Two days ago, he'd withdrawn the cash from his bank account and placed it in his bedside table until he'd need to take it with him to the club on Saturday night.

It was already Friday, and Evelyn needed that money.

The next morning, Matthew left the house at his usual time, precisely nine o'clock.

It was the first Saturday of the month, when many of the household servants took their personal day, leaving the household as close to empty as it would ever get.

Evelyn snuck into her husband's bedroom, took the stack of bills from his bedside drawer, slipped it into her pocket, then wandered out into the garden where she sat reading on a bench in the back, as was her habit.

She sat there for nearly an hour doing what she could to give the impression that nothing at all was out of the ordinary. Everything in her was ready to flee. But she had to wait the full hour so anyone her husband had watching her wouldn't see her behavior as odd. The whole time, her heart beat so heavily and quickly that she worried she might faint. It was all she could do to keep her hands from trembling while sweat dripped down her back, stinging the fresh wounds.

Finally, it was time.

Taking a slow, steadying breath, Evelyn lifted her gaze from the book. Matthew's money was tucked in her pocket, burning against her thigh. The hansom cab that passed by the back alley every day on its route through the neighborhood would be making its way down the street at any moment.

Casually closing her book, Evelyn rose to her feet and strolled her usual path through the garden. Her breath practically stopped as she neared the back gate, tucked behind the fall of a weeping willow tree.

It was now or never.

Two

Union Pacific Railroad Line
Wyoming Territory

The shriek of the train's brakes being applied with violent force split the air. Several passengers were thrown from their seats by the suddenly halted momentum.

Evelyn gripped the armrest of her bench seat, in part to retain her perch, but mostly in resistance to the terror sweeping through her body like a dousing of icy water. A frantic glance out the windows indicated they were nowhere near a train station. They were nowhere near anything at all. Barren, brown wilderness spread in all directions.

The only explanation that came to mind was not a rational one. Yet Evelyn couldn't shake it.

He's found me.

Murmurs of concern and annoyance erupted from the strangers surrounding her. Some rose to their feet and craned their necks to look out the windows, trying to determine the reason for their abrupt halt.

Evelyn did her best to remain calm and poised—in appearance, if nothing else. Clasping her hands in her lap to keep them from shaking, she sat silent and unmoving while a chilling sweat broke out beneath the heavy layers of her traveling dress.

The likelihood that Matthew had already caught up with her was near impossible. She had been so careful—every detail attended to—to ensure her disappearance from Boston left no trace.

She knew the absurdity of her suspicion, yet she could not shake the gripping fear that her escape had been foiled, her race to freedom ground to as complete and deafening a halt as the train.

They had been stalled for only a few minutes when the door to their car slid open and two men sauntered in. Evelyn held her breath as she took in their appearance from her corner seat at the far end of the car.

They were dressed in dust-coated denim and leather. Wide-brimmed hats shadowed their eyes, bandannas covered their faces, and their steps jingled with the sound of spurs. These men were undoubtedly the roughest characters she'd seen so far on this journey, but she had already acknowledged that the farther west she traveled, the less the people looked like anyone she was accustomed to seeing back in Boston.

Still, there was a bold look of danger about these men.

She was not the only one to think so. Their arrival inspired gasps from the other passengers as faces tightened with fear.

And then she saw the guns.

The terror that had been burgeoning beneath her serene demeanor surged to the surface. The burning of her lungs alerted her to the fact that she'd stopped breathing. The next breath she took was shallow and weak, but it cleared some of the sudden fog from her brain.

Matthew had found her, and he'd sent these men to bring her back.

The certainty sent a sharp numbness through her body. She stopped feeling anything at all. It was a strange sort of disassociation, as though she watched her story being played out from some distance.

She had finally gotten up the courage to flee, and she had failed.

There was nothing left for her to do.

"Hiya, folks," the smaller of the two gunmen said almost jovially. "I know what y'all are probably thinking, but this here ain't a robbery. If y'all just sit tight and don't make a fuss, we'll conduct our business and be on our way."

Evelyn almost laughed. She hadn't even considered a train robbery. Her odd bout of humor was short-lived, however, as the two men started making their way through the car, examining each passenger as they went.

For a second, Evelyn considered running. She sat at the far end of the car from where the men had entered. She was very close to the opposite door, which led to a cargo car. If she could make it into the next car, perhaps she could find a place to hide.

The man on her side of the train car was getting closer. He was only a few rows away now.

The numbness that had pervaded Evelyn's body helped to act as a sort of shield against her fear. Keeping her calm, allowing her mind to work. There had to be something she could do. She had gotten so far.

She couldn't just give up.

But even if she hid in the cargo car, it would only be a matter of time before the men found her. There had to be something else…

And then it was too late to run.

The smaller man had reached her row. His gaze was hard and direct as he peered at her from between the low brim of his hat. She noticed the flicker in his eyes as he took in her appearance.

Her heart stopped.

"What's yer name?" he asked. His voice was softer than she expected. It threw her off for a moment, and she didn't acknowledge his question right away.

Could it be that easy?

"I asked yer name, sweetheart."

Evelyn found herself uttering the first name she fell on that wasn't her own. It belonged to a young woman who had gotten on the train in St. Louis. The stranger had taken a seat beside Evelyn and had proceeded to declare herself Evelyn's traveling companion. Though she was heading west to marry a man she'd never met, she was currently enjoying the dining car with a gentleman passenger with whom she had started a light flirtation. Evelyn didn't think the woman would mind if she borrowed her name.

With a clear and steady voice she replied, "Sarah Cummings."

The man narrowed his gaze for a moment, then turned toward his partner. "I've got her."

"Then let's get the hell outta here," the other man replied.

The gunman grabbed Evelyn's arm in a punishing grip

and hoisted her out of her seat. Some of the other passengers gasped in shock as they saw what was happening.

Horror overwhelmed her. How had he seen through her lie?

One man dressed in a brown suit rose to his feet. "Now, hold on a minute. You can't just take her," he challenged.

"You wanna die today?" the other gunman asked, his voice cold.

The man shook his head, his eyes darting to Evelyn.

"Then sit down."

The brave man stood for a second in indecision until the woman seated beside him grabbed his sleeve and gave a sharp tug. Evelyn could see the fear in the woman's eyes and couldn't blame her.

She was a stranger to these people. She had been very careful over the last few days to make sure she gave them nothing to remember her by. She'd done all she could to be forgettable.

The man holding her arm gave a rough jerk and spun her around until her back was against his chest. Then he started backing toward the door that led to the cargo car, keeping his gun trained on anyone else who might think to interfere.

"Now, don't none of you good folks worry. We ain't gonna hurt this pretty lady, so just relax and we'll be on our way."

A voice deep inside screamed for her to fight.

Even if it kills you, Evie. You must fight with every last breath.

But another voice—quieter, but stronger—urged her to be silent. The grip on her arm was tight. The guns frightening. But as long as she was alive, there was a chance of escape.

The door on the far side of the passenger car suddenly

opened, and a passenger charged in with a pistol leveled straight toward Evelyn and the two retreating gunmen.

The newcomer didn't hesitate to shoot. The bullet sang past Evelyn's head to slam into the wall behind her.

The man holding her muttered a vicious oath before shoving her behind him. Lifting his gun, he fired off a round of his own a second after his partner did the same. Both shots hit the floor of the train, splintering wood and keeping the would-be hero back for the moment. Screams and shouts filled the air as people dove for cover and husbands threw themselves over their wives, shielding them with their own bodies.

Evelyn couldn't help but think it strange that anyone would sacrifice himself in such a way, but the thought barely finished in her mind before she saw a flash of movement coming at her from the side as someone lunged toward her and her captor in misguided bravery. They all went down together. Evelyn heard a resounding crack as her head hit the edge of a bench. Pain exploded in her temple and everything—the gunmen, the other passengers, the screams, and the fear—suddenly ceased to be.

THREE

Consciousness invaded slowly and with great discomfort.

A thudding pain resounded in Evelyn's skull, making it difficult to form cohesive thoughts. And a raw, burning pain spread across her back, while everywhere else she experienced an invasive cold. The harsh chill weighed down her limbs, making it impossible to move. She couldn't even feel her fingers or toes.

Evelyn wished she could slip back into oblivion, but an intense feeling of urgency spreading from the far reaches of her awareness wouldn't allow it.

Why was she so cold? Why was she in so much pain?

The panicked questions were swiftly followed by another—where was she?

Becoming more aware, she realized she was lying on her side on what felt like rough, uneven ground. Not far away was the murmur of multiple voices—all male. The words were too soft for her to make out what was being said.

A racking shiver slid through her bones as memories flooded her brain like pounding waves, each one crashing over the one before.

The train.

The two men carrying guns.

She'd claimed to be Sarah Cummings, but they'd grabbed her anyway.

Gunshots and the reckless passenger who'd lunged for them.

She'd fallen and hit her head. Obviously, losing consciousness.

Had she been saved or taken?

Gathering what shreds of courage she could find, she opened her eyes.

At first, all Evelyn saw was fire. The red flames, dancing in the darkness several feet away, had her sucking in a frightened breath before her addled mind recognized that she was looking at a campfire. A campfire surrounded by a half-dozen men.

So she had been taken.

There was a momentary flash of relief when she did not see Matthew's pale-blond head and lean form amongst the rough gathering of strangers. Not that it mattered if he wasn't there. It was only a matter of time before she was back under her husband's control.

She closed her eyes. Tears pricked hot at the back of her eyelids. Soul-aching regret and a surprising dose of fury rushed through her. To be so close to freedom only to have it snatched away. It was painful. Heartbreaking. She wished for oblivion once more.

But only more clarity awaited.

So far, none of the men around the fire had noticed she'd awakened. If they thought her unconscious, perhaps she might be able escape them.

A subtle attempt at movement revealed that her hands were tied together in front of her, as were her ankles, which explained why she hadn't been able to move her limbs. With her heart thudding so loudly she was amazed they couldn't hear it, she risked opening her eyes the barest degree so she might observe her captors unnoticed.

She was pretty sure she recognized the two from the train by their clothing and voices. The one who had grabbed her was the smaller of the two and appeared to be younger as well. With the bandanna no longer covering the lower half of his face, he looked to be little more than a boy with his lanky frame, rounded facial features, and shaggy hair brushing his collar. The other one was older, taller, and wider across the shoulders. The grin that flashed across his bearded face as he replied to something one of the others said was startlingly amicable. Pleasant even.

Evelyn shifted her gaze.

Two others sat at the fire with them. One was much older with thick, white hair and a bushy beard of iron-gray. The other was a younger man with dark skin and a calm, watchful expression.

A fifth man sat off to one side of the fire, lounging back against a saddle as he carved at a small chunk of wood with a sharp little knife. His feet were outstretched and crossed at the ankles, and unlike his friends, he did not wear the wide-brimmed hat she'd seen on so many of these westerners. His hair looked to be only a slightly paler shade of red than the flames.

The last man in the group was more difficult to see since he stood in the shadows directly across the fire from where Evelyn lay curled on the ground. He wore dark pants and a light-colored button-down shirt beneath a leather vest that had been left open. The man leaned back against the thick trunk of a tree with his arms crossed over his wide chest. His hair was parted in the middle and two long black braids fell over his shoulders, reaching nearly to his belt.

She sucked in a tight breath of astonishment. Not because he looked frighteningly large and intimidating in the flickering light of the campfire, though he did that. No, it was because as she glanced over his broad, shadowed features, she discovered that he was staring straight back at her, his focused gaze cutting easily through the darkness and distraction between them.

An intense flare of caution ignited across her nerves and sped her heart rate. The numbness in her hands and feet was forgotten, as was the discomfort of her position on the ground. All sensation—every bit of her awareness—was suddenly overwhelmed by the intensity of his direct and silent regard.

He knew she was awake. Yet he said nothing.

He just stared at her across the distance. No expression on his face, no change in his position.

Evelyn couldn't look away. Despite the panic inside her and the rising acknowledgment of her perilous situation, she could not break his steady gaze even to blink.

"Looks like she's awake." The words came from someone at the fire.

Evelyn's attention flew to the bearded man with the wide grin as he rose to his feet and walked toward her. She stiffened with fear as he lowered himself next to her and reached for her shoulders.

"Here, let me sit you up a bit," he muttered.

Evelyn tried not to flinch under his touch. She hated showing them even an ounce of the fear coursing through her. But she couldn't help it when all she wanted to do was shrink away and fade back into the darkness, beyond their notice.

He repositioned her quickly and easily, settling her into a seated position with her back against a tree she hadn't realized was behind her. She ground her teeth against the flash of searing pain as her back made contact with the rough-textured bark. He either didn't notice the way her body tensed, or he didn't care.

To her minimal relief, he withdrew his hands as soon as she was settled. But he didn't leave.

"Better?" he asked, and she wondered if he truly expected her to answer.

It seemed he did since he stayed crouched there, his elbows resting on his knees while he looked her over.

Forcing herself to maintain a steady expression, Evelyn studied him in return. He couldn't have been more than twenty-five, if that. The short beard covering half his face did nothing to hide the strong line of his jaw or his pleasantly shaped mouth, which appeared prone to smiling. His nose was straight, as were his brows, and his eyes were a shade of blue that could only be called pretty.

In short, he was quite handsome and not at all what Evelyn expected a ruthless gun for hire to look like.

But then his expression shifted. The subtle smile slipped from his lips, and it wasn't exactly anger she saw darkening his eyes, but it certainly wasn't good.

She stiffened against the desire to shrink away from the sudden coldness in his manner.

"Hey, what was that description again?" he shouted back to his companions without looking away from Evelyn's face.

"What description?" the red-haired man asked as he glanced up from his wood carving. Though he looked the part of an outlaw, he spoke with a cultured British accent infused with the rolling sounds of a Scottish brogue.

"Of the woman."

"Jesus Christ, Eli," exclaimed the gray-haired man in exasperation. "She's sitting right in front of you."

"What's the description?" the bearded one—Eli, apparently—repeated.

"Aged thirty-five, slim figure, yellow hair, brown eyes," someone offered.

Evelyn watched with growing tension as the man in front of her closed his eyes for a second, then rose swiftly to his feet. "We've got the wrong woman."

"Like hell we do!" The young one who had asked Evelyn her name on the train leapt to his feet and came to stand in front of her. He stood looking down at her with a fierce expression.

"This woman's eyes are blue, not brown," Eli declared. "And if she's a day over twenty, I'll eat my hat."

Evelyn held her breath as all eyes focused on her.

"But she said she was Sarah Cummings," the young one insisted. "It's gotta be her."

Eli muttered something under his breath before straightening up and stalking back to the fire. "It's not her."

"Bloody hell," the red-haired one said.

Evelyn felt like repeating the expletive as she finally accepted that these men had not been sent by Matthew after all. They truly had been seeking Sarah. The why of it made absolutely no sense, but there it was.

Relief and an unstable rush of elation swept through her.

She hadn't been found.

She was still free…sort of.

Well, not really at all. But she would take this over being dragged back to Boston in a heartbeat.

FOUR

While Evelyn reveled silently in her unexpected alteration of circumstances, the others erupted in a heated argument. Some voices berated the young gun, named Ramsey as she swiftly discovered, while others debated what to do with her now. Someone opted to bring her to the next town and drop her off, but the dark-skinned man they called Jackson argued it was too risky so soon after the kidnapping. The old man seated next to him agreed, then voiced concern for what their boss would say when he discovered the mistake.

She was distracted enough by the heated words that she didn't realize someone had skirted the reach of firelight, approaching her through the darkness to suddenly appear at her side.

A harsh inhale expanded her lungs as her gaze flew up to meet dark, unreadable eyes.

The tall, muscled man who'd stared at her across the fire was even more intimidating up close. He had expansive shoulders, thick arms barely contained in his pale-colored cotton shirt, and powerful legs encased in worn denim. In a graceful economy of muscle and movement, he folded his large body into a crouch, bringing his face even with hers.

And what a face it was. Strong and beautiful in a way she'd never seen before. He had a broad forehead and a long, straight nose. His jaw was sharply angled, as were his cheekbones, but his mouth was wide and his lips were soft and full.

But unsmiling.

Startled by his unexpected proximity, Evelyn flinched when he lifted his hand, realizing belatedly that he held a canteen and was offering it to her.

He did not react to her obvious fear. Instead, he remained still—his expression flat as his eyes held hers. "It's water," he said.

His voice matched the rest of him—richly complex and powerful. Something strange rolled through her at the sound. Like anticipation of a storm when you hear the rumble of distant thunder, but warmer.

Her lashes flickered as she glanced down at the canteen. She was unbelievably thirsty, but how could she trust anything offered by men who held her captive?

"If you want to survive, you'll drink the water and eat the food," he said quietly. The words were just between them. Still she did not reach for the canteen. "You want to live?" he asked, raising a brow.

Evelyn lifted her chin, regaining eye contact with the man, despite her uncertainty and fear. "Yes, I want to live," she replied, surprising herself by the conviction in her words.

With a single, short nod, he extended the canteen a bit more. "Then drink."

She lifted her hands to take the water, but because of the binding rope and her frozen fingers, she couldn't grasp it.

Realizing her predicament, he gave a quiet grunt, then set the canteen on the ground and reached for her wrists. His large, warm hands surrounded her curled fists. He held them in silence for a moment—as if his only intention was to share his heat and offer comfort.

Though Evelyn felt the icy stiffness in her fingers dissipating, she resisted the instinctive desire to accept anything more. But she didn't pull away.

And she wasn't sure why.

"Don't be scared," he stated, still in a private tone. "You won't be hurt."

She searched his gaze in the darkness. She wanted to believe him, but she knew far too well how easily a man could hide wicked intent. "I am not so naive," she replied, her voice barely more than a murmur of sound.

He did nothing to indicate he heard her reply as he released his hold on her hands and deftly loosened the ropes. He did not remove them altogether, but he allowed for a bit of freedom to use her hands more effectively. Then he picked up the canteen and offered it once again.

Evelyn managed to bring it to her lips this time and took a few long drinks. The water soothed her throat, but it also made her very aware of her empty stomach. Lowering the canteen, she offered it back to the man who remained patiently beside her. Watching her in silence.

His nearness was discomfiting. As were his size and his quiet manner.

She had no idea what to make of him. There was strength in him, something his muscled form attested to without effort, but he displayed not the slightest hint of temper or violence.

Of course, Matthew hadn't either...until something set him off.

The outlaw took the canteen, never shifting his gaze from hers. Not even when the voices around the fire rose higher in discord.

"Shit," the young one named Ramsey exclaimed, frustration clear in his tone. "We can still ransom the woman. I mean, look at her."

Evelyn stiffened under the sudden flood of attention. The man crouched before her was still watching her carefully, and she feared she might have revealed her trepidation when his brows lowered over his gaze.

Did she really believe she was better off with these outlaws than in her husband's hands?

Yes. Yes, she did. But that didn't mean she was not in danger.

He stared at her for a moment longer before he rose to his feet and walked away without a word, leaving the canteen on the ground beside her. She couldn't keep her gaze from following his powerful form as he melted into the darkness beyond the fire while the others continued discussing her fate.

She expected to release a breath of relief at being left alone again, but it didn't come.

"With her fancy clothes and fine airs, there's gotta be someone somewhere who'll be willing to pay good money to get her back."

Evelyn listened to the exchange with increasing tension. These men were right about one thing. Her husband would no doubt be willing to pay a small fortune to get her back. But there was nothing in the world that would convince her to tell them that.

"You bloody pea brain," the redheaded British man interjected. "We don't just go around kidnapping any lady we come across. We had a mark, and we missed it."

"Well, we've got *her* now," Eli noted. "And Ramsey's right about her people. We could still get a payday off her." He shrugged almost apologetically. "I know it's not how we normally do things, but it could be an opportunity we'd be stupid to pass up."

"I say we take her to Luke and let him make the call," Jackson suggested in a rational tone that seemed to resonate with the others as several of them nodded in agreement.

Evelyn did not like the idea of continuing in the company of these men, but it was becoming apparent that she wouldn't be able to convince the entire group to let her go. Not when they couldn't even decide amongst themselves what to do with her. She might, however, have a chance at convincing their leader. Since they hadn't intended to take her in the first place, maybe he'd be reasonable about it.

But if he ended up agreeing with some of his men that she would be worth a ransom, he would end up disappointed.

She was never going back. She would do anything in her power to avoid that.

She couldn't fight these outlaws—not in a physical way—but she could listen and learn and plot and plan. And when the right opportunity presented itself, she'd take full advantage.

She had to.

Nothing about her current situation could be considered

fortunate, but whatever might befall her now, as least she hadn't landed back into Matthew's cruel hands. He hadn't found her. She remained out of reach. Perhaps even more so with this bunch.

A deep shiver ran through her as the encroaching chill of night crept around her. Her spot against the tree was some distance from the fire—too far for her to get much benefit from the heat of the flames. She didn't think it was the intention of the outlaws to freeze her to death, but she considered the possibility of it happening anyway.

The dress she wore was perfectly suited to traveling by train in the spring. Though designed with draping layers and a sizable bustle as was the style, it was of light material to be comfortable for long days. Her undergarments were of cotton rather than flannel or wool since they were intended for comfort, not warmth. And her boots were serviceable, but made of soft suede, not thick leather. It was not an ensemble designed for spending great lengths of time out of doors...at night...near the mountains where the temperature had seemed to drop dramatically now that the sun was out of sight. And her shawl was still tucked into her traveling bag.

Dreadful panic swept through her on an icy wave.

Her traveling bag had been left behind on the train, tucked safely beneath her seat. All her money was in that bag. It was everything she had to start a new life. Without it, she was completely adrift.

That money was her lifeline. The one thing that gave her a little security as she faced the prospect of going out into the world alone. It was her link to survival. And now it was gone.

She steeled herself against the hopelessness that threatened to claim her. She could not allow its weight to crush her. She would find another way. She had left Boston because she wanted to live without fear and degradation. She wanted to be free.

She wouldn't give up, but another bone-chilling shiver coursed through her, punctuating her thoughts with the reality of the challenges she faced. She swept a glance over the men gathered near the fire. Every one of them was a threat to her well-being…

But they weren't Matthew.

She noticed that the large, quiet man had not yet rejoined his friends, and just as she had the thought, he appeared from the shadows directly in front of her.

She stilled, practically holding her breath as he approached.

He moved with an unusual combination of purpose and stealth, emerging from the night as though he were a part of it. It was fascinating to see such a large man move with such silent grace. So fascinating that it took her a moment to realize he carried something in his hands. When he reached her, the breadth of his shoulders completely blocked the light of the fire, and his face fell into total darkness.

She wanted to ignore him and the intense awareness she experienced in his presence. An awareness that was astoundingly similar to fear but remained a different thing entirely. She didn't understand what it was. Something about him compelled her gaze. She couldn't look away. Her pride—that damnable thing inside her that had so aggravated Matthew—forced her to sit straight and unflinching against the tree, though her muscles tensed sharply, drawing the injured skin taut across her back.

Looking down at her, the man seemed to pause. Just for a moment. And though he did nothing to suggest it, Evelyn suddenly felt like he could see right through her facade of courage and fortitude. As though his hidden gaze could see everything she tried to conceal. Her uncertainty. Her weakness. Her pain.

She wanted to deny it. To prove she was stronger than she appeared. But it would have been pointless.

He released a heavy sigh that she nearly didn't hear. Then he gently shook out the blanket he carried and draped it over her. It covered her from chest to toe and smelled faintly of horse and leather. It was made of rough wool that gently abraded the skin of her hands, but its weight and warmth was decidedly welcome.

Again, he offered comfort.

Warmth rushed to her skin as she experienced a flash of embarrassment, though she wasn't exactly sure why. She parted her lips to say *thank you,* but the man straightened to full height and walked away as silently as he'd arrived.

A few minutes later, Eli approached with a loose swagger and a plate of food.

"I'll release your hands so you can eat, but I'll have to tie you up again after. Can't have you running off in the night."

As if she would head out into the wilderness on her own.

Evelyn nodded and lifted her hands from the blanket so he could undo the ropes.

He left her to eat the beans and crust of dry bread in peace, returning a bit later to take her plate and replace the ropes. "You'd best get some sleep. You've got a long day of riding tomorrow."

Evelyn could not relax for a long time.

Instead, she watched and listened to the men around the fire. With their decision made on what to do with her, they talked of inconsequential things: a new saddle, a woman named Marion with large breasts from some unnamed town, a foal that had just been born.

None of them seemed to take much note of Evelyn other than to send a glance in her direction every now and then to assure themselves she was still there.

After a while, despite the tension and uncertainty riding high within her, her eyes drifted closed of their own volition and the men's voices became more muted. The crackle of the fire lulled her into a strange state of wary half-consciousness.

That was when she finally heard the quiet man's voice. "I will take her." He spoke softly, but his tone was clear and strong in the midst of so many others. He hadn't joined the conversation until that moment, so the low timbre immediately drew her sleepy attention.

"Why you?" someone asked. She thought it was young, impulsive Ramsey, but exhaustion had claimed her mental acuity along with her physical strength, and she couldn't be sure.

"Because it makes sense," came the even-toned reply she now associated with Jackson. "We have to split up anyway, and Gabe's horse is best suited to carry two riders through the pass."

Someone chuckled—Eli probably, since the sound brought to mind his wide grin and blue eyes. "It'll be a mighty dull ride. That woman talks even less than you do."

"There're other things to do beside talking," Ramsey offered with lascivious suggestion, making Evelyn's muscles tighten beneath the wool blanket.

"Shut the bloody hell up, Ramsey," the Brit admonished in a sharp tone. "We don't hurt women."

"Right," Ramsey grumbled. "I's just joking."

"Well, don't bother. The only thing funny about you is the size of your ears."

The others laughed at that, and the rolling sounds finally managed to send Evelyn into a reluctant and uneasy slumber.

FIVE

The man narrowed his steely gaze and read through the message for the fourth time.

Despite its length, it provided very little detail, even fewer facts, and a whole lot of speculative assumptions. Either the sender knew next to nothing about the circumstances for which they expressed their deep concern, or they were purposely trying to conceal the whole truth of it.

For a man who liked to know all there was to know about a job before he agreed to take it on, the situation was less than ideal. He did not like working under supposition and theory, but he'd done it before. Most often, that was when his instincts and intuition came to the fore, leading him in a straighter line to the prize than if he followed a path laid by someone else.

Regardless of how it'd come to him, he'd have to take the job.

His stubborn and insistent partner hadn't exactly given him a choice in the matter, but even if they had, he'd rather see the task completed himself than pass it on to anyone else.

The message didn't reveal any clear and obvious threat of danger, but it was heavily implied, and that was enough for him.

Six

Gabriel Sloan, known by most as Gabe and by a spare few as something else altogether, sat cross-legged on his blanket, staring across the smoldering coals to where the young woman slept. She still sat upright against the tree but had curled herself into a ball beneath his blanket. Her legs were bent and drawn in snug to her chest, and her face was tucked down toward her knees.

She'd probably been cold through the night.

More than once he'd considered bringing her nearer to the fire, but that would have brought her closer to the men, and something about her suggested she preferred the distance.

Also, moving her would have required that he touch her. Something she definitely wouldn't have welcomed.

He sipped his coffee, figuring he could afford to let her sleep a while longer. The others had all taken off some time ago, and it was just the two of them now. Old Pete and Jackson were taking the long way back and would hopefully lead anyone who'd thought to track them from the train on a bit of a journey. Eli had a job to take care of in South Pass City before heading home, and Gentleman George had been tasked with seeing that Ramsey got back to camp and explained his error to Luke.

The kid was going to catch hell for taking the wrong woman.

Luke chose their jobs carefully based on specific criteria. His methods had served them all pretty well over the years. Sarah Cummings was to have brought in a hefty ransom. Ramsey's mistake cost them all.

After draining the last of his coffee, Gabriel tossed out the grounds still sitting in the bottom of his cup and rinsed it clean. There was a bit more coffee being kept warm on the last of the coals in case the woman wanted any, but she'd have to use his cup. It was all he had.

He sat back to wait.

It wasn't much longer before the woman stirred. She lifted her head first, letting it rest back against the tree trunk. Then she straightened her legs in a limited stretch that drew a soft, breathy moan from her lips.

She was going be stiff, her muscles tight. Riding all day was going be tough on her.

Gabriel watched in silence as she drifted into full consciousness. He saw the moment she recalled her situation. Her body tensed beneath the blanket. Her spine straightened, and her hands came up as her eyes opened. Then her stark, clear blue gaze slammed straight into his.

Everything in him tightened. Painfully. Instantly. Just as it had last night when she'd stared at him across the fire. The only difference was that today there were no wavering shadows or flickering firelight.

He expected more of the fear he'd seen in her the night before. Most women would be horrified to awaken in his company with their limbs bound and no one else around for miles.

The woman took a second to scan the camp with a sweep of her lashes. When her gaze returned to him, he couldn't quite make out what he saw in her eyes, but there was something unusual hidden in the soft blue. Something deeper than basic fear, something complex and curious.

He couldn't believe Ramsey had thought this woman to be anywhere near thirty years of age. Her brow was smooth, her skin completely unmarked. And her cheeks were still soft with youth. Though she had a rather strong jaw, her mouth with its lush fullness and elegant arches balanced the effect. As did her large, light eyes shining from a frame of thick lashes. Her hair was a very pale shade of blond that made him think of sunlight on a winter day.

As he analyzed her appearance, he noted her growing discomfort. He should probably say something to put her at ease, though he doubted anything would.

"Coffee?"

The single word, spoken after the length of silence, sounded aggressive even to him. So, he wasn't surprised when her eyes flickered in reaction. But then she gave a small nod.

Her blue eyes followed his every movement as he rose to his feet and approached the fire, poured the coffee into his cup, and started toward her. He'd long ago learned to move slowly and deliberately around people who might see him as a threat. It didn't help that he had grown to an intimidating size.

As he neared her, he was surprised to note that she did not look away or cast her gaze downward. Despite her obvious fear, there was an innate strength inside her that preferred to face him directly.

He had seen courage like that before. When he'd been a boy.

He crouched down to offer the steaming cup, and she took it from him with both hands still bound. "Hungry?"

She nodded again.

Gabriel returned to the fire for the leftover salt pork and fetched some dried fruit from his pack. After setting the food beside her, he went about cleaning up camp and readying his horse.

He was tamping down the last of the coals when he heard her speak. "Excuse me." The polite words were not altogether unexpected. The woman's gentility was abundantly evident in every inch of her appearance. What did surprise him was how the tone of her voice—the almost crystalline quality—resonated through him.

He turned to look at her and noticed the color in her cheeks. She had set aside the cup and plate, having finished the limited breakfast, and for the first time, her gaze was slightly averted.

"I need a moment of privacy," she said.

He should have thought of that.

Gabriel approached her slowly. Still, her entire body tensed.

Intentionally avoiding a glance at her face, he lifted the blanket to her knees and then raised the hem of her skirts so he could get at the rope around her ankles. Once it loosened and fell away, he reached for her hands.

Her fingers were chilled, and her skin was soft beneath the callused brush of his fingers. Though the rope hadn't been tight, its rough fibers had still rubbed her skin to an angry red.

She sat unnaturally still as he completed his task, but the layer of tension beneath her silent demeanor was obvious. Despite the cheery morning sunshine, he'd bet anything that if he took a look into her eyes, he'd see shadows there.

If he had to guess, he'd say the darkness sitting silent inside her had nothing to do with her current circumstances. This woman's distress went too deep.

Keeping his gaze averted, he leaned over her to grasp her arms just above her elbows, then lifted her easily and swiftly to her feet. She was a small woman, light and slim. But Gabriel realized his mistake instantly.

The gasp that slid from her lips was more than surprise at the swift change in position. The way her body stiffened beneath his hands and the sudden intense burst of energy he felt through her was indicative of only one thing. The woman was terrified.

Her stoic manner had completely disguised the truth of how frightened she actually was.

Gabriel accepted her resistance and softened his grip on her arms, but he couldn't release her. In her current panic, she could do something stupid—run off and get hurt. It was important she understand the situation. For her own safety. "Relax," he said quietly.

Her fierce tension slid away almost immediately. As though she had only momentarily forgotten herself. The rush of panic was replaced once again by the calm, controlled regard.

Her wide blue gaze collided with his, causing that fierce tightness to twist harder inside him. The faint scent of roses clung to her, mixing with the smell of the earth she'd slept on and the bitter aroma of campfire coffee. He could see the effort it took to remain still while his hands held her. The shadows swirled quietly in her gaze while she stood strong in front of him.

Fear and courage were a stark contradiction inside her. Stark, yet silent.

"I'll give you a few minutes," he stated. "Don't run."

"I won't run," she said. The clear, melodic tone of her voice flowed like a song through his blood. "I have nowhere to go."

"If you take too long, I *will* come for you." He hoped the warning would be sufficient to prevent that possibility. The flicker in her soft blue eyes suggested she would hurry. But there was a spark of rebellion there as well. Hidden deep, barely acknowledged, perhaps even by her.

She nodded, and Gabriel released her. Stepping back, she put some distance between them before she turned her back to him and walked sedately toward the nearest cluster of trees.

"That's far enough," her captor called after she'd gone several paces. Evelyn stopped and turned to look back and caught only a glimpse of the clearing she'd left behind.

If she defied his dictate and continued farther into the wilderness, she had no doubt he'd come after her. She had no desire for that to happen.

It took some creative maneuvering to take care of her needs. She'd never had any practice with having to do such a thing in the middle of nature and hadn't exactly dressed for it. In the end, she managed the deed, though with a distinct lack of efficiency and grace.

Once her skirts were smoothed back into place, she took a few moments to breathe. His warning about not taking too long rang in her ears, but she could not resist the need to center herself.

Pressing a hand flat to her chest, she closed her eyes and tipped her chin up to feel the scattered drops of sunlight that filtered through the trees. With a straight spine, she took lung-filling inhalations. The expansive movement of her chest aggravated the tight burning across her back, but it was worth it.

The air felt exceptionally free out here. Less contained—fresher, wilder—than the air back in Boston. It filled her up and chased away the last foggy remnants of sleep.

In a silent inner discourse, she reminded herself that she had endured a great deal in the last year, and this new challenge would not be enough to break her. She might no longer have her money, but she had her wits and her determination.

If, for now, she had to take her chances with these outlaws, so be it. She might be their temporary captive, but she was still far freer than she had been in a long time. She intended to hold on to that freedom with all her strength.

Her body tensed with a swift flash of awareness as she realized she was no longer alone.

She did not hear anything beyond the movement of the wind and the birds in the trees, but she knew with a certainty that came from deep in her bones that he had come to fetch her.

She lowered her chin and opened her eyes.

He stood several paces away.

Though his distance and physical stance were neutral and unthreatening, the sight of him caused an intense and sudden...expansion. It was like taking a full, deep breath with her whole body. It was life spreading outward from a point in her center in a sudden rush.

It was...alarming and confusing.

Strange that his simple, quiet presence—his silent, focused attention—could affect her so completely. Especially since he seemed so totally unaffected himself. Though his gaze was direct, it never revealed his thoughts. His expression revealed even less.

"Time to go," he said.

The low, earthy quality of his voice had a distinctly grounding effect on her as it reverberated through her center and out to her fingers and toes.

She nodded and stepped forward to follow him.

Rather than leading the way, he turned to the side so she could go ahead of him.

As she passed him and noted the incongruity in their size and strength, she couldn't help but acknowledge her physical vulnerability. She was alone with this stranger in the wilderness, completely at his mercy. Her safety, her dignity—her everything—rested entirely in his hands.

And yet the idea didn't completely terrify her.

He was intimidating in his size and strength and his quiet, assessing manner. And though her awareness of him in a physical sense was intense and flowed straight from the core of her being, it did not carry that icy-cold sense of fear she had gotten so familiar with in her marriage.

Rather…it was warm, hot even; the way her senses—her body—reacted to him.

In her brief absence, the camp had been completely dismantled. If she hadn't known they'd just passed the night in the small clearing, she never would have suspected anything had disturbed the spot. Even the remains of the campfire had been effectively reclaimed by the earth.

The outlaw nodded his head in the direction of his horse, which stood patiently waiting without needing to be tied. He was a large animal with withers nearly at Evelyn's eye level, solid muscle tone beneath his dusty-gray coat, and a long, curling mane and tail. He was beautiful in a raw, untamed way. Daunting in his size and power—much like the man who rode him.

Evelyn had never spent much time around horses. She possessed a basic knowledge of riding but had most often walked or took the carriage when getting from one place to another in the city.

She was likely about to endure something quite beyond a simple pleasure ride through the park.

Her escort swung up onto the horse's back in one fluid motion, and it was only then that she realized there was no saddle. None at all. Just a wool blanket and a sheep hide secured to the horse by thin leather straps. Yet he sat confident and proud, one hand holding thin reins and the other extended toward her as he waited for her put her hand in his.

Evelyn held her breath and looked into his broad, strong features. He showed no emotion, no impatience, no clear intention. His complete neutrality was unsettling, but Evelyn had to take a chance.

"Let me go," she said softly. Nothing changed in his expression, nor did he lower his hand, but she knew he'd heard her. "I understand I was taken off the train by mistake," she continued. "You could just return me to the nearest town and ride away."

He was silent for a long moment with his hand still outstretched. Then he said simply, "No. You will come with me." His words were solid, his tone unbendable. Final.

"Where are you taking me?"

"An unmapped valley protected by the mountains."

"Why?"

His brows furrowed over that question, just slightly, and his head tilted a notch to one side. "Your questions will be answered when we arrive. You will not be harmed."

Feeling defeated, she allowed a tremor of frustration to enter her voice as she replied, "I should believe you?"

"Yes."

The assurance in his voice and the steady way he looked down at her with his hand still waiting to take hers struck a deep chord. She was desperate to believe that in going with him, she was not being led into something worse than what she'd left behind in Boston.

Although she'd discovered in the months since her marriage that she could endure a great deal, she was not so stupid as to think she could survive on her own in the wilderness. Even if she could somehow manage to escape him, she had no idea how far or in what direction she'd find the nearest town.

She met his dark gaze, wondering if there was anything she could say that might sway him. For a moment, she thought she saw a flicker of subtle emotion in his dark eyes.

Her breath caught and held before she realized she must have been mistaken.

"Come," he said. One word. Filled with assurance and command.

She had little choice.

Taking a step forward, she lifted her hand. There was a moment of breathlessness when she slid her palm against the outlaw's much larger one. She had only a second to acknowledge the warmth of his skin, the encompassing strength of his grip, before she was lifted off the ground and set down in front of him on the horse. Giving her no time to adjust her seating, he set the horse in motion, heading straight toward the mountains at a swift lope.

SEVEN

THEY RODE IN SILENCE FOR SEVERAL HOURS OF TEDIOUS discomfort.

At first, Evelyn was focused on trying to keep as much distance between herself and the man seated behind her as possible. But it quickly became far more important to keep from getting bounced off the horse. She sat with both legs and the bulk of her skirts draped to one side. Since there was no saddle, all she had to hold on to was the thick mane of the horse—and she did, at times quite desperately, as they flew steadily across uneven terrain.

Horse and man seemed barely bothered by her added presence, while Evelyn couldn't seem to figure out how to maintain straight posture and proper physical distance from the man behind her while also retaining her seat and her sanity. Every time his chest bumped against her back, or his thigh pressed firmly beneath hers, she tensed.

Aside from his earlier declaration that she wouldn't be harmed, he did nothing further to try to put her at ease. In fact, he didn't say a single thing to her once they left the camp. Even the commands he gave his horse were done without words as he used the pressure of his knees or an occasional clicking sound made with his tongue. He didn't use a proper bridle, having only a leather halter to guide the horse's head. That he was able to control the animal with barely any sound and the strength of his will alone was unsettling.

She'd never met anyone like this man.

Or was it just that she had grown so accustomed to Matthew's manner that anything else seemed unnatural?

In public, Matthew was effusive in his charm and flattery. In private, he could strip Evelyn of her confidence and self-worth with a few choice words. Every conversation had been a practice in discerning the crooked, twisting path he loved to lay for her with the intention of undermining her every thought and belief. The longer she was away from him, the more she realized just how great his influence had been, down to even the smallest detail of her life. He had manipulated her to the point where she no longer trusted her own judgment.

But that was all she had now.

Around midday, they finally stopped to rest.

The outlaw dropped to the ground first, then turned to reach both hands up to her. His expression was neutral, his eyes direct and unreadable. She got the sense he did that without even really thinking about it—closed his thoughts off from her view.

Did he do it with everyone?

Though she would have preferred to avoid direct physical contact, she couldn't dismount from the tall horse on her own. Holding herself rigid despite her exhaustion, she leaned forward and placed her hands on his shoulders. The hard, curved muscle bunched beneath her palms as he grasped her waist and lifted her from the horse's back.

An odd feeling flew through her as he lowered her carefully to the ground: a moment of breathlessness, a flash of heat, a strange tightening inside her. She tried desperately to conceal her reaction as her eyes met his. But there was something similar flickering in his gaze—a spark quickly doused as he released her and turned away.

She stared at his broad back as he walked to the edge of the creek they'd stopped beside. His horse followed him without urging. Both man and animal bent to drink from the clear water. She didn't know what had just happened, but it left her unbalanced and flushed. As though a warm wind had just passed through her.

Perhaps her overwhelming exhaustion and uncertainty were causing the disorienting reactions in her body.

Evelyn walked unsteadily to a large rock and took a seat. Her back felt as if it had gone up in flames, her rear end was surely bruised, and her legs felt watery and weak. The chance to rest was a welcome relief.

A few minutes later, the outlaw walked toward her to offer the canteen he had just refilled in the creek. After only a brief hesitation, she took it and eased her thirst with the cold water. It had a mineral taste but was infinitely refreshing. When she would have passed the canteen back to him, he gave a short nod indicating she was to keep it. Then he pulled a dry piece of bread from his shoulder bag and offered that as well.

"Hardtack."

The bread was as hard as it looked and as lacking in flavor, but it satisfied the ache in her stomach. While she ate, he retreated a few paces to lean his shoulders back against a nearby tree and silently waited. Rather than pretend he wasn't there, she deliberately turned to meet his steady, impenetrable gaze.

After a few moments, he lowered his chin and spoke. "You are not Sarah Cummings. What is your real name?"

Evelyn stiffened. The subtle movement pulled at the wounds on her back, forcing her to clench her teeth to keep from grimacing. Nothing would convince her to give him her name, not when it would afford them the means to ransom her back into her husband's keeping.

"If not your true name," he said in a rich, lowered tone, "is there something I can call you?"

How had he so easily seen into her thoughts? It was disturbing and tilted her off axis. But she found herself grateful for the minor reprieve. She could give him any name now, and he wouldn't be certain if it was true or false.

Her closest friends called her Evie. But she couldn't bring herself to give this stranger such intimacy.

"I am known as Gabriel," he offered into the lengthening silence.

It was not at all what she'd expected him to say. She had heard the others refer to him as Gabe. That he was actually named for God's messenger angel surprised her and ignited a spark of inspiration.

"You may call me Eve."

He tilted his head as he replied. "Why did you claim to be Sarah Cummings on the train?" he asked, and his voice was low and calm, suggesting infinite patience, while his eyes stared bold and direct into hers.

Feeling increasingly vulnerable, Evelyn—*Eve*—replied, "If I had known it would get me kidnapped, I wouldn't have done so."

His brows lowered fractionally as he crossed his arms over his wide chest and gave a short nod. "Yes. Then why did you?"

She didn't answer. There was nothing she could say that wouldn't put her at greater risk.

An image of Matthew flashed through her mind. His face drawn tight and flushed with exertion as sweat rolled down from his temples. And there—crouching within in his refined features as he gazed at the destruction he'd wrought upon her naked back—pleasure.

A shudder passed through her at her recollection of that moment. But directly on its heels came a steely spear of determination. Because she had gotten away.

And nothing in the world would ever bring her back.

She returned the outlaw's—Gabriel's—questioning stare with a rebellious one of her own.

His brows furrowed. "You will not be harmed, Eve."

Tension—and something else—rose up in reaction to his words. The deep intonation in his voice and the quiet, steady look in his eyes stabbed straight to her center. She wanted so badly to believe him, to believe that she was safe in his company when she hadn't felt safe for so long. But how stupid would she have to be to trust an outlaw, a man who was committed to escorting her against her will to a stranger who would decide what was to become of her next?

Would she ever be free to decide her own fate?

A flash of willful frustration had her stating in clear defiance, "I will not be ransomed."

Her declaration did not seem to surprise him. In fact, he did not appear to have any reaction at all. He just stared back at her. Though his physical appearance gave the impression of barely contained power and strength, his demeanor was calm and still. It was clear that his thoughts ran deep, but his focus did not falter.

Uncertainty threatened to overwhelm her practiced facade. The man before her promised she wouldn't be harmed, but she recalled the last time she'd trusted a man with her well-being, her future. She'd not only trusted Matthew; she'd believed for a short time that she could grow to love him.

How stupid. How dreadfully weak and naive she'd been.

It was her shame and regret that finally had her lowering her gaze. For some reason, she did not want this man to see such things in her.

While she kept her gaze trained on the canteen grasped tightly in her hands, he walked away. His steps were so quiet that they could barely be heard above the trickling sound of the creek and insects buzzing nearby. But she felt his retreat as much as she heard it, and relief flowed through her. She expelled her breath, and tears pricked fiercely at the back of her eyes.

After a few moments, she managed to gather herself back together. She would not fall apart now. It served no purpose. She had accepted that she would have to fight for her freedom, and she would do so. The current situation she faced was a temporary detour. She would find a way to endure her time with the outlaws until she was on her own once again.

EIGHT

After a while, Gabriel returned. Without a word, he swung gracefully onto the back of his horse, then urged the large animal forward as he extended his hand to her. With a sense of calm acceptance, she put her hand in his and gasped a breath as she was lifted into place in front of him.

The solid wall of his body behind her and the power of the animal beneath had become familiar. Though she didn't completely relax her posture, she at least found a way to sit that was less jarring and bruising to her backside. A good thing since the rest of the day continued with more hard riding and more silence.

A raw, open expanse of wilderness spread out to either side as the imposing rise of the Rocky Mountains filled the horizon ahead of them. As the hours passed, Eve acknowledged that they never once came within sight of a town or any kind of human establishment. They never even passed another traveler. The world they rode through was more barren and isolated than anything she'd ever experienced.

As night approached, they stopped to make camp in

the shadow of a collection of large rocks that rose from the rugged landscape. Gabriel dismounted first, then turned to assist her to the ground. Eve could not escape the rush of sensation that claimed her in the brief moments when his hands were around her waist.

It seemed silly when she'd spent the day sitting in front of him atop the horse, doing her best to limit their contact to the press of his thighs on hers and the occasional brush of his arms as he handled the reins or a brief bump of his chest against her back. But this was different. This was face-to-face intentional contact.

She should have been grateful when he released her as soon as her legs were steady beneath her, but that wasn't exactly the right word for what she was feeling.

As he attended to his horse and then started to gather wood to build a fire, Eve found herself wandering around camp, trying to bring proper life back into her stiff legs and aching back. Once the worst of the kinks seemed to be worked out of her body, she found a place to sit on a boulder with a somewhat flat surface.

Despite the fact Gabriel remained busy with his tasks and never glanced her way directly, she felt herself constantly in his awareness.

With nothing else to do, Eve found herself watching him rather intently as he crouched before the pile of dead sticks and dried branches he'd collected from beneath the spare bushes and trees. He expertly struck a spark with the flint he carried, then leaned in close to blow gently at the newborn flame, coaxing it to life.

Once the fire was going strong, he removed something from his shoulder bag and rose to his feet. His dark eyes met hers the moment he turned toward her, a length of rope in his hand.

Everything inside her rebelled at the thought of being bound again, but she remained strong and unmoving. She would not let him see how vulnerable she felt in that moment.

When he reached her, he crouched before her, and she realized he did that a lot—condensed his great size when he was close to her.

His gaze penetrated the gathering dusk as he studied her face. She remained silently resistant, her attention fixated on the rope in his hands. She thought she heard him sigh before he spoke. "It's necessary. Until I can trust you."

Her gaze flew up to meet his at the words.

He spoke of trusting her? She was his captive. What need did he have to trust her? She found the idea so odd that it threw her off for a moment, and she didn't realize he hadn't moved to tie her up but seemed to be waiting. For her permission?

"I won't run," she stated firmly. "I'm not that stupid."

"Stupid, no. But desperation can push us to do many things." He lowered his chin while holding her gaze. "I need to be sure. For your safety."

It bothered her that he could see her desperation, though she did her best to hide it. What else could he see?

She searched his face for some indication of what he might be thinking, but there was nothing to read in his strong features, dark eyes, or wide, unsmiling mouth.

She suddenly wondered how a smile might alter his appearance. Her belly warmed strangely at the thought.

She was disturbed by her wayward thoughts; her gaze

jumped back up to meet his, and her breath caught on a shallow inhale.

His straight brows had lowered over his eyes, shadowing any glimmer of what might be running through his mind. But there was a new intensity in his expression that caused heat to rise instantly in her cheeks. As though he were asking some harsh and quiet question that had nothing to do with the rope in his hands.

And then the question was gone, replaced by that neutral calm she had come to expect from him. "Your foot," he said simply, reminding her of his purpose.

She swallowed hard past the uncertainty in her chest. With a small nod, she shifted her gaze to the fire glowing bright in the gathering dusk. Despite his show of waiting for her permission, she didn't truly have a choice in the matter.

Having received her assent, he reached beneath the hem of her skirt. His large hand encircled her ankle just above the edge of her boot as he drew her foot toward him. She felt the rope slip against her stockinged leg before it settled around the top edge of her boot. After securing the tether with a tight knot, he rose to full height and circled around behind her to loop the rope over a nearby boulder, knotting it around the base where it couldn't be slipped free.

The indignity of the situation quickly chased away her previous awkwardness.

"I'll be right back," he said from behind her.

Panic flared. He was leaving her? Tied to a rock with no means of protection against...whatever might come out of the wilderness?

"Wait. Where are you going?" she asked, twisting

around to glance behind her. But there was no one there. He had already gone.

As full darkness started to descend, so too did the chill of night. The warmth of the fire beckoned, and after several minutes of staring into the deepening shadows and wondering when the outlaw might return, Eve became cold enough to discover just how long a leash he had given her. Rising slowly to her feet to accommodate the soreness that remained after riding all day, she approached the fire.

Her tether allowed her to get close enough that she could make use of the heat of the flames, but not so close that she could use the fire to burn through the rope. Not that she would have bothered to do so. She had absolutely no experience in traveling through a remote mountain range. She had no idea where they were exactly, where to find water or someone else to help her. Not to mention, she had no means of defending herself against wild creatures or the elements.

She wouldn't try to escape. She had accepted that she would be in Gabriel's company until he handed her off to the leader of the outlaw gang.

She was still kneeling in the dirt in her fine traveling dress with her hands extended toward the flames when her silent captor returned with a large rabbit in his hand. He had been gone less than fifteen minutes.

She had not even heard a shot.

Her eyes narrowed as he approached the fire. In fact, he wasn't carrying a gun.

Kneeling on the ground across the fire from her, he efficiently dressed the rabbit before fashioning a spit over the flames and putting the animal on to roast.

Then, still without saying a single word, he shook the travel dust from the sheepskin and blanket that had been on his horse. He laid the blanket out on the ground and set the sheepskin aside. From his shoulder bag, he pulled out the wool blanket he'd covered her with the night before and set it next to the sheepskin. Then he lowered himself to sit cross-legged in the middle of the horse blanket, resting his large hands on the surface of his thighs. Only then did he look in her direction.

Eve didn't realize how intently she'd been watching him until his gaze slammed suddenly into hers. This time, the heat spread beyond her cheeks as her entire body warmed with a flush of awareness.

He did not seem surprised to find her staring. In fact, it was almost as though he'd expected it. His gaze steady, he gave a short lift of his chin. "Where do you come from, Eve?"

She remained silent.

He could ask all the questions he could think of. She would never provide information that might connect her back to Boston. And Matthew.

Rather than pressing her for a response, he remained silent as well, his back straight and strong, the two long braids falling over his shoulders to his waist, his hands resting on his muscled thighs, his expression calm.

After spending the entire day together, she knew nothing about him beyond the obvious. He was clearly of native blood but went by the name of a biblical archangel. He was an outlaw, and as such was likely capable any number of dastardly deeds, yet he assured her she wouldn't be harmed and had done nothing to belie the statement. In fact, he seemed intent on keeping a physical distance from her unless it was necessary to do otherwise.

"You will not answer my question," he stated simply.

Her instinctual wariness slowly eased as she realized he would not force the issue. At least not now. "I will not be ransomed," she said firmly, repeating her earlier declaration.

There was no change in his expression as he responded with a deep rolling sound that briefly lifted his chest. "Hmm."

Then he rose smoothly to his feet and approached the fire to check the rabbit. The scent of roasting meat called to the clawing hunger in her belly. After removing the animal from the spit, he tore off a piece of the meat and extended it toward her.

Eve looked as it with a dubious expression.

"If you're hungry, you'll eat it."

Without a plate or utensils or anything? She looked up into his eyes as he waited patiently. Her hunger was fierce. Fierce enough to set aside the proper manners ingrained in her being. Reaching out, she took the meat from his hand.

It smelled wonderful and tasted even better.

By the time she finished that piece, he was there, offering water from his canteen, then another piece of the savory meat.

Eve never would have expected to appreciate such an unrefined meal so much. But such things were relative, she supposed, like so many other things in life—as she had come to understand since the day of her wedding.

When the rabbit was fully consumed, Gabriel doused a handkerchief in water and offered it to her to clean her fingers and wipe any remaining grease from her lips. When she handed it back to him, he did the same. For a moment she was fascinated by the sight of the cloth swiping across his wide mouth before he tucked the handkerchief away.

"If you need privacy, the rope will reach around behind those bushes," he said, nodding toward the edge of the outcropping where some craggy foliage created shadows from the firelight.

Beyond that, the darkness was total and endless. What dangers lurked outside the flickering light? What perils still awaited her on this journey?

What did it matter?

Her exhaustion was making her maudlin and philosophical when she needed to be pragmatic and focused.

Rising to her feet, she felt every protest in her body: the tightness of the muscles in her legs, the stiff, burning soreness across her back, the constant tension in her shoulders, and the uncertainty in her chest. With as much grace and dignity as she could manage, she left the light of the fire behind.

As she crept slowly past the bushes, her eyes began to make out vague outlines of her environment—the thick, solid lines of more rocks and the rustling shapes of the bushes. She continued forward until the tug of the rope advised she could go no farther. Then she turned around and looked back toward the camp. A warm orange glow spread across the rocky terrain and gently illuminated the distant sky overhead.

It was oddly beautiful.

Then the sound of some wild creature howling in the distance reminded her she was in the middle of a vast wilderness. She addressed her needs quickly and returned to the fire.

While she was gone, Gabriel had laid out the sheepskin on her side of the fire and set the wool blanket beside it.

"Tomorrow is another long day," he said from his spot in the center of the horse blanket. "You should sleep."

Eve lowered herself carefully onto the sheepskin, grateful for its softness and the added warmth it would provide against the cooling earth. Lying on her side, facing the fire, she unrolled the blanket and drew it up around her shoulders.

How strange life had become in such a short time! That single moment when she'd decided to claim Sarah's name had sent her path spiraling off in a direction she never could have anticipated.

The rope around her ankle did not bode well for freedom, but hope and desperation were powerful motivators. At least she was alive.

NINE

Gabriel waited until the woman's breathing eased to a deep and steady rhythm before he lay down. Stretching out on his back, he folded his hands over his abdomen and gazed up at the endless stretch of stars above.

The sight usually soothed him. It was familiar and comfortable and felt as much like home as anything else in his life.

But tonight he was restless. He'd been restless and unsettled from the moment the woman sleeping across the fire had opened her eyes the night before and marked him with her quiet, seeking stare.

Gabriel resisted the urge to glance her way.

She was fine.

Better than fine. She seemed to be handling her kidnapping with an exceptional amount of resilience. Far more than would have been expected of anyone. He should feel lucky he didn't have the task of escorting a hysterical woman into the mountains. Instead, her calm acceptance made him wary.

Beneath her quiet, complacent manner was something unbreakable. He could see it in her eyes. Her fear was apparent, but so was her courage. From the beginning, he knew not to underestimate her.

So, it didn't surprise him when she declared she wouldn't be ransomed. He had been waiting for her to reveal the resistance rooted inside her.

Unfortunately, what became of her was not his decision to make.

His job was to bring her to the valley. Luke would decide the rest.

Though Luke could be hotheaded and reckless with his personal safety, he chose the gang's jobs with particular care and expected his men to follow certain rules when it came to innocent bystanders. Motivated by far more than greed or the simple need for survival, Luke never led his men into unnecessary danger, but his word was final.

Gabriel had never been given cause not to trust him. But for some reason, the idea of Luke deciding the fate of this small, pale-haired woman who called herself Eve did not sit well with Gabriel.

That morning, when she'd asked him to release her, he'd almost been tempted. The determined desperation in her eyes was hauntingly familiar...which was exactly the reason he had to refuse.

After being separated from his family in childhood, Gabriel had deliberately avoided becoming attached to anything. Not to the men he lived and worked with. Not to any idea of home. Not to anyone.

Gabriel's path was fated to be a solitary one.

It was a difficult lesson he'd been forced to accept as a young man when he'd finally returned to his tribe, only to discover he no longer belonged. His time away had changed him—not for good or bad, but enough for him to realize his path had diverged from what it might have been if he'd never left. His experience in the ceremonial sun dance had confirmed that it was his destiny to make his way alone.

When he'd later joined up with Luke and the others, it was with the knowledge that his loyalty would always be to himself first. Eventually, he would part ways with the gang. His path was not destined to run parallel to anyone for long, but for a time at least, the gang provided a place where he could exist on his own terms.

Terms that did not involve personal relationships of any kind.

Which was why his reaction to Eve was so disturbing. When he'd met her wide, glistening gaze across the fire that first night, he'd felt something—a hard, swift tug below his rib cage. Even when he'd seen her fear, he hadn't been able to stop himself from going to her.

He experienced that same inexorable pull whenever their eyes met. She drew on something inside him that he'd thought no longer existed. The desire to understand. To protect. To know the secret fears and yearning another person carries.

He should feel no such desire. It served him no purpose and her even less.

By all appearances, she should have someone willing to pay handsomely for her safe return, yet she'd stated twice that she wouldn't be ransomed. She clearly had no wish to be returned to the place from which she'd come, but why? Where was she heading on that train?

And why did her eyes seem to hold so many shadows?

They were questions Luke would need to have answered before he decided what he'd do with the woman. But Gabriel felt a need to know for other reasons entirely.

Whatever power this young woman held over him, he needed to keep it under control. His responsibility for her well-being would be short-lived. Her fate would soon be passed into someone else's hands.

The next morning dawned with a crisp, white sun.

Gabriel moved silently about camp as he spread out the glowing coals and kicked dirt over them to smother their heat.

There would be no coffee this morning. Only hardtack and jerky with what water he had left. He would have gone a bit out of his way to fill his canteen last night if he hadn't been worried about pushing the woman past her endurance.

He was settling the blanket on his horse's back when he suddenly knew she was awake.

She hadn't made any sound—no shifting in her blankets or swift breath, but Gabriel knew all the same. One moment there was silence inside him, and in the next, a surge of awareness, like the tumbling of swift rapids, flowing from head to toe.

He continued at his task as he said, "We leave soon."

Silence greeted his words, but after a bit, he heard her moving. A moment later, he knew she had stepped beyond the bushes for privacy. He had removed the rope that secured her to the rock earlier. Though he didn't believe she would run, he still listened intently for her return.

Gabriel was kneeling on the ground, rolling up the blanket she had used, when she stepped back into camp several minutes later. He looked up and allowed himself a moment to take in her appearance.

The fine dress she wore—proof of her wealth and the likelihood of a promising ransom—now held very little of its original elegance. Dusty from riding and wrinkled beyond repair from sleeping on the ground, its quality was still evident to anyone with eyes. The woman herself was looking just as worn and ragged. If she'd once had gloves or a hat, they'd been left behind on the train, and dirt had started collecting under the perfectly curved crescents of her fingernails. Her pale-blond hair was still held securely in a twisting bun at her nape, but wispy tendrils had slipped free to brush against her face and neck. Dirt smudged the crest of one fine cheekbone, and her weariness was evident in the downward turn of her mouth.

Still, she walked into camp with a serene and regal air that defied her rough appearance. No matter what this woman wore or how trying her circumstances became, there would be no mistaking her worth, a diamond in the dirt.

There was a great deal of dignity and pride contained in her slight form.

Her gaze was unwavering as she approached. He found it unsettling how she looked directly at him. Even when he returned her stare, she did not glance away. Many others would have.

He knew the fear was still there, carefully banked behind a calm facade, but there was determination in her as well. And that subtle thread of strength and courage never wavered.

Gabriel finished tying up the blanket and rose to his feet.

Her gaze flickered as he stood.

He tried to ignore the clenching in his stomach at her reaction.

Even if his size was not capable of making people wary of him at a glance, there were many people who distrusted and feared him based solely on his native heritage. He'd grown to accept it, refusing to assist people in altering their prejudices. He'd created balance in his life that didn't rely on other people's opinions of him. It had been a long time since he'd wished he could be judged by his actions rather than appearances.

There was no reason to wish the woman approaching him might see him in a way many others could not.

He tucked the bedroll beneath his arm, then scooped up the sheepskin and gave it a few hard shakes to dislodge the dirt. With a nod, he gestured toward the hardtack and jerky he'd set aside for her. "Food and water. We head out in five minutes."

He expected to reach Bitter Creek that night, but it would require some hard riding. He hoped the woman was up for it after the long day yesterday. Something told him he wouldn't hear a word from her even if she wasn't.

She stepped up beside him just as he got everything strapped into place. Her sudden nearness and the charge of physical awareness it brought had his core tightening and his muscles tensing.

Her lashes swept down over her gaze just before she reached him and handed him the canteen. There hadn't been much water left in it, and he'd figured she'd need it all. When he took the canteen, however, it wasn't empty.

She'd left some for him.

He acknowledged the gesture with a spread of warmth in his chest as he raised the canteen to his lips to claim the last swallow. Lowering the canteen again, he noticed that she'd watched him drink. His body reacted instantly to what he detected in the depth of her soft blue eyes, despite her carefully controlled expression.

He quickly tried to douse the flames that leapt to life within him. It was the second time he'd caught a glimpse of that quiet, smoldering look in her eyes. And the second time he'd had to forcefully deny his natural reaction to it.

He thought he knew what desire looked like in a woman's gaze. He'd seen it frequently enough. He'd become accustomed to seeing that gleam of excitement and understood what it meant.

But what he saw—what he felt—in this woman's gaze was different. It hit him deeper, struck harder. Because it was quiet and gentle and filled with uncertainty.

If it *was* desire, it was the reluctant sort. It was quite possible she didn't even know that's what she was feeling when she looked at him.

Or she knew exactly what she was feeling and preferred to deny it.

With a flicker of her lashes, the glimmer in her eyes was dulled once again.

After tucking the empty canteen into his shoulder bag, Gabriel turned and leapt up onto his mustang's back. Keeping the eager horse under control with a gentle command for patience, he extended his hand to the woman still standing on the ground.

With only a brief hesitation, she placed her hand in his.

Gabriel lifted her easily to sit in front of him. She settled into place with her spine straight and her gaze trained forward. He knew she was doing all she could to avoid touching him any more than was necessary, and he did his best to respect the boundaries she'd set. More than once the day before, he'd wanted to suggest that she relax back against him. As the hours had gone by and her fatigue had become more and more apparent, he was tempted to offer himself as support. But the words never rose to his lips.

She would have refused.

Her pride would never allow her to take even that simple comfort from him.

The landscape they traveled through was rough and rugged, but Gabriel knew the terrain well. He refilled their water supply at the first available stop and knew just where to find food worth scavenging. By late afternoon, they'd reached the twisting banks of an ancient creek that was fed by a spring high up the mountains. From there, they continued to follow the creek upstream into the foothills. Just a few more hours of hard riding, and they should reach Maddy and Jane's before nightfall.

The original plan had not included taking Sarah Cummings all the way to the valley. A separate location had been set up from which Jackson and Old Pete would have managed the ransom. But with Ramsey's ridiculous mistake, the plan had changed. While ransoming this woman appeared to be a good idea at a glance, nothing was done in Luke's gang without his say-so.

Taking the woman up through the mountain passes to their hideout would not be a simple task. She'd need a horse of her own—a hardy mountain horse. And she'd need proper clothing.

That meant a stop at Bitter Creek Ranch.

Maddy and Jane were as close to allies as anyone they had outside the gang, but the two women had limits on what they were willing to risk for Luke and his men. And they didn't take kindly to unexpected visits in the dark of night.

The sun was already low in its descent as Gabe crested the ridge that overlooked the ranch. The woman seated in front of him tensed at the first sight of civilization they'd encountered in more than two days.

"We'll stop here for the night," he said.

She didn't ask any questions, but her tension was evident as they neared the cattle spread.

They'd been spotted some way out, so Maddy and Jane were already waiting on their front porch to greet them as they rode into the yard stretching between the ranch house and the fenced riding arena.

Maddy watched their approach with a faint smile of curiosity. She was the older of the two, in her midforties. A tall woman with a full figure and stately bearing, her tightly curling black hair was liberally threaded with gray and pulled back into a bun on the back of her head. Wearing an apron over her blue flowered dress and wiping her hands on a towel, she looked like she'd just stepped from the kitchen.

Jane stood beside her with her hands planted in narrow hips and no smile on her face. She was younger than Maddy by nearly ten years, and where Maddy was all friendly warmth and open smiles, Jane was fierce grit and ready action contained within a compact frame. She preferred pants and men's shirts to skirts and kept her hair cut short like a boy's. She was straightforward in her speech and sparing in her trust.

Jane was the first to speak as Gabriel approached. "We weren't expecting you, Gabe."

He nodded. "Sorry to impose. I would've sent word if I'd been able."

Before Jane could reply, Maddy said, "You're always welcome, Gabe. Is there something we can do for you?" Her gaze slid to Eve with a lift to her brow.

"A bed for the night. A bath maybe. And we'll need some proper attire for the lady and another horse."

Jane frowned. "You're taking her into the mountains?"

Gabriel nodded. "Everything borrowed will be returned."

"Of course. We know that," Maddy assured him as she sent a pointed look in Jane's direction. "Why don't you both come on in. There's just enough time to wash up before supper."

Without dismounting, Gabriel offered his hand to Eve. After only the briefest moment of hesitation, she settled her hand in his. He clenched the back of his teeth together to keep from showing how the soft, warm slide of her palm against his pulled something tight inside him. With care, he eased her to the ground.

When he didn't dismount after her, she looked up at him in question. "Maddy will get you settled," he said. "I've gotta see to the horse."

There was a flicker of something deep in her gaze as she glanced toward the women on the porch. But then she turned away from him to stride toward the house with the grace and dignity he'd come to expect from her. Gabriel watched as Maddy led Eve inside with a wide smile of welcome.

When he would have urged his horse toward the barn, Jane spoke in a stern tone. "Just a minute, Gabe."

He waited, figuring he knew what the woman would say.

"Now, you know Maddy and I are willing to help you boys out when we can. But you also know there are certain things we won't stand for." Her black gaze turned hard and flinty as she crossed her arms over her chest. "Because I trust you, I won't ask what you've got going on with that lady in there. But if I find out the situation is less than civil, our association will come to a full stop. You hear me?"

Gabriel had always admired Jane's forthrightness. Though nearly half his weight in muscle, she'd never hesitated to speak her mind to him or any of the others. If it came down to it, Jane wouldn't hesitate to enter a fight either for or against them, depending on the side of the line where her sensibilities and conscience landed.

He gave a short nod.

Jane smiled. The act brightened her face, showing a softness to her features that she didn't often reveal. "Good. Now get your horse settled and come in for some supper. And don't forget to wash up first. You know how Maddy is about dirt at the table."

Ten

Eve allowed herself to be guided into the neat and tidy little home. The woman beside her exuded warmth and kindness, and it baffled Eve why she would be associated with an outlaw.

Unless she didn't know of the man's criminal behavior.

"This way, honey," the older woman said with a smile. "My name is Maddy Jones. And you are?"

"Eve."

Maddy lifted her brows at the lack of a surname but did not press the issue. They passed through a parlor that contained a couple sofas, a desk in the corner, and two cozy reading chairs.

"Supper will be a little while yet, but I'm thinking you might like a bath first."

"That would be lovely," Eve replied as they started down a hallway, passing a kitchen on the right. The idea of a bath honestly had her heart racing with anticipation. Her last real bath had been so long ago she could barely imagine what it'd feel like to be clean again.

"The bedrooms are this way. I'll let you get settled in while I draw some water from the well and set it on the stove to heat. I'm afraid you'll have to make do with a hip bath."

"That will be just fine, Miss Jones. Thank you."

The corners of her rich brown eyes crinkled with her smile as the woman replied, "Just Maddy, please. And here we are." She turned and entered a bedroom with a narrow bed set in the corner. A small chest of drawers rested against the wall across from it, and a chair stood in between. A single window over the chair let in the rich golden light of the dying sun, and a red handwoven rug covered the wooden floor.

"Go ahead and have a bit of a rest while your bath is readied. We'll see you freshened up in no time."

Eve had never been so grateful for such a simple kindness. Surely, this woman would not condone kidnapping and whatever other criminal activities outlaws engaged in!

As the older woman started to back from the room, Eve stepped toward her. "May I ask you something..." she began but hesitated, unsure how to properly broach the subject.

"What is it, honey?"

The unmistakable compassion in the woman's voice convinced Eve to continue. "Do you know Mr...ah... Gabriel well?"

Maddy sighed and gave a warm smile. "I'm not sure anyone can say they know Gabe well, but we've been acquainted for several years now." She tilted her head in concern. "Are you in some sort of trouble, honey?"

"I'm not sure," Eve answered honestly.

The older woman smiled again. "Well, if it's any help, I can tell you Gabe is one of the most honorable men I've ever met. If you're looking for someone to trust, he's a good choice."

A weight settled heavily in Eve's stomach. Maddy was clearly loyal to Gabriel. Of course, she should have known he wouldn't bring her somewhere there might be potential for her to escape.

"Now," Maddy said as she crossed the room, "I'll be back soon to get that bath filled for you."

She left the door open, and Eve didn't bother going to close it. Instead, she walked to the bed and sat down on the edge.

She was alive.

Matthew was far, far away.

And so far, Gabriel had done nothing to negate the promise that she would be unharmed.

There was still hope.

Not quite five minutes later, Jane appeared in the doorway, carrying a copper hip bath. She nodded toward Eve as she set the tub in the middle of the room and left again. She returned several times carrying buckets of water. Cold water first, then the water that had been heated on the stove, until the tub let off a gentle, beckoning steam.

Maddy reappeared with a cake of soap and a towel. "I'll just set these here for you. Jane went to look for some clothes more appropriate for heading up into the mountains this time of year. I'll make sure your dress is cleaned and packed for you before you go."

"Thank you. I appreciate your kindness."

"It's no problem, honey. We take care of each other out here. Life is tough, but it can be made a little easier every now and then by good friends."

The woman's words made Eve ache desperately for her own friends. But Alexandra and Courtney had left Boston for new lives of their own. As much as she wished to, Eve couldn't risk contacting them. It's exactly what Matthew would expect of her, so she had to stay as far from her old friends as possible. It was undeniably the hardest thing she'd had to do.

"Are you gonna need any help with your things?"

All her life, Eve had had a personal maid to assist her with bathing and dressing. After her marriage, only Lettie had been allowed to attend her.

Eve shook her head. "I'll manage."

"All right then. Once you're finished, we'll sit down to supper." With another warm smile, Maddy left the room, closing the door softly behind her.

Anxious for a bath and a real meal, Eve quickly started to shed her layers of clothing. Doing her best to keep the dirt from ending up all over the clean floor, she carefully folded each item after she removed it and set them all in a pile on top of her boots. It didn't take her very long. She had intentionally kept her wardrobe simple the day she'd left her Boston home for the last time.

Standing in the last of her undergarments, she carefully lifted her camisole over her head, hoping it wouldn't stick to the wounds that were still raw and open.

"I think I found something that'll fit you."

Eve jolted and spun around at Jane's entrance, but it was clear by the other woman's expression that she had already seen Eve's bare back. Jane's face darkened with fury, and her eyes flashed as she muttered vehemently, "That goddamned son of a bitch." Tossing the clothes to the bed, the suddenly furious woman spun on her heel and strode swiftly down the hall.

Eve's stomach dropped. Every instinct made her want to

hide. Or run. But all she could do was stand there, clutching her camisole to her chest as embarrassment burned under her skin.

She was still frozen in place in the middle of the room when Maddy came rushing in. "What on earth?"

Eve could only stare back at her in wretched silence.

"What happened?" Maddy asked again, her tone gentle despite the sharp concern in her eyes. "Jane can be a bit hot-headed, but there are only a few things that'll get her that fuming mad."

Tears gathered in Eve's eyes, and she closed them tight to hold them at bay.

The older woman came forward. "What is it?"

There was no point in hiding it. Jane wasn't likely to keep what she'd seen from the other woman. With a deep breath, Eve turned around.

"Oh, honey." Maddy's compassionate response was nearly more than Eve could take. She bowed her head and allowed the tears to fall.

Gabriel had just finished in the barn and was approaching the house when the screen door flew open and Jane stepped from the house onto the front porch.

The small, lean-muscled woman was clearly furious, and her fierce gaze was pinned on him. "You better have a damn good explanation for what I just saw, or you'll be staring down the barrel of my gun," she stated through gritting teeth, her hand hovering over the Colt strapped to her hip.

Gabriel stared back at her, every muscle in his body

primed. But he was not one to take action without knowing the cause. "What did you see?" he asked.

"You think I don't know what a beating looks like?"

His blood suddenly ran ice cold, and his lungs seized as though he'd just been dunked in a mountain stream after winter thaw.

He took ground-eating strides across the porch, stepping past Jane into the house. He knew which room Maddy and Jane reserved for guests, having made use of it a time or two in the past. He didn't stop until he filled the doorway.

Maddy must have heard him coming. She stood sentry a few steps inside the room, blocking further progression. A quick glance over her head revealed a hip bath steaming in the corner, a neatly folded pile of the woman's clothes on the floor by the bed, and Eve standing in the center of the room with a blanket wrapped around her shoulders.

He met Maddy's gaze and saw sympathy there...and silent pity.

What the hell?

Jane came up behind him. He could feel her angry tension, but he didn't bother turning around. He took another step into the room. The short shake of Maddy's head had him stopping his advance.

"How long has this young lady been in your company, Gabe?" Maddy asked. Though her voice was gentle, there was a thread of something stern and unbendable beneath it.

"Two days."

The older woman shifted her attention to Jane and gave a little shake of her head before she took a step back and to the side. The gesture seemed enough for Jane to relax her defensive stance beside him but did nothing to ease the grinding dread stuck in the back of Gabriel's throat.

He quickly took in the appearance of the woman standing still and silent before him. She was barefoot; her small feet peeked out from beneath the quilted blanket that looked as though it had been grabbed off the bed and tossed over her shoulders just before he'd arrived. She stood in profile, facing the bath. Her chin was level, and she stared straight forward as though she'd prefer not to acknowledge the drama around her.

"Show me."

His words hung in the room for a long moment before Maddy said softly, "You don't have to..."

"Show me," Gabriel repeated, speaking directly to Eve.

She turned her head, and her gaze slid to meet his. She looked...defeated. Shamed and weary.

His stomach tightened, and his hands clenched in fists as a sudden urge to fight claimed him. He couldn't protect her if he didn't know what threatened her. "Trust me," he urged in a low tone.

The truth shining from her gaze was like a knife to his gut.

She didn't trust him. Not even a little.

But she still moved to obey. It was more likely that she had no strength left to resist than that faith in his protection had her turning in place until she faced away from him.

Her pale hair was still loosely pinned up at the back of her head, but several strands had slid free. The slight dishevelment only added to her vulnerability. He almost stopped her, hating the indignity of the moment. But then she squared her shoulders and lifted her chin, and in the next second, she opened the blanket and let it fall the floor.

The knife in Gabriel's gut twisted harshly as he took in the sight before him with furious disbelief.

She wore only her white cotton pantalets, the waistband resting on the feminine curve of her hips beneath a trim waist. All down the full length of her narrow back—from her shoulders to the swell of her hips—were crisscrossed marks that could only have come from a whip.

Gabriel took a deep breath to dispel the heat in his lungs and pushed down the bile rising in his throat. He forced his hands to uncurl from tight fists as he took a measured step closer. Maddy muttered a stern sound of warning, but he ignored her and took another step.

The most obvious wounds were several days old. A few of the slashes had broken the skin. Scabs had formed and cracked in an effort to heal the exposed flesh. Other stripes were raised and swollen welts, still deep purple in color, while some milder ones were turning green and yellow around the edges.

And beneath these was evidence of older wounds—long healed, but still visible on her pale skin.

Gabriel took another step closer, and her slim body tensed with a subtle flinch. She feared his approach, and yet she did nothing to protect herself or to stop his advance.

That is what he had seen in her expression before she'd turned around, and perhaps at other moments in the last few days.

He had mistaken it for resignation. But he knew better now.

It was a strong determination to endure.

He knew that feeling well.

"Who the hell did that to you, girl?" Jane asked angrily from the doorway.

There would be no answer. He knew well enough now that Eve kept her secrets close, tucked safely behind the shadows in her blue eyes.

Fury rolled hot and wild through him. Instead of unleashing it as he wished to, he crouched down to pick up the blanket she'd dropped. Standing again, he gently placed it back over her shoulders. She grasped the edges and enclosed herself in the soft covering, but she did not turn around.

Then he turned away and strode from the room.

He heard Maddy speaking softly behind him, but he didn't bother making out her words as he continued down the hall and back out into the fresh air.

He felt sick and angry as hell.

The repeated, deliberate violence inflicted upon Eve was nothing shy of evil. Whoever had done that deserved the worst punishment imaginable. It didn't matter that she was safe now, whether she believed it or not. If she were his woman—

Gabriel stopped, bringing a sudden halt to his angry, ground-eating strides and the racing direction of his thoughts.

She wasn't his woman.

It was not his responsibility to avenge past wrongs against her. His job was to take her to Luke. Luke would decide her fate—her future. And if she asked it, he might even see a way to claim justice on her behalf. Though he went about it in unexpected and often unlawful ways, Luke was dedicated to seeing righteousness prevail when more conventional methods failed amidst the lawlessness of the western territories.

Gabriel preferred to remove himself from such things. He had been content to accomplish the tasks set for him. It was easy then to remain unattached to the outcome of their endeavors. He never interfered with Luke's role as leader and never questioned the man's decisions.

At the moment, it took far more effort than he liked to admit to remind himself of that.

ELEVEN

After Eve finished her bath, Maddy insisted on applying a salve to her back. Eve tried to refuse the offer, but the older woman was adamant. Her touch was soothing, but it was difficult for Eve to relax under the gentle ministrations.

She had always been an easygoing child, naturally kind and agreeable. Her mother often brought it up as contrast to her older brother's stubborn determination to go his own way. As an adult, she knew what was expected of her, and she did what was required in order to avoid disappointing anyone. Most people assumed her acquiescence was due to a biddable nature.

In truth, it was an overabundance of pride that most often guided her.

She hated feeling as though she might not live up to other people's standards. That she could fail in anyone's expectations, however unreasonable.

Her pride had kept her from revealing to her friends that her marriage was not the fairy tale it appeared. And pride had kept her under Matthew's thumb...believing she could change things. Believing she could change him. If she could just figure out the right things to say, the right things to do.

Such a fool she'd been—for far too long.

She closed her eyes as she thought of Gabriel gazing upon the evidence of her weakness and her shame. He had been all fire and fury when he'd come into her room, yet she hadn't felt the slightest bit of fear. Because he was always so obviously in control of everything he did and everything he felt. The two words he'd uttered—*Show me,* so low and commanding—had resonated deep in her bones. And when she'd met his gaze, something strange had happened to her. It was an odd rush of strength. As though he had gathered his stoic resolve and conveyed it to her with a look.

In that moment, she saw no point in denying his request.

She had been surprised, however, by the low sound that had issued from his chest. It was like the growl of a fierce predator. Instead of frightening her, the sound had reverberated within her, making her muscles tighten and her belly clench with a strange, elemental reaction.

And then, when he'd stepped up behind her and replaced the blanket, she'd felt the brief weight of his hands on her shoulders and had almost wanted to lean back against him.

It made no sense.

"That should do for now," Maddy said as she rose to her feet. "More should be applied in the morning, and I'll send a jar with you for your journey."

"Thank you," Eve said.

"Would you like to come down for supper, or would you rather eat up here?" the older woman asked.

"I think I'd prefer to take my meal here, if that is all right."

"Of course, honey." Maddy walked to the door, but before leaving, she turned back. "You know, I'm likely overstepping, but I figure I've reached an age where I can claim that prerogative. I'm not going to make any guesses as to who might have done that to you. But I can see this incident wasn't the first. Some scars take a while to heal, even after they've stopped hurting. I know that truth very well."

Eve didn't respond; she had no idea what to say. But Maddy didn't seem to be expecting any sort of reply.

The other woman smiled sadly and continued. "When I was young, my father decided it was his duty to purge me of my sinful ways. He did it for my own good, he said. For a while I believed him. I believed I deserved those beatings." Soft brown eyes met Eve's with firm intent. "I was wrong. No one deserves that kind of treatment. I ran away and never looked back. Now, I'll say again that I don't need to know how you came to be traveling with Gabe, but if you're running from the person who did that to you, Gabe and those boys up in the mountains might be able to help you."

Eve could see the sincerity in the other woman's expression. Maddy truly believed what she said. But Eve could not imagine seeking help from anyone, let alone a gang of outlaws. The last time she had placed her faith in someone, she'd wound up nearly broken by the experience. Still, feeling a need to somehow set the woman at ease, she replied, "I will consider it."

Maddy smiled and left the room.

Eve rose to her feet and removed the towel she had used to cover herself while Maddy applied the salve. She replaced it with the soft flannel nightgown from the pile of clothes Jane had gathered to lend her.

Tomorrow, she was expected to ride into the mountains, getting farther and farther away from the reach of civilization. If Matthew were looking for her, he was not likely to find her where she was going, but she was still heading toward the outlaws' hideout, and she had no assurance of what would happen to her once she got there.

The next morning, Eve woke to a curt knock on her door.

"Twenty minutes."

The sound of Gabriel's voice had her coming to full wakefulness in an instant. She dressed in the flannel undergarments, woolen stockings, split riding skirt, and flannel shirt she'd been given. After her bath the night before, she'd secured her hair in a single braid to keep it from getting tangled as she slept. She decided to leave it as it was, rather than try to twist it in a chignon, and stuffed her remaining hairpins into the deep pocket of her skirt, in case she'd want them later.

A wave of reluctance flowed through her as she left the room. Facing everyone after what had been revealed the day before was not something she relished. Aside from the embarrassment she already felt at having been so exposed, she dreaded seeing a look of pity in anyone's eyes. But she couldn't hide forever. So, she decided to face them with as much dignity as she could manage.

As she reached the kitchen, the smell of coffee mingled with the savory scent of bacon. Maddy was at the stove, stirring something in a pan as she spoke to someone else in the room. "The sun has barely topped the horizon. You can spare enough time to eat a full breakfast and enjoy some coffee."

"It's best we be on our way."

It was Gabriel. The sound of his voice and the way he reduced his sentences to the shortest possible form were becoming too readily familiar to Eve. She stopped outside the door, where she still couldn't see him and he couldn't see her.

A flash of heat swept through her as she recalled his heavy gaze on her bare back.

She could endure this. She had to.

Forcing herself past her hesitation, she stepped into the kitchen.

"Ah, good morning," Maddy said, waving Eve forward with a plate in hand. "Come have a seat at the table and eat some breakfast."

She set the plate down in front of the chair across from where Gabriel was seated, which meant Eve could no longer avoid looking at him.

He seemed too big for the table. He sat upright with his feet braced wide beneath it and his shoulders completely obscuring the back of his chair. A steaming mug of coffee was wrapped in one hand while the other rested on his thigh.

Eve looked for any sign of pity or curiosity. But his expression gave away nothing of his thoughts. His eyes were another story. Though she couldn't read anything specific in their dark depths, she felt something in his intent gaze that made her insides tighten.

She did her best to ignore the odd reaction. Or at the very least, to not reveal it.

"Coffee?" Maddy asked, approaching with a mug.

"Yes. Thank you," Eve replied, accepting the hot brew gratefully. She preferred tea but would accept anything that might fortify her for the journey ahead.

She had learned from Maddy the night before that it would take them a few more days to get where they were going and the way would be difficult.

Though Eve was a passably good rider, she had never done anything of this sort.

"Now, eat your breakfast. Jane is just making sure your saddlebags are packed with everything you'll need over the next few days," Maddy said. "It can get quite cold at night. Be sure to keep your coat secured and your head covered."

"Maddy," Gabriel interrupted quietly, firmly. "She'll be fine."

"Oh, I know you'll take good care of her. It's just gonna be rough for someone who's not used to such travel."

"She'll be fine," Gabriel repeated, and Eve got the strangest sense he was speaking more of her capabilities than his own as escort.

No. He was not an escort. He was her captor and an outlaw. She needed to keep thinking of him as such.

Not ten minutes later, they were ready to head out.

A large gray gelding had been readied for Eve, already loaded with full saddlebags and a blanket roll. Jane had come into the house just as they'd finished breakfast and handed Eve a large coat made of sheepskin. "It'll keep the chill away," she'd said gruffly before she'd turned away to grab a piece of cooling bacon off a plate on the counter.

Eve was immediately grateful for the warmth of the coat—and her woolen stockings and flannel underclothes—as she stepped out into the early morning. There was frost on the grass, and her breath left her lips in visible puffs.

"This here is Ranger," Jane explained as she released the gray horse from where his reins had been looped over the porch railing. "He's strong and sure-footed and knows his way through these mountains almost as well as Gabe."

Eve eyed the height of the horse's back with trepidation. Though he had been fitted with a solid western saddle that had stirrups, she wasn't sure she'd be able to get herself up there.

And then Gabriel was at her side. "I'll help."

Eve stiffened for just a second as she thought of his large hands on her body. But it wasn't fear that coursed through her in a warm wave. She took a breath to steady the swirling inside her and reached for the saddle. His hands came around her waist, and he lifted her clear off the ground. "Swing a leg over," he said.

As soon as she was seated astride in the saddle, he released her and turned toward his own horse. Jane handed her the reins as the horse adjusted his stance to accept her added weight. It was only then that she noticed the thick rope tying her horse to Gabriel's.

She wasn't surprised. Now that she had a mount, she would have a better chance at making it away on her own.

If she assured him that she had decided to take her chances in speaking with the leader of the outlaw gang, would he untie her? Did it even matter? She was a captive either way.

After some swift goodbyes, Gabriel turned his horse away from the ranch house, and Eve's horse followed obediently behind. In front of them, the Rockies rose fierce and impenetrable. Eve had never seen or felt anything as imposing and intimidating as the mountainous landscape. And she was about to ride right into it.

TWELVE

LOCATING A MISSING WOMAN WAS NOT THE KIND OF JOB HE typically took on. Not even back in the days when he'd been more active in the hunting of various prey.

The fact that the woman he was chasing down was a fancy-stepping lady of Boston society should have made him more than reluctant to take the job.

But here he was.

It seemed he could be motivated by something other than revenge and bloodlust after all.

Considering the task was a bit outside his usual experience, he'd been forced to reach out to an associate for assistance. He hated it, preferring to work alone—or at least, that had always been his way in the past. But he figured it couldn't hurt to call in a long-owed favor, especially since he was feeling an intense amount of pressure to locate the missing woman as quickly as possible.

As it was, his former professional acquaintance was able to narrow the search significantly. He'd determined that the woman had definitely left Boston, alone and apparently in a covert manner. There was an infinite number of places for a person to hide out in the more populated areas of the eastern

United States, but it appeared the greatest likelihood was that she'd headed west.

This news was both good and bad.

The western territories would not be an easy place for a tenderfoot lady from the big city to hide.

But there was a helluva lot of ground to cover.

Thirteen

The day was far more arduous than Eve could have imagined. She hadn't realized how much effort and discomfort she'd been spared by riding tandem with Gabriel the first couple days. Since she was unaccustomed to the western saddle or riding astride, soreness set in after only a few hours. Her general discomfort was compounded by the difficult terrain, which required a great deal of physical effort to maintain a proper seat while maneuvering along the occasionally treacherous trail. By the end of the day, her bottom was nearly numb, while the muscles of her back and limbs screamed in exhaustion.

At least there was plenty to see to keep her mind occupied. She never would have expected the mountains to be so beautiful. Alexandra had often waxed poetic about the years when she'd grown up in Montana, but Eve had always wondered if her cousin's descriptions were exaggerated by her nostalgia. But the farther they went into the rugged rise of the Rockies, the more awed she became by their surroundings. She felt tiny in the midst of the sheer scale of what surrounded her. Towering peaks that appeared just up ahead remained far distant throughout the day, never seeming to get any closer. That sense of smallness was strangely comforting, but also rather disconcerting as it forced her to see herself in a way she'd never had the opportunity to do before.

There was no doubt about it. The world was far larger and bolder than she'd ever realized while ensconced within Boston's elite society. Could she truly survive on her own—without family or friends for support?

When she'd left, her only goal had been to get as far away from Matthew as possible. The train she was on would have taken her to Sacramento, California. And from there, with the money she had saved, Eve had thought she might continue on to San Francisco or one of the other cities growing rapidly along the western coast. It didn't matter where she settled exactly, as long as it was somewhere she could start anew as someone else and get lost in a crowd of strangers.

But now...

With her money lost, California seemed so far away. Her plan was completely derailed. She had no other choice than to see where her current path led.

Or rather...where Gabriel led.

That was another thing that had managed to keep her preoccupied throughout the day.

He rode ahead of her most of the time, picking his way along the trail, obviously making an effort to find the safest route through a landscape that often went straight up the rocky face of the mountain or came ridiculously close to the edge of a cliff.

As she was starting to expect of him, he never showed the slightest bit of impatience or frustration, though she had to be slowing him down. His steady forward focus only wavered when he sent swift, assessing glances in her direction.

Even when riding silently several horse lengths ahead of her, the man could not be ignored. His presence filled her vision...and far too often, her thoughts. She spent more time than she would have liked to admit wondering about her very odd and consistent reactions to him.

She finally decided to acknowledge to herself how acutely aware of him she was...in a physical sense, but also in a way that went much deeper.

It wasn't just the way her gaze kept sweeping over the broad span of his shoulders, the straight fall of his black hair, or his thick muscled legs as they hugged his horse without need of a saddle. It was more than her admiration for how alert and attuned he was to every shift in the wind or the subtlest movement in the trees as they passed. He once brought their horses to a quiet halt, moments before a deer and her fawn crossed their path in the distance, as though he knew they were coming.

What affected her most was something that ran beneath all that.

It was his steady calm and quiet regard. It was the strength and assurance in his dark gaze. Though it made no sense, it was the way he made her feel safe and protected just by being near.

It unsettled her.

As the day continued toward evening and the scenery became more starkly beautiful and intimidating, the air became crisper and cooler. By the time the sun started to descend behind the rocky walls around them, she was huddled in her coat, tired and sore from the saddle and the effort it had taken to stay seated all day through the occasionally treacherous terrain while her thoughts careened wildly from the man riding in front of her to the past she had left behind and the freedom she desperately yearned for.

She barely noticed when Gabriel took them off the rugged trail they had been following to lead them up the side of an incline into a dense grouping of pine trees. Sharp branches brushed against her legs and arms, but her horse dutifully continued on behind the mustang. After a while, the path opened to a little clearing where they came to a slow stop.

Eve could hear the bubbling flow of water over a shallow rock bed, but she couldn't see the source.

"We'll camp here," Gabe said as he swung easily from his mustang's back.

Eve felt his flickering glance before he turned away from her to attend his horse. Carefully sliding her feet out of the stirrups, she felt a twinge of pain in her knees from having maintained the unfamiliar position all day. There would be no easy way to dismount. All she could do was try not to embarrass herself by revealing her weakness.

Leaning forward over the saddle horn, which she clutched in both hands, she swung her leg over the horse and tried to lower herself to the ground. She hadn't expected her arms and shoulders to be as weary as they were, and instead of a graceful descent, she dropped, landing hard in her borrowed boots. The jolt sent more pain through her knees, while her bruised bottom throbbed in protest and the skin across her back tightened painfully.

Forcing slow breaths through her nose, she rested her forehead against the smooth leather of the saddle. Her hands still tightly gripped the saddle horn. It was the only thing keeping her upright.

"What is it?" His voice came from directly behind her. It was a testament to her distress that she hadn't sensed his approach. But now that she knew he was there, her body reacted with a burst of heat and awareness.

She squeezed her eyes closed, refusing to acknowledge him. She simply needed a few moments to reclaim her balance and poise.

He issued a low mutter of words she didn't understand—though they sounded like something that was part growl, part apology—as he swept her off her feet to lift her high against his chest. Embarrassment at revealing her weakness burned beneath her skin. But the pain receded from her limbs, leaving only the discomfort of his arm pressed to her back.

She glanced at his face.

His broad features were set in a harsh expression with his heavy brows low over his gaze. He pressed his full lips together firmly in obvious irritation as he strode swiftly and powerfully away from the horses to set her down on a patch of grass.

Eve tensed in anticipation of a reprimand...or worse. Despite her pain and exhaustion, she sat stiff and proud, awaiting the consequences of his anger.

He crouched in front of her. His strength was evident in the muscles of his forearms as they braced atop his thighs and in his large hands, only inches from her. Her attention fell to those hands. His long, blunt-tipped fingers were deft and efficient in dressing a rabbit or starting a fire. His grip was strong enough to lift her easily off the ground with one hand.

He could do a great deal of damage if he curled his fist in anger.

A low sound rumbled in his throat, and it was all she could do not to flinch. His brows lowered over his gaze, and the muscles in his jaw bunched. "You have no need to fear me, Eve."

She met his gaze with more courage than she felt. "You're angry."

"I am," he admitted. "I failed to detect your discomfort. I should have allowed more rest today." Something flickered across his face, something unreadable. "You thought I was angry with you?"

Eve returned his questioning stare. What could she say? Experience had taught her to be wary of a man's displeasure, that frustration often led to fury, and to always anticipate retaliation.

She remained silent as his gaze slid past the barriers she'd long ago erected in a desperate attempt at self-preservation. He seemed to see right down into the heart of her fear, to know it was as much about doubting herself as about distrusting others.

He sighed, long and deep. The sound slid past her defenses, curling through her insides. "I would never hurt you. Not in anger or for any other reason," he said darkly.

Eve sat in stunned silence as he stood and strode back to their mounts.

She had initially thought Gabriel's stoic manner was reflective of a lack of emotion. Every moment in his company proved that that assumption was ridiculously far from the truth. His thoughts and feelings were certainly deeply concealed, but they were there—rich and complex. What she'd seen in him just now had been entirely unexpected.

Compassion. It was not something she was familiar with.

She had been cared for, protected, and guided by her family and a household of servants. She knew she was loved by Alexandra and Courtney, the two people in her life who knew her best.

But compassion was something else. It was kindness for the simple sake of it. Receiving the consideration from such an unexpected source left her unsure how to respond.

She tensed when Gabriel reappeared before her. She wasn't sure if he'd moved that silently or if she had been that distracted by her thoughts. But one moment he was just there, and her breath caught on a stifled gasp.

Lowering himself in front of her, he offered something wrapped in brown paper. "Maddy packed some food." His gaze dropped to the ground for a moment before he lifted it again to her face. "There's also some salve. If you need—"

"No," she blurted out quickly. She would not be able to manage applying the healing salve herself, and just the thought of baring her back to his gaze again—let alone his touch—sent waves of fire and ice through her. "There's no need," she asserted.

He studied her for a long moment, his eyes slightly narrowed. Then he gave a short nod.

Eve shifted her attention to the small paper-wrapped parcel, which revealed some cold chicken and a biscuit. Though she was ravenously hungry, she somehow resisted the urge to grab it with both hands and devour it immediately. She hadn't quite forgotten the manners that had been drilled into her.

While she imagined sinking her teeth into the plump chicken breast, Gabriel remained crouched before her, balancing effortlessly on the balls of his feet, his knees spread wide.

She lifted her eyes to his in question.

"Do we need a rope tonight?" he asked.

Eve was surprised by the question. If she said no, would he really take her word for it? Now that she had a horse of her own and supplies in her bags, she was much more prepared to strike out on her own than she had been before.

But she still believed talking to the leader of the outlaw gang was her best option. Her only option, really. And that meant remaining in the company of this man, despite the odd way he made her feel.

"I will go with you to the valley." She met his stare, trying to show more courage and conviction than she might have felt. "But I will not be ransomed," she said.

Nothing changed in his expression, and he didn't try to argue the point. Instead, he seemed to study her. His presence was calm, steady, and immovable. "Who hurt you?"

He asked the question in a low and private tone, as if he wished to keep the conversation just between them. As though he would not even share it with the wind or the trees or the horses that stood several paces away.

"It doesn't matter," she replied, her voice as quiet as his.

As she said the words, they felt like a lie.

She wanted it to be true. She wanted the past she left behind to be unimportant. She had put her life, her person, her trust in a man who had betrayed and dishonored her. The wounds he'd inflicted upon her body would heal. They might leave scars, but the wounds on her soul bothered her more. No matter how far away she got from Matthew or how long she continued to run, she doubted she'd ever be able to heal the damage he'd done to her soul.

"Will this person come for you?"

The idea of Matthew finding her made her stomach

twist with a specific kind of fear. A fear he had instilled in her minute by minute, day by day from the moment she became his. He had convinced her of his right to treat her as he saw fit. He had convinced her that she existed only as an extension of himself. He believed her to be his property, purchased and formed to suit his needs—and his needs alone.

There had been a time, not long ago, when she had believed a wife's place was at her husband's side. She'd believed that once such a commitment to honor and obey was made, nothing could tear it asunder.

Until she realized the man she'd married had never honored the words he'd spoken that day in the church in front of hundreds of their family and friends. He'd broken every vow he'd uttered.

To save herself, she too had to forsake her marriage vows, and she felt not the slightest bit of remorse about it.

Would he come after her?

Yes. Most definitely.

She had done all she could to ensure he would not have a trail to follow, but Matthew was clever and well connected and utterly ruthless.

Though she provided no answer to Gabriel's low-spoken question, he did not bother to repeat it. Instead, he made a short sound in his throat and rose to his feet. He seemed to have gleaned an answer despite her lack of response.

And he was not pleased by it.

FOURTEEN

A FRIGID CHILL SWEPT UP EVE'S SPINE. SHE CURLED deeper into the tight ball of warmth beneath the woolen blanket. She was lying on her side, facing the low-burning campfire with her knees drawn up close to her chest and her hands tucked between her legs.

But still, the chill of night pervaded her bones.

It felt as if she had slept for only a short while before she'd been awakened by cold pressing in around her. She couldn't fight it off to fall back to sleep, no matter how hard she tried. Cold had invaded her body, making her muscles tense and tremble with an involuntary effort to produce some warmth. She shifted closer to the fire, and though she could feel its heat against her face and knees, the warmth did not go further and she continued to shiver.

As her teeth began to chatter, there was a soft sound of subtle movement across the fire. She stilled instantly.

In the hours she'd lain awake in the darkness, fighting off the cold, the man who made up the large shadowed form beyond the low flames had barely moved. All she had heard from him had been the slow, even rhythm of his breath.

But now he rose to his feet in a solid, graceful movement.

Eve closed her eyes, not wanting him to know she was awake. He made no noise, and she did not realize he had approached her until she felt a disturbance of the cold air against her back.

She flinched sharply at the sudden tingling rush his nearness triggered across her nerves.

"I offer warmth. Nothing more."

"I'm fine," Eve replied, but her voice was too tight, and the words barely made it past her chattering teeth.

He muttered something roughly beneath his breath that she didn't understand as he stretched out on the ground behind her. Alarm lit across her nerves. Her body tensed for flight, but she had nowhere to go. She couldn't get any closer to the fire without rolling right into it. If she tried to rise, he could easily grab her and pull her down.

"Sleep. I won't harm you." His words were low and gruff in the night.

Eve's muscles began to ache, and her heart pounded with trepidation and the acute intense awareness of *him*. Solid. Male. Close, but not touching. He lay there, still and silent behind her while the warmth of his body started to reach out to her. He might not be touching her, but she felt him nonetheless.

Anticipation and anxiety rode high in her chest as the seconds turned into minutes. She had never lain in such intimate proximity with someone. Her brief experiences in the marriage bed were not even remotely comparable to what she felt lying between the low-flickering fire and Gabriel's large body.

Eventually, the initial shock wore off and she found

herself relaxing, as though her body accepted the lack of risk and danger well before her mind came to the same conclusion. He'd said he wouldn't hurt her. And it seemed she believed him.

From that first time he offered her water and in each instance afterward, unless he had a reason to be near her, he deliberately kept himself at a certain distance. Even when they'd shared his horse, he'd allowed a space between them. Aside from when she'd nearly fallen to the ground after riding all day, he'd never put his hands on her without expressly obtaining her permission or giving her an opportunity to refuse.

In truth, he had shown her as much courtesy as the gentlemen she'd known back home. Perhaps even more.

And as warmth slowly spread through her body, she could not resist the softening of her tense muscles. Her eyes drifted closed, and she snuggled a bit deeper beneath her blanket.

For a while, she listened to the sound of the crackling fire and the deep, steady breaths rising and falling behind her. But eventually, against her better judgment, she was lulled to sleep.

She didn't trust him.

She feared him.

But now he understood why. Her fear was her protection.

From the moment she'd awakened after being dragged from the train, surrounded by strangers and outlaws, she had shown a resilience and courage to be admired. She never once panicked or screamed, despite the terror in her gaze. She'd listened and observed.

While the men had discussed what to do with her once they'd realized Ramsey's mistake, Gabriel had watched her. Her eyes had been closed. The others likely thought her asleep. Gabriel had known better.

She had been gaining information.

Before she'd fallen asleep just a moment ago, instead of jumping to her feet when he settled beside her, as he knew she likely wished to, she had remained still and thoughtful.

He wished he knew what had traveled through her mind until she'd relaxed. But at least she'd let herself fall asleep.

Gabriel remained stretched out on his back. With his eyes closed, he was acutely aware of the cold earth beneath him and the chilling brush of the night air. Night birds called in the trees above; the whispered dance and crackle of low-burning flames and the soft, occasional movements of the horses filtered through the dark. And he felt the silent tension of the woman beside him. Though she'd slipped into sleep, her body still possessed a shell of steady resistance, like a quiet, constant barrier.

He'd known she wouldn't like him lying next to her, but he couldn't let her freeze all night when he could prevent it. It wouldn't do her any favors tomorrow if she was dead tired on her horse, her body too stiff to move. Today was a tough ride, but tomorrow would be worse. He'd have to take things slower, stop more often. She'd be sore, and he now knew she wouldn't say anything about her discomfort.

There was also the matter of her injuries.

His stomach turned at the thought of the marks that scored her slim back. Significant force had been used to cut so deeply into her skin. Her ability to conceal what must have been very painful for the first couple days in his company had him wondering just how long she had been practicing such concealment.

The anger he felt on her behalf surprised him.

From the day he'd been taken from his family as a boy, he had deliberately cultivated an attitude of detachment from the people around him. It was easy to do. Those years with the Sloans, the missionary couple who had taken him in as part of their *good work*, had only reinforced his desperate desire to keep himself protected from the harm people could inflict with their good intentions.

And when he'd finally started to make his way in the world alone, it had been second nature to keep others at a distance. He trusted Luke and most of the others with his life, and he was loyal to them, but he could not call them friends. That required something he was no longer capable of.

Yet his reaction to seeing what the woman who called herself Eve had endured was not one of detachment. He hadn't felt such intense fury over someone else's pain since he'd been a boy. And he had seen plenty of suffering in the years since.

But it wasn't just her pain he felt like a lightning bolt to his chest. It was her spirit. Her fear, her strength, and her silent resistance. He'd never seen anyone who held so much inside. It required a supreme amount of discipline to maintain such control.

He knew that well enough.

Realizing dawn would be coming soon, he willed himself to sleep.

It seemed like only moments later that he had awoke

with a rush of alarm sliding through him. He immediately knew the cause as the woman beside him moaned softly in her sleep. Though he was not touching her, he could feel the tension in her body.

He turned toward her and lifted himself to his elbow. She was curled tightly into a ball, burying her face in her raised arms.

His instinct was to wake her from the nightmare she seemed to be trapped in. But his touch would likely cause terror rather than comfort.

Instead, he spoke in a gentle tone so as not to startle her. "Wake up."

She moaned again, then gasped, arching her back sharply.

"Wake up, Eve," he said, more firmly this time.

His voice must have reached her, or perhaps the dream had reached its end, because she drew a swift breath and came to sudden awareness. Her gaze flew around her as she desperately tried to place herself in the correct time and place. When she finally turned her head enough to see Gabriel leaning over her, she froze.

Her breath stopped passing through her parted lips. Her eyes widened, and her pupils dilated until the blue around them was no more than a thin ring. Her pulse thrummed swiftly at the base of her throat.

Gabriel didn't move, and he didn't speak.

He could have risen to his feet and given her some distance, likely frightening her further until she realized he was walking away. But some silent instinct told him to remain where he was, urged him to prove he was no threat by showing her she was safe in his proximity.

As they lay there locked in the moment, their gazes unwavering, he noted the slow rise of her chest as she drew a breath. Then a shift in her eyes as the terror slid back into the shadows she so carefully protected.

"Are you all right?" he asked.

Her lashes fluttered over her gaze, but she did not look away. "It's morning."

Gabriel was not expecting that response, and he lifted a brow as he replied, "It is."

"Did you sleep?" she asked.

"Enough."

She said nothing more as she continued to stare into his eyes. He saw the uncertainty swirling behind the blue, but he saw something else as well. Curiosity, resistance, heat.

Bare inches separated them, yet it felt like miles. Inside himself, Gabriel could feel the call of her soul to his. He could see by the pulse in her throat that their hearts were beating in unison. Any other woman, any other time, he might have lifted his hand to touch her. He might have rested his hand on her hip or brushed his thumb over the curve of her cheek.

But not this woman.

After what seemed like a second stretched to an age, her eyes swept to the side as she pushed to a seated position. Her expression tightened with the movement; a subtle reaction, quickly controlled and concealed. But Gabriel had seen it.

Self-directed anger coursed through him. He should have insisted on treating the wounds the night before. But he had been reluctant to challenge her barriers.

"You need salve," he said as he rose to his knees and reached for the saddlebags.

"No," she argued, the word tight and short. "I'm fine."

Gabriel paused, holding the small jar Maddy had packed. He said nothing, just looked at the tense line of her back, which appeared far too slim and gentle to be carrying such a painful burden.

"You would rather go through the day with your skin feeling like it's being stretched over hot coals?"

His challenging words forced her chin up a notch, but she did not refute him.

"The damaged skin will continue to tighten as it heals. It'll burn and sting. You know it's true," he added roughly, noting the way her jaw tensed in acknowledgment of his words. He couldn't see her face as he kneeled behind her, but he knew her expression would give away very little of what she was feeling or thinking. "The salve will help."

Gabriel waited.

As the horses began to stir with soft huffs of breath and a gentle shifting of weight. As birds sang from the trees that surrounded the small clearing, and the water flowed joyfully nearby. As the small, pale-haired woman sat silently in front of him.

If she refused again, he would let it be.

He watched and waited. Another minute passed, and he saw her chin lower by the smallest degree. Then her hands came up, and she started to unfasten the heavy coat Jane had lent her.

Gabriel remained unmoving, but something inside him gave a hard, swift twist. And that twist opened something else, releasing a wave of warmth through his muscles and over his nerves.

In this one small thing, at least, she had decided to offer him her trust.

She lifted the coat off her shoulders and let it fall down her arms to settle on the ground around her hips. Then she did the same with her shirt, releasing the buttons, then lifting and sliding it down her bare arms. The tails remained tucked into her skirt, but her back was bare now except for the soft flannel undergarment.

Swollen lines in shades of red, purple, and green disappeared in an angry pattern beneath the edge of the soft flannel. Her shoulders were curved forward protectively.

Gabriel's stomach tightened, and his jaw ached from clenching his teeth against the snarl that rose inside him. If he did not regain his self-control before he touched her, she would feel the fury inside him. She might misunderstand his anger, and he would lose the sliver of trust he'd gained.

He watched as she brought her chin back up and straightened her spine, just before she slipped the straps off her shoulders and lowered the undergarment to her waist.

FIFTEEN

He hesitated.

She wished he wouldn't. Now that she accepted his assistance, she needed it done and over with—before she lost what scraps of courage she'd managed to gather around herself.

The last few days had been intensely uncomfortable. But Maddy's salve had helped. Beyond her expectation. And in the hurry to leave the house yesterday morning, there hadn't been time to apply more.

Unfortunately, she couldn't possibly spread the salve herself.

Her decision to accept his offer had been an act of pure self-preservation.

It was also a risky test of sorts.

At some point the night before, she had decided to believe his declaration that he wouldn't hurt her. This was his chance to prove it.

Keeping her arms crossed over her naked chest, she closed her eyes, refusing to acknowledge the tear that slipped free as she did so. Her stomach turned with dread and fear and a glimmer of quiet hope as she waited for his touch.

The salve had been cooled through the night, and at the first sweep across her skin, a chill swept down her spine, causing gooseflesh to rise. Eve kept her teeth tightly clenched against the urge to gasp. Almost immediately, the medicinal elements of the mixture started to take effect, causing a slight tingling where it was applied. The smell of the ointment drifted around her, making her nostrils flare.

He applied the salve swiftly and with long strokes. Though his touch was nearly as gentle as Maddy's had been, her tender flesh felt every pass acutely. She tried to imagine what he was seeing and wondered what he was thinking. Did he see her as weak and foolish? Did he guess at the shame each stroke of the lash had embedded in her skin?

When he reached the worst of her wounds, Eve held her breath and forced herself to remain still and unflinching.

In her mind's eye, she saw his large, capable hands carefully spreading the salve in slow, deliberate strokes. She saw his effort at keeping his touch as light as possible to avoid hurting her further. It was odd to be so vulnerable as she sat still and half-naked beneath his touch. Was she only imagining that she could sense his consideration, his focused care?

Matthew would have exploited the moment in every way possible. He'd have expressed his disappointment in her inability to be stronger and less needy. He'd have subtly and expertly reminded her that her place was to serve him, not the other way around.

Yet Gabriel said nothing. His presence was calm and quietly assuring as he continued to apply the soothing salve. He was thorough, quick, and gentle. The strikes of Matthew's whip had reached as low as the flare of her hips, and she sat up straighter as Gabriel's fingers feathered across the small of her back and lower.

And then he was finished.

She heard the lid of the jar being replaced and the soft sounds as he returned the salve to her bags.

"I'm sorry." The two words were uttered in a low, rough tone that seemed to rasp over her taut nerves.

Before she could determine what he was apologizing for, let alone figure out a proper response, he had risen to his feet and walked away.

Eve tensed with a flicker of irrational panic.

Then she heard the low tones of his voice as he spoke to the horses where they had been secured beyond a collection of bushes. The salve required some time to soak in before she could replace her clothing. He likely knew that and had left to afford what little privacy was possible.

Opening her eyes, she glanced around.

The camp was lit by random patterns from the morning sun as it filtered through the trees. The campfire had been reduced to black ash releasing lazy tendrils of smoke that lifted lightly in the breeze. Looking behind her, she saw the horse blanket he had lain on through the night, and a shiver danced down her spine—a shiver that had nothing to do with the cold air of morning.

Not only had she managed to fall asleep beside him, but she had slept quite deeply in the proximity of his added warmth. Heat infused her cheeks. It was unfathomable.

He did not return until nearly thirty minutes later. She had already redressed and was waiting quietly for him. The moment he came back into camp, his eyes sought hers, a question in their depths. Without conscious consideration, she understood what he was asking. Warmth rolled through her. She calmly returned his watchful stare to assure him she was well.

After the moment of silent communication, he went about starting the coffee and digging out something to eat before they started on their way.

That day progressed much as the one before except for the fact that they continued at a near-steady incline as they made their way back and forth up mountainsides or through deep, cavernous ravines. The air grew colder and thinner as they ascended farther into the mountains, yet their horses barely seemed affected by the more challenging conditions. Another difference was that Gabriel orchestrated brief yet frequent stops throughout the day, instructing Eve to dismount and walk around to keep her legs and back from getting stiff.

Despite the occasional rests, it was still a physically trying day. By the time they stopped for camp that night, the sun descended beyond the mountain peaks, painting the sky in lovely shades of pink and purple, and the night air was quickly growing colder.

After their meal of roasted grouse was finished, Gabriel met her gaze across the fire.

"Shall I apply more salve?" he asked.

The words were warm with consideration. That he asked rather than insisted was not lost on Eve. The choice to refuse him was present in the air. But she didn't want to refuse. The salve would make her more comfortable through the night and already seemed to be accelerating the healing process. Refusing served little benefit.

But accepting meant she would have to bare herself again to this man's touch.

Not completely unexpectedly, the thought did not give rise to fear or trepidation.

He had gained her trust in this at least. He would not harm her. She believed that.

Meeting his patient gaze, she gave a small nod.

As he rose to his feet to fetch the salve from her saddlebags, she removed her coat and slipped her shirt and undergarment from her shoulders. Sitting straight with her legs drawn against her chest in an effort to preserve some modesty, she wrapped her arms around her knees and waited.

She felt more than heard him as he settled behind her.

The warmth of his presence was becoming too familiar.

He did not have to touch her for her to know he was there. She did not have hear or see him to imagine his movements.

"It looks better," he said in that low voice.

"It feels better," she acknowledged.

The first cool touch of salve on her upper back had her drawing a swift breath, but the cream was soon warmed by the spread of his fingers, and a sigh slid from her lips. After a bit, she turned her head and rested her cheek on her knees as she allowed her eyes to close.

She wasn't sure whether the physical challenges of the day, the tingling effects of the medicinal salve, or the soothing comfort of his touch was what had her body slowly relaxing. One moment she was breathing softly and steadily, listening to the sounds of night animals and the flow of the nearby creek, and in the next moment, she felt Gabriel rising behind her and heard him replacing the jar in the saddlebag.

"I'm going to see to the horses."

Eve remained unmoving on her blanket long after he left her alone.

There had been something odd in his voice when he'd spoken. The low, soothing rhythm had been layered with a new roughness. It was subtle, but Eve had heard it. She'd *felt* it. Like the brush of raw silk over bare skin—soft and textured.

She remained as she was for quite a while, knowing he wouldn't return until the salve had soaked into her skin and she was returned to a state of full dress. She also knew he was close enough to be at her side in a moment if she called out a need for him.

Outlaw. Captor. Protector.

Eventually, the chill of the night mountain air urged her to replace her clothing and don the thick coat. Curling up on the bedroll, she tucked her blanket snugly beneath her chin and drew her bent legs close to her chest. Already, a persistent nighttime chill crowded around her. Once the campfire died down, she would have a difficult time keeping the cold at bay.

Would Gabriel insist on sleeping beside her again?

Did she want him to?

A swift tightening in her belly did not give her the answer. Carrying with it a feeling of trepidation and anticipation, it only gave rise to more questions.

Though her eyes were closed and his steps made no noise on the soft forest floor, she knew the moment Gabriel returned. She knew his silent, measured approach by the acceleration of her heart rate and the way her senses seemed to reach for him, seeking the sound of his breath, the scents of cedar, horse, and wool she had come to associate with him.

So, she was not surprised to find him so close when he finally spoke.

"The night will get colder. Will you accept my warmth?" he asked. The low timbre of his voice rolled gently over her nerves, eliciting delicate chills that had nothing to do with the mountain air.

Refusing the warmth he offered out of pride would only hurt her. It was the logical and practical choice to accept. An act of prudence. Of survival.

Then why did it feel so intimate?

Her response was no more than a whisper. "I will."

He must have heard her since he lowered himself to the ground behind her. Again, he was careful not to touch her, but remained close enough to block much of the night wind.

She should probably be worried about allowing him to get so close. She should be more discerning in regard to the comfort and security he offered in multiple ways, both obvious and subtle.

But she was tired, and the heat from his body quickly soaked through her blanket and the layers of clothing she wore. Within minutes, she drifted to sleep.

Gabriel woke slowly the next morning, just as the sun was starting to send its light into the sky, the golden rays framing the eastern mountaintops like a crown.

The air was cold enough for him to see his breath, but he was quite warm.

Some hours ago, the woman sleeping beside him had shifted closer. He had been awakened by the subtle movement, his muscles tensing as he waited for her to become aware of what she was doing. But she never did. And as her body met his, she curved her spine to better fit her slim back along the length of his side.

It had taken him a while to fall asleep again as the quiet passage of her breath matched the rise and fall of his chest.

She had stayed there—snug to his side—the rest of the night. But now it was morning, and Gabriel sensed she would not wish to awaken in such a position.

Carefully, he eased himself away from her and rose to his feet.

He went first to check on the horses, then stepped off to relieve himself. They would reach the valley tonight if they made good time. Tomorrow, if the way was difficult. Then Gabriel would explain the situation to Luke, and his responsibility to Eve would be at an end.

He should feel relieved.

He felt many things, but relief was not one of them.

Taking a deep breath to dispel the uncomfortable tension in his chest, he lifted his gaze to the swiftly lightening sky. He frowned and drew a long inhale through his nose. Though the stretch of pale blue overhead was without clouds, there was a sense of something approaching on the wind.

He returned to the camp to see that the woman had risen and was seated close to the smoking embers of the fire. Her bedroll had already been tied up.

She looked up at his approach, and he saw nothing in her gaze to suggest she was aware of how closely they'd slept. He quickly cut off the keen prick of disappointment. She had not intentionally sought solace from him in the night.

It had been nothing more than a body's instinctive craving for warmth.

He understood that. It was senseless to imagine anything else.

He went to his shoulder bag and withdrew some hardtack and jerky. She rose to her feet as he came toward her and accepted the meager offering from his hand.

"Bad weather is coming," he said. "We'll need to get ahead of it."

She tipped her head back to look up at him. Her gaze was thoughtful, searching. Then a faint blush pinkened her cheeks.

Perhaps she recalled something of the night before after all.

"It'll be a rough day," he added.

"I understand."

"Your back?"

Her gaze flickered, but she did not look away. "It's better. I do not need the salve this morning."

He searched her features for any indication she was not being truthful. He saw none.

"Ten minutes."

She nodded, and Gabriel walked away to ready the horses.

SIXTEEN

THE BAD WEATHER HIT MIDDAY AND GRADUALLY worsened. Wind and rain slanted and swirled as they trudged along narrow paths and steep inclines. For several hours, the horses fought to keep their footing on rain-slick rocks or slogged through mud that sucked at their hooves.

Eve was soaking wet down to her skin and cold clear through her bones. While her oiled coat did much to ward off the wetness for a while, even that lost its usefulness when her hair became wet and water dripped down her neck to soak everything beneath. Her teeth chattered, and her hands were nearly numb as they gripped the reins. But she'd been in this state for so many hours now, she wasn't sure she could remember how it felt to be otherwise.

And still they trudged on.

Eve found herself grateful for how dutifully her horse followed Gabriel's while allowing her to lower her head and tuck her chin toward her chest to keep the pelting rain from her face. It became all she could do to hold on to the saddle horn and keep her feet in the stirrups as they inched their way around rocky outcroppings before starting a winding ascent along a narrow, rocky ledge with the mountain rising high on one side and dropping off sharply on the other.

Water not only fell from the sky, but also flowed down the mountainside in swift streams that crossed the trail on its way down. Gritting her teeth and closing her eyes against the sight of just how swiftly they could slip or stumble and fall to a certain death, she placed her faith in Gabriel's guidance and her horse's abilities. If continuing onward got them out of the elements that much sooner, she could endure the wet and cold and a terrain that grew more and more treacherous as the rain continued to fall.

Finally, they had reached a slight broadening of the path. Pine trees cropped up along the trail, providing intermittent shelter. A sudden, fierce gust of wind swept against them, sending the rain in a slant. If Eve hadn't found the strength to grip hard to the saddle horn, the wind might have sent her toppling from her horse's back.

Gabriel kept them close to the mountainside, but he must have given his mount some added encouragement because their pace picked up by half.

Sometime later—though perhaps it was only a few minutes—they turned toward the mountain face. It took Eve a moment to realize that they weren't riding straight into a hard rock wall; that there was a crevice that angled into the mountain. As soon as they entered it, the flurry of wind softened, though she could still hear it whirling against the rock, and the rain continued to fall from above in great torrents.

The crevice was perhaps ten feet wide at its opening but continued to narrow with each step. When they got to a point where the horses could go no farther, Gabriel stopped and turned back to her. Water ran down the planes of his face in never-ending rivulets. "We'll stop here for the night."

"Here?" Eve's voice came out tight and short from her chattering jaw.

"There's a small cave."

She nodded stiffly.

After dismounting, Eve followed Gabriel into the recesses of the crevice. The muscles in her legs trembled with every step, and her spine ached from fatigue.

What he had called a cave was little more than the end of the crevice where the mountain formed a rocky overhang to shelter beneath.

Gabriel lowered himself to settle his back against one wall of the cave while he propped his foot against the opposite wall. Looking up, he lifted his hand toward her. "Come."

Exhausted and cold, she put her hand in his. He gently drew her down to sit between his legs, positioning her so she rested sideways against him. Her lower back rested against his braced leg and her head fell against his shoulder while her legs curled between his.

With one of his arms wrapped around her shoulders and the other across her hips, he served as a source of comfort and warmth in that tiny cave.

"We'll stay here until the rain lets up," he murmured roughly. "Rest. Sleep if you can."

The words, spoken low and so close to her ear she could feel the brush of his breath against her neck, caused a roll of heat in her center. For a second, she was tempted to burrow deeper into his arms and nearly turned to nestle her face against his warm throat. It would have been an instinctive attempt at seeking comfort. But even understanding the base need that motivated the desire to get closer to him, she was stunned by how deep the longing went.

Of course, she refrained from acting on the impulse. But not without a twinge of regret for all the things that held her back.

Unable to do much of anything except shiver for a good long while, it was some time before Eve began to experience an easing of the tension in her limbs. With the mountain sheltering them from the worst of the weather and the horses standing sentry at the entrance to the little cave, she soon began to feel almost cozy.

Admittedly, a great deal of that was due to the man who cushioned and cradled her body with his own. She could not imagine that the rocky wall at his back was very comfortable, but at least the body heat shared between them made the heavy wetness of their clothing nearly bearable.

All notions of propriety dictated that she should be resisting the physical contact. She should at least feel some trepidation at being held so intimately. But all she could acknowledge was a pervading sense of peace.

And as soon as she felt that, she slipped into sleep.

She had no idea how long she'd slept when she was awakened by Gabriel's warm, dark voice. "Time to be on our way."

Eve stirred slowly and with great effort. As she came to full wakefulness, she realized that although she could still hear the rush of wind against rock, there was no rainfall.

Opening her eyes, she saw that it was full night. A glance outward from their shelter showed a faint glow of inconstant moonlight trying to push through swift-moving clouds.

"It's still night," she stated, though of course, he knew that.

"It will be dawn soon. We must make our way over the rise before the skies open again."

"You expect more rain?"

She took the low sound that rolled from the back of his throat to be a yes.

Reluctantly and tentatively, she shifted her legs and tried to sit upright.

Gabriel's arms fell away. He remained still and patient as she struggled to bring life back to her limbs and strength to her spine, while holding back the groan of pain as the soreness in her body became apparent.

"Can you rise?" he asked.

The thin layer of concern in his voice was enough to awaken Eve's pride. "I'm fine."

With clenched teeth, she pushed herself to her feet, bracing her hand on the rocky wall to steady herself as the stiffness in her body started to ease.

Meanwhile, Gabriel rose beside her in one graceful, effortless roll of his large body.

After a brief glance, likely to ensure she wouldn't collapse, he went first to her horse, checking the animal over for any distress. Then he looked to Eve and nodded.

His expression, though stoic as usual, still somehow conveyed subtle and patient concern, a slight question, and confidence all at once.

Eve shook off as much of her physical discomfort as she could manage and walked toward him.

Within minutes they were on their way again, heading ever upward along the twisting, turning trail. Making their way by the shifting light of the moon and Gabriel's knowledge of the path. After maybe an hour or so, the sky started to lighten with shades of lavender and gray. And shortly after that, they crested a dramatic rise.

Gabriel brought his horse to a stop and waited for Eve's mount to come up beside him.

Together, they gazed out at the misty landscape spread out before them. Imposing peaks rose all around, their sharp angles a striking contrast against the cloudy sky. And far below, deep, shadowed crevices cut through the rock to make space for pine trees and hidden wildlife.

It was a severe landscape and a forbidding one.

Eve never would have imagined such a place existed. It was beautiful and frightening. But the fear it inspired was invigorating because she was going be passing through those rocky passes and over the harsh ridges. The smell of the pines was already becoming familiar to her, as were the movement of her horse over the uneven terrain and the sight of Gabriel's broad shoulders leading the way.

She turned to look at the man beside her.

He sat straight and still on his horse. His eyes gazed outward, surveying the path ahead, but Eve suspected a greater focus was directed inward. He seemed to be contemplating something that went beyond the question of what route to take.

She wanted to ask him what he was thinking.

She shouldn't care.

She did.

Then he turned his head, and his steady gaze found hers.

Warmth unfurled in her center. Warmth and a strange but undeniable sense of assurance. Despite the difficult way ahead, he would see her safely through it.

"There will be more rain, but today, we will reach the valley," he said.

Eve swallowed down the small rise of trepidation. "I'm ready."

Gabriel gave a nod. Turning back to the path ahead, he uttered a soft command, and his horse started down the rise.

SEVENTEEN

They made it a few hours through the hazy morning before the clouds darkened overhead and rain poured down in steady, unrelenting streams. Within a short time, Eve was once again soaked through to the skin and shivering from head to toe.

Despite the miserable conditions, she decided quite forcefully to be grateful that at least they were not being buffeted by constant swirling wind. She was also becoming more and more grateful for the sure-footed horse that continued to carry her through the rocky mountain passes with very little direction from her as the hours spread out in an endless practice in endurance.

As expected, Gabriel said very little throughout the day. But his presence remained a strong reminder that she was not alone along the forbidding trail, even though he seemed barely affected by the harsh conditions.

As the heavy gray of day started to make way for the dark of night, the path they were on began to take a sharp descent. Lifting her chin from where it was tucked in toward her chest, Eve saw that they had entered a long and narrow valley. The rain and quickly darkening sky made it difficult to see much, but as they continued forward, she could vaguely make out the shape of a building tucked against the far end of the valley, where thick, dark pines rose not far beyond.

Her relief was intense. Shelter. Warmth.

Outlaws.

As they got closer, Eve realized that the large building she'd glimpsed through the rain was actually two. The first was a barn, and beyond that stood a long building made of logs in a single story. There was a door in the center that was covered by a short little roof, with a row of windows stretching out to either side. Only a couple of the windows were lit from within, but that was enough to confirm the building was occupied.

Gabriel dismounted as soon as they reached a hitching post to the left of the door. Without even bothering to tie up his horse, he strode to her side.

Releasing her feet from the stirrups, she tried to swing her leg over the saddle, but she was so waterlogged and fatigued that she couldn't manage it. Instead, she nearly tumbled from the horse into the arms of the outlaw.

He caught her with a soft sound of displeasure.

"You don't have to carry me," she protested, hating that this was the second time she'd been unable to find her feet after riding. She hated the physical weakness and the vulnerability that required she rely so heavily upon his strength and greater fortitude.

His response was a short sound that managed to be both an acknowledgment and a signal of disagreement. Adjusting her into a more secure position, he turned and carried her toward the building.

Eve kept her chin down as he carried her past the horses. If she'd had any strength left, she would have declared she could make it on her own, but it would have been nearly impossible to walk when she couldn't feel anything below her knees. Upon entering the building, she felt an immediate blast of warmth that contradictorily triggered a fresh bout of uncontrollable shivers.

Gabriel kicked the door shut behind him and strode down a short hall into a large room where an impressive stone fireplace roared with glorious flames. Spread before the hearth in a rather haphazard fashion were various chairs and sofas and end tables.

Beyond the chaotic seating area, Eve caught a glimpse of a long dinner table surrounded by mismatched chairs set in front of a row of windows. And farther past that was a large, open kitchen area with a heavy black stove and broad cupboards lining the wall. The last things she noticed were the two hallways that extended in opposite directions from the great room.

Gabriel strode toward one of the sofas nearest to the fireplace and carefully set her down. She felt terrible that her wet clothes would soon soak through the furniture, but he didn't seem to care.

"Whoa-ho! What's this?"

Gabriel straightened and turned at the question. Eve looked past him to see a lanky young man entering the great room from one of the long hallways. Wearing a thick coat, baggy trousers, and a wide-brimmed hat, the very young man cast a swift and curious glance in her direction.

Gabriel ignored his question. "She needs to get warm. Can you get a blanket?"

"Sure thing." Booted steps sounded on the wooden floor as the newcomer retreated down the hall.

Gabriel crossed to the fireplace and grasped a couple of logs from the stack beside it to toss onto the already healthy flames. A moment later, the slim outlaw returned and handed a blanket to Gabriel. "Here ya go. Have your horses been seen to?"

"Not yet."

"I'll take care of it."

Gabriel didn't offer a response as he stirred the fire to greater life. But the lanky young man didn't seem to expect much more as he tossed another curious look toward Eve, then crossed the room and headed outside.

She sat in a tight ball in the corner of the sofa—teeth still chattering, hair dripping, and hands numb. Gabriel came forward and draped the blanket over her. "Stay here."

She nodded. She wasn't planning on moving an inch away from the fire. He crossed the room to a door near the dining table. As he stepped outside, a blast of rain and wind disturbed the growing warmth of the room before he closed the door securely behind him.

Then she was alone.

But only for a moment.

Someone was coming down the hall behind her. The steps were unhurried, but she noted a slight unevenness in their cadence. A limp. It was subtle but there nonetheless, and in her exhausted and mind-numbed state, Eve couldn't help but focus on that subtly uneven rhythm as the steps came closer. Her body tensed with a frisson of dread, and she wished Gabriel would return quickly.

As a man came into view around the end of the sofa, she

lifted her chin with as much dignity as she could manage in her trembling, exhausted state.

The man before her was somewhere in his late twenties with medium-brown hair that fell in haphazard waves over his forehead. His slim but well-muscled form was dressed in woolen trousers held up by a pair of red suspenders and a loose-fitted cotton shirt that had been rolled up to his elbows. He didn't necessarily look much like an outlaw until Eve met his gaze.

His eyes were an odd mix of light and dark—but mostly dark—and sparked with unpredictability. He assessed her with a sharp and fleeting glance, taking in everything he could see in a brief instant. As his gaze narrowed on her face, something odd flickered in his eyes.

Her heart gave a tiny stutter.

For a second, there appeared to be a fleeting hint of recognition in his eyes.

But then his expression shadowed over with a fierce scowl, and she figured it was a trick of her exhausted mind.

"What're you doing here?" the man asked in a hard tone.

"I was taken from the train." With her jaw still stiff from cold, the words came out in a tone that was slightly sharp and accusing.

The man's scowl deepened. "You're not Sarah Cummings."

He said it with such strong conviction, Eve wondered if he had known the woman. But then, he would have recognized in an instant she wasn't Sarah since they didn't resemble each other much. More likely he was going off the same description of the woman the others had had. He'd just come to the correct conclusion much quicker.

A moment later, the slim young man who had gone out

to see to their horses came inside. He shook the rain off his shoulders and hat much like a dog as he came into the main room.

"Do you know anything about this, Johnny?" the scowler asked.

The young man shrugged and tossed a casual glance toward Eve. "Nope. She came in with Gabe."

That brief explanation seemed to satisfy the newcomer a bit.

With a last glance over at Eve where she still huddled in the corner of the couch, he crossed behind the sofa and headed toward the stove. At the same time, Johnny came forward to stand just off to the left of the fireplace. Crossing his arms over a narrow chest, he lowered his chin and settled a steady gaze on Eve.

She glanced away, resting her head on the back of the sofa.

These men could stare and intimidate all they wanted. She was too weary to care.

She might have drifted off for a bit, because the next thing she knew she was jolting to awareness as the front door opened again and Gabriel swept back inside.

Eve turned to see him striding across the room to reach her side, ignoring the others while rain dripped from his hair and clothes. He parted the edges of his coat to produce a neatly folded stack of clothing.

"Dry clothes," he explained simply, not bothering to say where they came from.

Eve shifted to withdraw her arms from the blanket and took the stack of clothes.

"Can you walk?" he asked.

Eve nodded and proved it by setting the now-damp blanket aside and carefully rising to her feet.

Gabriel stood nearby, not moving until he seemed assured she wouldn't collapse to the floor. Then he turned and led her toward the hallway Johnny had initially emerged from. Eve sent a quick glance behind her before following him down the hall and saw the other two outlaws, Johnny and the scowler, staring after them with the oddest of expressions.

She didn't have time to wonder what had them so perplexed as she continued after Gabriel's large form to the door of a darkened room. She waited in the doorway while he lit a small lamp on a corner table. In addition to the table, the room held a single narrow bed, a short wooden bench, and a small chest of drawers.

When he turned to face her in the confining space, he looked larger than ever. His stance spanned the space between the bed and the dresser, while his wide, solid shoulders completely blocked the window behind him. He filled the room entirely with his presence. The lighting was dim and soft, yet she could see him quite clearly, his taciturn expression defined by a hard-angled jaw, broad nose, and wide forehead. His generous mouth was held in a firm line, and his eyes stared back at her with silent depth.

Eve couldn't breathe. Her chest felt as though it were being constricted by a too-tight corset, and her throat thickened with an odd urge to cry. It was as though everything inside her tightened up in a fierce spiral of emotion that came out of nowhere. It was sadness and fear and uncertainty and pride and a pure sort of fatigue that left her feeling defenseless.

Though she knew she had done nothing to alter her

expression or manner, Gabriel seemed to sense her disturbance. His expression tensed and his brows lowered in obvious concern as he stepped forward, his hand lifting to reach for her.

Though she felt a strong desire to accept the comfort she suspected he wished to offer, she feared what it might do to her in her present state. An instinct for self-protection had her taking a step back.

Noting her retreat, he stopped immediately. His body stiffened as his gaze went flat and unreadable. "There is a lock on the door. You should sleep," he said.

Eve, ashamed of revealing her weakened state, retreated farther into the hall to allow him space to leave the room. He did not pause as he passed her but continued toward the well-lit front room.

Eve watched him go, the tightness inside her refusing to release.

Gabriel stepped into the great room to find Johnny lounging in one of the chairs, staring wide-eyed at him with a smirk barely concealed at the corners of his mouth. Gabriel ignored him. It was Luke he needed to talk to.

The leader of their gang stood leaning back against the kitchen counter with a coffee in one hand. He didn't smirk, but his stare was just as curious as Johnny's.

Gabriel crossed to the stove to pour himself some coffee before speaking. His clothes were still soaked through, but he'd see to his comfort later, once the business of Eve was taken care of.

Luke was one of the few people who understood Gabriel's way and never rushed him into conversation. He stood patiently sipping his coffee.

Finally, Gabriel turned to him and met the other man's direct stare. "George and Ramsey didn't make it back yet?"

"No."

Gabriel frowned. The two men should have returned to the valley well ahead of Gabriel and Eve.

"Ramsey took the wrong woman."

Luke's intent hazel eyes narrowed. "How?"

"She said she was Sarah Cummings."

"She isn't."

"The kid didn't verify the description."

"Why is she here?" Luke asked pointedly.

"Her original clothing suggested wealth. The others thought you might still want to ransom her."

There was a pause as Luke studied Gabriel in silence. Then he said, "You don't agree."

Gabriel held his tongue. He might be Luke's right-hand man, but it wasn't his place to agree or disagree. It was his job to follow orders and make sure the others did the same.

"We don't kidnap random women," Johnny offered from his chair, clearly listening in on the conversation. His tone was sharp. Johnny had been with the gang nearly as long as Gabriel and knew how Luke operated.

Now that the matter was in Luke's hands, there was nothing to keep Gabriel there. He should go to his place to dry off and warm up and finally get some solid sleep.

But he waited.

Noticing Gabriel's hesitation, Luke tossed a quick, subtly questioning glance toward Johnny, who Gabriel imagined was staring in amused fascination. He understood why they were confused by his behavior, but he couldn't bring himself to care what they thought of it.

He met Luke's hard gaze.

The man was the closest thing to a friend Gabriel had had since he was a boy. He trusted Luke with his life as he did the others.

"She's running from something," Gabriel finally stated.

Luke's expression darkened. "The law?"

"Doubtful."

"Husband?"

Gabriel gave a short shrug in response, ignoring the harsh twist behind his sternum.

"A high-stepping lady like her must have a damn good reason to leave the comforts of home for the western wilderness," Luke noted, his expression intense. "All on her own?"

"Seems so."

"Any ideas?"

Gabriel hesitated. Saying more felt like a betrayal to the woman he'd been tasked with protecting the last few days. But Luke would need to know all of it if he were to make a solid decision on the woman's fate. "She's been hurt."

A spark flickered in Luke's hard gaze. "Hurt how? In some sort of accident?"

"No."

Silence filled the room.

Luke frowned, his hazel eyes narrowing as he became thoughtful. When Gabriel first met him more than seven years ago, Luke had been reckless and angry. He'd learned to rein in his temper since then, but a few things could still tip him into a state of fury.

Mistreatment of women and children was one of them.

Sarah Cummings's kidnapping had been planned to ensure the woman's comfort and safety until the ransom fee was paid by her intended and she was eventually turned over to him, none the worse.

Luke gave a nod and lowered his chin. "I'll talk to her."

Gabriel wanted to feel relieved at handing the issue of the woman's well-being into Luke's hands. Any other time, he would have walked away without another thought on the issue.

But this time...

He had to force himself to turn away. As he crossed to the front door and let himself back out into the pouring rain, he could feel Luke and Johnny's gazes burning holes into his back.

EIGHTEEN

GRANGER WAS A SMALL TOWN LOCATED ON THE SOUTHWESTERN *plains of Wyoming Territory. During its active history, the town had been used as an annual meeting spot for fur traders, a stopover for the Pony Express, a station on the Overland Stage route, and finally, an active stop on the Union Pacific rail line.*

The sheriff's office was a neat and tidy little room located in the front of the jailhouse. The sheriff himself was as neat and tidy as his office. A small man with white hair and a squinty gaze, Sheriff Fawkes did not seem too pleased to have a stranger invading his space and reviewing his reports.

But word sometimes spread quickly through the territory, especially when it dealt with the unlawful boarding of a train that resulted in a very strange abduction but not a single robbery.

The stranger glanced up from the neat script to pin the sheriff with a steel-eyed stare. "This is the full report?"

Sheriff Fawkes met his glare with one of his own. Though smaller by a foot or more, he wasn't intimidated. "There wasn't much to report. No one on the train knew the woman other than Miss Cummings, who stated only that her name was Miss Smith. She didn't know where the woman was traveling to or where she'd come from. The case she left behind held only a few items of clothing and a large amount of cash." The sheriff's bushy white mustache twitched in agitation. "There was nothing else to report."

Accepting the sheriff's explanation, the stranger lowered his gaze to reread the passage describing the abducted woman's appearance.

Early twenties in age, fair hair, blue eyes, quiet nature.

That was it. But it was enough. Instinct honed over years spent hunting men back and forth across the wild and endless territories told him this was the woman he was looking for.

"And the outlaws?" he asked.

"They're believed to be part of a gang that's been operating in Wyoming and southern Montana for ten years or so. They're known around here as the Green River Gang, but other places call them different things."

"How do you know it's the same gang of outlaws?"

The sheriff gave a snort. "They never take anything from individual citizens. The targets of their theft are always wealthy ranching operations or large companies with broad holdings."

"Thieves. Have they ever kidnapped anyone before?"

"Never."

"Any idea where they're holed up?"

"The farthest anyone's ever been able to track them is up near the Absaroka Range. We figure they've got a hideout somewhere in those mountains, but no one's ever found it."

Shit.

If the woman had been taken by these outlaws, she'd not be easy to find.

He set the report on the sheriff's desk and rose to his feet. "I appreciate your time."

"You gonna find that girl?" the sheriff asked with a sniff.

The stranger didn't bother answering as he strode from the office and crossed the boardwalk to his horse.

He was familiar with how easy it was to disappear in the forbidding stretch of the Rockies. If Mrs. Preston had been taken by a group of outlaws—and he believed she had—the task of locating her had just gotten a great deal more difficult.

But he wasn't the type to give up when things got tough.

He'd been tasked with finding the woman. And that's what he'd do.

NINETEEN

Eve was awakened by a sharp knock on her locked door and Johnny's voice on the other side saying the boss wanted to talk to her. She blinked away her lingering sleep and sat up. Through the single narrow window beside her bed, she could see that although the sky was lightening to a pale gray-blue, the sun had not yet risen above the mountain range that surrounded the private little valley.

Just over five minutes later, she opened the door. Still wearing the simple cotton dress she'd been given the night before, she knew she looked wrinkled and weary, though she'd rested well through the night. It was uncertainty that wore on her now.

Johnny was leaning against the wall across from her door, one boot braced on the wall behind him and his arms crossed loosely over his chest. At her appearance, he pushed off from the wall and led her down the hallway, across the quiet and dusky great room, then down the opposite hall to the last room, where he left her without a word.

She took a breath and straightened her spine as she crossed the threshold into a room no bigger than the one she'd slept in. Instead of a narrow bed and chest of drawers, this room had a scarred and battered desk holding a half-full bottle of spirits and nothing else.

She had to force down a rise of nerves when she recognized the man seated behind the desk as the one who had briefly questioned her the night before. If she had known then that she was facing the leader of the outlaw gang, she might have responded to his questioning differently.

Then again, maybe not.

For certain, she hadn't expected the man known only as *Luke* to be so young.

Facing him now, it wasn't difficult to imagine him as the leader of an outlaw gang. There was no denying his calculating gaze or the fact that he didn't even bother to conceal the assessing nature of his thoughts. Once again, she couldn't shake the sense that the man was far more dangerous than he appeared.

The only chair in the room was the one behind the desk, so she was forced to stand awkwardly in the middle of the room as she waited for him to address her. She was not oblivious to how she likely appeared in her borrowed dress with her hair a tangled mass tied back at her nape. Ragged, worn-down, vulnerable, and alone.

She couldn't allow that to matter. Keeping her head high and her gaze direct, she waited.

After a few minutes of silence, he spoke, as curtly as he had the night before. "Who are you?"

Eve steeled herself for what would likely be a challenging confrontation. This man didn't know yet that her stubborn determination was all she had until she gained her freedom.

"You can call me Eve."

Something flashed in his eyes, then was gone. "But that's not your name," he replied.

She said nothing.

"Why did you claim to be Sarah Cummings?"

"My reasons are my own."

"How did you know her?"

"We met on the train."

He paused, as though deciding whether to believe her answer. Then he leaned back in his chair, causing the weathered wood to creak beneath him. "What do you know of her destination?"

"Just that she was going to Montana to be married."

"The name of the groom?"

Eve paused. She hadn't expected this line of questioning, and she began to worry that her answers might put Sarah in further danger. She had obviously been a target of this group—perhaps of this man specifically—and might still be.

"His name?" Luke prompted.

"I don't recall."

She could see in an instant he didn't believe her. She was surprised he didn't press the issue as he abruptly changed direction instead. "Where're you headed?"

She kept her mouth closed and her gaze steadily forward.

"Where are you from?"

She said nothing.

"From the Eastern style of your talk, I'd say you came a pretty long way."

"I will not be ransomed," Eve said firmly.

There was a lengthy pause as his brows lowered and an odd tension seemed to settle across his shoulders. "What do you see happening here?" he asked after a while.

Though anxiety trembled through her, Eve answered firmly. "I expect you to let me go."

A smile teased at the corner of his mouth. "Really?"

Eve plunged forward. "I am not the woman you'd intended to…kidnap." She may as well call it what it was. "And since I have no intention of providing any information to assist in a ransom, I am of absolutely no use to you. All I ask is for an escort to take me to the nearest train station so I can continue on my way."

"And alert the first sheriff you see to where we're holed up."

"I assure you, Mr.… Luke. I haven't the slightest idea where we are, other than the fact that we're surrounded by giant rocks. But from what I've seen on the journey here, that appears to be the norm rather than the exception."

He chuckled at that. The sound was incongruent with his hard gaze. "You've got more spunk than you like to let on, don't you?"

Eve lapsed back into silence. *Spunky* was certainly not a term anyone who knew her ever would have applied. But desperation did things to a person. And right now, she was desperate for this man to grant her freedom. "Just let me go."

With a low sigh, he interlaced his fingers and rested them on his abdomen as he crossed one ankle over the opposite knee. "If I agreed to your request…where would you go?"

Eve lifted her chin. Even if she had an answer, she wouldn't give it to him. Her original plan had been to get as far from Boston as possible, but without her money, what options did she have left?

Eve's stomach twisted. She had nothing. No means. No real direction.

Unless she could somehow reclaim her money. As

long as no one else stole her bag as their own, it was likely being held by the railroad. Her abduction had surely been reported to local law enforcement. If she could get to the nearest station on the Union Pacific line and explain what happened, she might be able to reclaim it.

But then again…

If Matthew had expended any resources to monitor the train system, he very well could have heard about a young woman with light hair who had been taken in Wyoming Territory. Even if he didn't suspect it to be her right away, such news would surely prompt further investigation. He could already have men watching the railway lines.

Matthew was nothing if not thorough.

Could she risk returning to the train station at all?

While her thoughts had been whirling through the full impact of these details, the gang leader had been watching her with narrowed focus. "What're you running from?"

Eve stiffened. "Who says I'm running from anything?"

He gave a brief chuckle. "We're all running from something, aren't we?"

She chose not to reply to the philosophical question.

"I just need to know if you've got the law on your tail."

That, at least, was something she could answer with abject certainty. Matthew would never be so indiscreet as to involve law enforcement. His primary priority would be to preserve appearances as much as possible.

She returned the outlaw's sharp hazel gaze with a flat stare. "I'm no criminal."

"Then what are you?"

She curled her linked fingers into a tighter grip as she tipped her chin to an imperious angle, but she didn't answer.

Luke rose to his feet. His limp was barely noticeable as he came slowly around the desk to stand directly in front of her. Folding his arms across his chest, he leaned back against the desk and crossed his ankles.

Rather than easing her trepidation, the relaxed stance only made her warier. Eve got the tingling sense that this man could present himself in countless different ways depending on what the situation called for.

"Look, whoever you are and whatever you're trying to escape, I might be able to help you...but you gotta tell me what you're up against."

Eve was taken aback. He was offering to help her? She eyed him with suspicion. "You do not intend to ransom me?"

He shrugged. "You don't wanna go back to where you came from, so I'm not gonna make you. Besides, a ransom gets awful tough to manage when we don't know who to contact for payment. As you likely already know, me and my men are outlaws. We rob stagecoaches and trains and, on occasion, kidnap wealthy young women in exchange for money," he said with a hitch at the corner of his mouth. Then he lowered his chin and something in his light-dark eyes shifted. "But that's not *all* we do. Sometimes, we come across people who need somewhere to hide out for a while." He swept his hand toward the window. "This valley is a great place for hiding."

Eve took in his words and what they seemed to mean. "Are you saying I can stay here?"

"For a time. You'll be treated with respect by my men until you have the means to continue your journey safely."

A rush of something like relief nearly washed through her but was swiftly cut off by her greater sense.

"And if I wish to leave immediately?"

"Well, that might be tricky. You see, the law will be looking for a young blond woman who was taken off a train. If any of my men are seen with such a woman, they'd be suspect. But I imagine we could find a way to get you to the nearest station in Granger."

Where Matthew might very well be waiting for her.

Eve hesitated in uncertainty.

Surely, it was better to keep pushing toward California—to keep putting as much distance between herself and Boston as possible. But if she failed in reclaiming her money...

"Think about it. There's no real hurry," Luke said as he straightened and walked back to his chair. He took a seat, stretching one leg out in front of him. "In the meantime, feel free to make yourself at home," he added with a nod toward the door, essentially dismissing her.

Eve turned and left the room. Her chest felt tight, and her stomach churned.

She seemed to be facing two equally uncertain options: return to the Union Pacific line with the hope that she might somehow reclaim her bag with her money still inside *and* that Matthew hadn't heard news of the kidnapping of a young, fair-haired woman.

Or remain in this outlaw hideout for an undetermined time until her trail went cold, so to speak, and she felt safe enough to continue.

Either way, the risks were great and the future totally uncertain.

TWENTY

EVE STEPPED INTO THE GREAT ROOM. THE SAVORY SCENT of food reminded her of how little she'd eaten the day before.

Gabriel had eaten even less.

The thought of him caused a twist in her belly.

Where had he gone the night before? Was he sleeping in one of the other rooms she had passed in the two hallways? Now that he had delivered her to his boss, had he left the valley altogether?

Johnny stood at the stove scooping something from a large iron skillet onto a plate.

The lanky outlaw glanced her way. "You want some breakfast?"

Eve was far too hungry to even consider turning down the offer, and the food smelled unbelievably good. "Yes, I would. Thank you."

"Have a seat," the outlaw said with a gesture toward the long dinner table.

"Coffee?" Johnny asked as he set a full plate on the table, then went back to the stove to fill another.

"Yes, please," Eve replied as she eyed the heaping pile of food. She saw scrambled eggs, fried potatoes, some onion, mushrooms maybe, thick chunks of bacon, and some other things she wasn't sure of, all thrown together and covered in a light-brown gravy.

"The food I make never looks too pretty, but it sure tastes good," Johnny declared as he set a mug of coffee down and then slid his lean body into a chair across from Eve. He didn't bother waiting as he picked up his fork and dug into his own heaping plate.

The outlaw hadn't been boasting without cause. The food tasted even better than it smelled. Rich and savory and utterly satisfying.

"You're not one to talk much, are you?" Johnny asked around a mouthful of food. "Not that I'm saying you have to. If you don't feel like talkin', don't. I prolly talk more than I should. At least that's what everyone says." Eve might have replied if the young man had given her a chance, but in the next breath he asked another question. "You waiting for Gabe to show up?"

Eve shifted her gaze to see the young man staring at her curiously from beneath a shaggy fall of light-brown hair that partially obscured his eyes.

"What?"

"You've been glancing at the door every couple of minutes since you sat down."

Eve's face heated. "No, I haven't."

"Sure, lady," Johnny said with a snorting laugh. "Whatever you say. Even though you *weren't* wondering, Gabe never comes by the bunkhouse unless it's to talk to Luke. He prefers to keep to himself, so you're not likely to see him much."

Eve couldn't deny the surge of disappointment. She

hated admitting it even to herself, but Johnny was right. She *had* been hoping to see Gabriel.

For some reason, she felt less...adrift when he was near. Safer, somehow.

It worried her that she had become so accustomed to his presence that she could so acutely experience the loss of his steady, watchful silence, his patience, and the way he managed to assure her with a glance.

As she sat there, struggling to understand the odd longing inside her, the front door opened, and Gabriel walked in.

He was dressed similarly to how he'd been on the journey—worn boots, denim pants, a cotton button-down shirt rolled up at the sleeves and open at the throat. He did not wear a vest or coat, and the soft cotton of his shirt did very little to conceal the broad muscles of his chest and shoulders. Today, he had drawn his long hair back into a single braid down the center of his back.

At the sight of him, it all came rushing back: the tingling through her blood, the sudden sense of being off-balance and grounded at the same time, the flare of warmth in her chest.

His gaze found hers as he shut the door. His hard-angled features revealed nothing of his thoughts or intentions, but something in his eyes managed to soothe the jittery sensations that had been awakened by his unexpected arrival.

"I'll be damned," Johnny mumbled under his breath.

Gabriel didn't spare the young man a glance. Nor did he come any farther into the room, but remained standing just inside the door.

"You slept well?" he asked Eve in a low, almost intimate tone.

She nodded.

"Talk to Luke?"

"Yes."

After a moment when he seemed to be searching for something in her eyes, Gabriel dipped his chin in what could have been acknowledgment, then strode toward the hallway that led to Luke's office.

As soon as the sound of his steps receded, Johnny gave a choked little chuckle. "Holy shit. I've never in my life seen two people say so much with so few words."

Eve looked down at her plate.

What was going on with her?

"Don't be shy about it," Johnny said in a near-whisper as he leaned forward over the table. "It's kinda nice to see Gabe taking an interest in something." He cocked his tawny head to one side. "What's yer story anyway?"

Eve met his curious gaze. There was something about the young outlaw that invited an easy sort of camaraderie, but she couldn't afford to be swayed by it. "I'd rather not say."

Johnny took another bite of food and chewed slowly while seeming to study Eve and her response.

She boldly stared back. There was no hint of malice or manipulation in the young outlaw's brown eyes—eyes surrounded by a thick fringe of lashes beneath eyebrows that had a gentle arch to them, giving an impression of natural amicability. Johnny's nose was narrow and straight, his cheekbones prominent, and his mouth softly curved.

Johnny lifted his mug to take a big swig of coffee before saying, "I ain't one to pry. Lots of people who end up in this valley have secrets. You wanna keep yers, that's fine. Just don't bring no harm to these men." Johnny's voice dropped to a flat note of warning. "I won't stand for it."

There was a pause as the words of warning settled between them.

"I have no intention of bringing harm to anyone," Eve replied.

"What *is* your intention?" the young outlaw asked pointedly.

For some reason, the truth bubbled to Eve's lips before she could stop it. "I just want to be free."

There was a flicker of acknowledgment in Johnny's brown eyes. "From what?"

"The past," Eve answered, surprised at her honesty.

The young outlaw gave a half smile. "I can understand that. Some pasts are easier to escape than others. It's okay to accept a little help along the way."

Eve met the outlaw's earnest gaze. "At what cost?"

Johnny shrugged. "I reckon that's up to you."

"I didn't expect to see you today. But maybe I should've."

Gabriel ignored the question in Luke's tone. "You spoke with her."

"Yep," Luke replied as he leaned back in his chair, a faint smile hovering on his lips.

Gabriel held silent against a flash of frustration at the man's amusement.

"Your woman's not real forthcoming," Luke said after a minute.

Gabriel refused to acknowledge the sensation that flowed through him when Luke called Eve *his woman*.

"We can only help her if she lets us, but it'd be nice to know what kind of situation she's in."

"You offered to help her?" Gabriel asked.

Luke met his stare with a hard one of his own. "We can't exactly ransom her if we've got no one to contact for the payout."

Gabriel's relief was like a swift unraveling of the tension that had been balled up inside him.

Luke braced his hands on the arm of his chair and rose to his feet. "Maybe Honey'll have some luck with her."

Luke's twin sister was a no-nonsense kind of person—stubborn, but empathetic and kind.

"Is your sister expected?" Gabriel asked.

Luke nodded. "But it depends on when the doc can get away." Honey's husband was the doctor for the closest town of Chester Springs and the only medical man in the region. "Let's hope it's sooner rather than later."

Gabriel wasn't too confident Honey would discover anything more about Eve than what they knew already. He'd never met a woman so closed off.

"What about Sarah Cummings?" Gabriel asked.

Luke's expression darkened. "She's probably reached Freeman by now. If ransom's no longer an option, I'll find some other way to damage the man's bottom line."

John Freeman, a wealthy land baron up in Montana, was one of Luke's frequent marks. Gabriel never bothered to ask why Luke held such a harsh grudge against the man and his wealth, but it seemed to have something to do with Honey, since she hated the man even more than Luke did.

"Maybe I'll give Ramsey another chance to make this right."

Gabriel frowned. "You think that's a good idea?" The kidnapping was not the first thing Ramsey had messed up with his carelessness and lack of attention to detail. In Gabriel's opinion, the kid was a risk.

Luke lifted a brow. "If we don't give him a chance to prove himself, he'll never be able to."

Something in Luke's tone had Gabriel wondering if their leader saw something of himself in the newest and youngest member of their gang.

Luke pushed his chair back across the wooden floor as he rose to his feet. "It smells to me like Johnny's been cooking. How 'bout some breakfast?"

Gabriel should have refused. Any other time the offer had been given, that's what he'd done, preferring to keep to himself even when in the valley. He'd built his place just so he wouldn't have to congregate in the bunkhouse. It wasn't that he specifically *disliked* the others' company; he just wasn't a sociable sort.

But this time, he found himself saying, "Sure."

The swift return of amusement in Luke's sideways glance was obvious and irritating, so Gabriel ignored it.

The two men made their way out to the main room.

"Anything left for us?" Luke asked as he strode toward the stove.

"You know I always make way too much," Johnny replied. "My eyes are always bigger than my stomach."

He had finished off the plate in front of him and was stretched out in his spot at the table with long legs spread wide and one elbow hooked on the back of his chair.

Anyone else would be in danger of toppling to the floor, but Johnny had a way of being comfortable with even the oddest arrangement of his limbs.

Gabriel stopped midway between the kitchen and the dining table. His gaze was lured to the woman seated across from Johnny. She sat facing away from him with the straight-spined posture and untouchable demeanor he'd become familiar with. She was still dressed in the blue flowered dress he'd borrowed from the clothing Luke's sister had left behind when she and her family moved into town. Her hair, the color of corn silk, was secured at her nape to fall in a tangle down the center of her back.

"You just gonna stand there, or you gonna eat?" Luke asked as he passed by with a full plate.

Gabriel turned to get himself some coffee. He'd already eaten. He'd been up since dawn and had needed to waste some time before heading over to the bunkhouse. It was bad enough Luke and Johnny would wonder at him being there—he didn't need to show up before anyone else had even rolled from their beds.

Turning to the table with his hand wrapped around a hot mug, he suddenly felt awkward and too large and completely out of place in the semidomestic setting.

The table could easily seat ten people, or more if need be, though that was usually only necessary during the Christmas holiday. Luke's sister, Honey, still insisted on coming back to throw a big feast every year, even though she hadn't lived in the valley for the last couple of winters.

Luke took a seat at the far end of the table in his usual spot where he had the best view of the front door and the short hall that led out back. As Gabriel pulled out the chair at the end of the table close to the door, Eve slid her eyes in his direction. The blue of her gaze, so soft and shadowed, tightened the muscles that wrapped his ribs and crossed his abdomen.

For the first time in almost twenty years, Gabriel felt a sense of responsibility for someone else. In all the time he'd been with Luke and the gang, his concern had never extended beyond whatever task he was assigned to complete.

Every now and then, he'd enjoyed the company of a woman eager to share his bed, but it had been a while since the last one. And the women had only been interested in knowing him in the most basic, physical way. Which had always been fine with him. He'd never had an interest in anything more either.

Gabriel preferred simplicity. And solitude.

So, why the hell was he here again?

The fringe of lashes that framed the poignant blue gaze lowered briefly as Eve glanced away again. Her attention had been on him for no more than a few seconds, but Gabriel's body responded with instant tension that ran from the back of his neck down to his heels.

Right. That's why.

He shifted his gaze to see both Luke and Johnny watching him again.

He should've stayed away.

Before he could consider sending a silent message to both of them to back off, the sound of horses approaching had them all scraping back their chairs as they rose to their feet.

"George and Ramsey," Johnny muttered from his

position near the window before turning away to swipe up his plate. "You done?" he asked.

Gabriel glanced over to see Eve giving a small nod.

Johnny grabbed her plate and headed to the kitchen while Luke resumed his place at the table. Gabriel saw it all in his peripheral vision because his eyes had locked on Eve and hadn't left.

She sat stiff and silent. Her face had been drained of all color, and her eyes were dark with an inner terror she was desperately trying to control as she stared hard at the window.

The sound of new arrivals had sent her into a petrified panic.

Gabriel willed her to look at him.

And she did.

Her eyes flickered toward him without her moving her head. She seemed almost frozen in place. Holding her frightened gaze, he noted the way she intently slowed her breathing, then forced herself to relax.

"You're safe." Gabriel didn't realize he'd said the words aloud until he saw her give a tiny nod before she looked away again.

He glanced toward Luke, who had witnessed the whole thing and was now staring at Eve himself. When he glanced back at Gabriel, his jaw was stern and his eyes hard.

Gabriel said nothing more as the front door swung open to admit a long-striding Ramsey into the bunkhouse with Gentleman George following at a more sedate stroll.

Gabriel stepped to the side and leaned back against the wall, crossing his arms over his chest as the youngest member of their gang gave a low whistle. "Dang, that food smells good," Ramsey declared as he made straight for the skillet still warm on the stove.

"Where've you two been?" Luke asked, shoving his empty plate forward and leaning back in his chair.

Gentleman George—named for the cultured British accent and the fine manners that were too ingrained in him to shake despite his line of work—offered an explanation. "We encountered a spot of trouble on our way back and had to take a bit of a detour."

"You weren't followed?"

George arched a russet brow. "Of course not."

Ramsey swung into a chair near Eve and gave her a wide wink. "Hiya. Don't you look fresh and pretty this morning."

Luke stood. "In my office," he said curtly.

Ramsey glanced up in surprise. "But I just sat down to eat."

Luke didn't wait for compliance as he headed off down the hallway, knowing Ramsey would follow.

"Shit," the kid muttered under his breath before he pushed off from the table.

"Excellent," George said, eagerly taking the seat Ramsey had vacated and lifting the discarded fork. "I bloody well love it when you cook, Johnny."

"Well, that's the last of it," the lanky outlaw replied. "Ramsey's gonna be pissed."

The red-haired Brit gestured with his fork as he spoke around a mouthful of food. "That pup has been a royal pain in my arse for the last few days. He owes me. I cannot understand why in bloody hell Luke agreed to let him join us."

"You know the kid's story," Johnny replied.

"Well, he's wild. And not too bright," George added,

sending a flickering glance toward Eve where she sat stiffly at the table, watching the others with tension still running high through her frame.

Johnny shrugged. "Luke'll set him straight."

With that, a muffled shout could be heard coming from the back office. A moment later, Ramsey came stomping down the hall, taking a turn toward the back door with his chin down and his shoulders tense about his ears.

"Where you headin', kid?" Johnny asked.

"Gotta muck out the horse stalls" was the grumbled reply.

George's hearty laughter filled the room. "That's the third time he's been given that chore out of turn since he got here. He'll either learn, or he'll spend more time in the barn than in the bunkhouse."

"I ain't complainin'," Johnny replied with a wide grin.

Twenty-One

Eve watched the others interact with wary curiosity. She wasn't sure what she would have expected if she'd ever considered wondering how outlaws might behave around each other. But it wasn't this. Despite the fact that every man wore a gun or two belted around his hips—with the exception of Gabriel who carried no weapon she could see—they seemed more like a rowdy little family than a gang of ruthless criminals.

She glanced to where Gabriel stood leaning against the wall, his arms crossed over the solid breadth of his chest. With his dark eyes assessing, his large, muscled body always seeming to be on the verge of action despite its steady stillness.

The fact that no one seemed thrown off by his silence suggested it was a typical occurrence. She had wondered if his lack of conversation during the journey here had been specific to her company.

But she realized now that it was his natural tendency.

She had often been accused of being too quiet and unsociable. Only Courtney and Alexandra had understood that Eve sometimes preferred to observe for a bit before engaging, and she had never really been an effusive person. She tended to internalize things rather than share them.

That was one of the reasons Matthew had been drawn to her. He'd admitted as much shortly before their wedding. At the time she'd been flattered by the idea that he appreciated her more inward nature.

Now, she knew better.

It had made it far too easy for him to isolate her from the people she had been close to in order to ensure he was the only one left for her to rely on.

She could see now that she had never been Matthew's wife. She had been nothing more than a possession for him to mold and toy with for his own amusement and to boost his grandiose sense of self-worth.

Eve only wished she had seen the truth sooner.

A strange tingling ran down the back of her neck. Having allowed her thoughts to drag her awareness inward, it took a moment to refocus her eyes. As she found herself meeting Gabriel's dark-eyed stare, the tingle turned to a fierce rush of heat that was part embarrassment, part something else.

Yet, she couldn't look away.

The good-natured ribbing continued, but the voices had faded to the background.

She was pulled in by the Gabriel's quiet regard—his intense, hooded focus. The depth of his gaze was infinite. As was the sense that he was seeing further into her than anyone else ever had. It was both frightening and exhilarating to be seen in such a way.

Whatever he saw when he looked at her like that, he gave nothing away in his expression or manner.

Eve did not want to analyze the subtle sense of loss she

experienced as he shifted his gaze back to the room as a whole. Trying to figure out exactly what the outlaw made her feel was not something she was prepared to delve into.

"Hey, I was thinking..." Eve turned to see Johnny standing beside her chair, an odd, almost sheepish look in his warm, brown eyes. "There's a river that runs through the valley, and not too far away is a spot where it's wide enough and deep enough to swim in. It's a little cold, but it's good for bathing. You want someone to take you?"

Eve tensed at the idea of stripping down to take a bath outdoors, surrounded by outlaws.

Johnny tipped his head and frowned. "No one'll bother you. You can have your privacy, but someone should be close enough to hear you shout if you get in trouble."

"What kind of trouble?" Eve asked.

The outlaw shrugged.

Eve considered the offer. She hadn't bathed in several days, and the thought of getting clean was unbelievably tempting, but she didn't think she had the courage to do so out in the open where wild animals might pose a threat with only an outlaw nearby to keep her safe. "I don't know..." she began hesitantly.

"She can use the cabin," Gabriel stated, entering the conversation without even glancing their way.

Johnny slapped his thigh. "Dang, that's right. I forgot about the cabin." He flashed Eve a wide grin. "It's got a nice, big copper tub and anything else you'd need for a proper bath. And you can lock the door. Gabe here can escort you."

Eve looked back and forth between Johnny and Gabriel.

Johnny offered a wide grin of encouragement, while Gabriel's dark eyes narrowed on the younger outlaw. Johnny seemed oblivious to the hard resistance in Gabriel's gaze. That, or he was choosing to ignore it.

But Eve saw it.

Gabriel didn't want to take her anywhere.

After a beat of silence, he looked down at her. "You want a bath?"

Eve's pride flared in response to his reluctance. She replied truthfully and not without a hint of challenge in her tone. "I do."

With a short nod, he pushed off from the wall and reached the front door in two long strides. Eve rose swiftly to her feet, anxious to follow. A real bath in a cabin with a locked door suddenly sounded like the greatest luxury she could imagine.

He held the door for her to pass through.

For the sake of her pride as much as her equilibrium, she kept her gaze forward as she walked past him, catching a brief whiff of his familiar scent before stepping outside.

A long, covered porch ran nearly the full length of the front of the bunkhouse, shading them from the sun that had risen above the mountaintops to bathe the valley in light.

Eve took a deep breath of the spring air. It felt so much crisper, cleaner here. She'd noticed that on the long ride into the mountains. The thinning air had made the way difficult since she was unaccustomed to it, but now, as she experienced the ease with which she filled her lungs, Eve appreciated the sense of lightness it gave her.

"This way." Gabriel stepped past her and started down the porch steps to the grass.

Eve followed as he led the way across the valley toward the tree line. Looking around his wide-shouldered form, all she saw were dark pines climbing up the side of the mountain where the forest held shadows and quiet, unseen movement. Soon they reached a path that had been worn into the earth from the frequent passage of footsteps.

Stepping out of the summer sunshine and into the cool shadows of the pines, where the sun reached the ground in small sprinkling patches of light, required a swift adjustment of the senses. The air chilled against her skin. The smell of the earth was richer, almost heady. Sounds of wind through the treetops and the subtle rustling of small creatures surrounded them as they continued deeper into the forest.

As she followed a step or two behind Gabriel on the narrow footpath, Eve couldn't help but acknowledge how he seemed so much a part of this environment. While she felt out of place and foreign.

As she glanced around, she thought she might learn to enjoy the deep quiet of such a place. It was all so very different from the brightly lit ballrooms and drawing rooms she'd left behind, but it held a unique kind of peace.

Just as she began to wonder how far they'd have to go, she saw a little cabin up ahead. It was made of logs, like the larger house in the valley below, and had a similar covered porch. But it was significantly smaller.

Gabriel stepped onto the porch and reached for the front door. It opened with a creak of unused hinges. He stepped to the side and looked back at Eve. "I'll have to get a fire going and haul up some water, but you can go in and look around."

Eve stepped forward cautiously. "Does anyone live here?"

"Not anymore."

She continued through the door into a room not unlike the great room in the bunkhouse, if only much smaller. The living space and kitchen were open to each other with the counter and stove off to the right and a fireplace to the left. In between, there was room for a small kitchen table and a sofa facing the fireplace with what appeared to be two rooms extending off the main one, most likely bedrooms.

For not being lived in, the cabin had a distinctly homey feel. Rugs of various shapes and sizes and colors covered the wooden floor. A lap blanket was thrown over the back of the sofa, and books were stacked up on the floor in front of a comfortable-looking armchair.

Gabriel strode past her to the fireplace where he crouched and started adding kindling from a wooden box beside the woodpile stacked neatly to one side.

Eve took advantage of his turned back to observe him freely. She wasn't sure why his movements fascinated her so. They were like his silence and his steady, unreadable gaze. He was so unlike anyone she'd ever known. There was so much grace and economy in his movements. No effort was ever wasted. He did nothing without direct purpose. But there was nothing stiff or calculated about it. His body possessed a fluidity that was rather beautiful considering the obvious strength and bulk behind it.

Eve had been raised—trained, actually—to be deliberate and reserved in her behaviors. It was the Boston Brahmin way, and Eve's mother had wanted nothing more than to see her daughter married into that society of the city's most elite citizens. With a constant focus on her posture, the proper tilt of her head and position of her hands, and the right-size step, Eve always felt so forced and unnatural in her movements. So…fettered.

Matthew had expected supreme propriety at all times—out in society as well as in the privacy of their home. Eve was forever conscientious about how she dressed and moved and spoke. Her gowns had to be perfectly fitted, her hair had to be styled in the latest fashion, her manners had better be flawless. Even the slightest misstep could be cause for repercussions.

It had been exhausting to exist on a knife edge of potential violence. It was difficult even now to shake that perpetual sense of trepidation.

Gabriel stood and turned to face her before Eve had a chance to glance away or shield her thoughts. His expression immediately darkened. Black brows lowered heavily over his eyes, and the strong line of his jaw becoming even more prominent.

Eve realized how stiff and unmoving she must appear. The muscles along her spine ached, and her fingers cramped from being clasped so tightly together. She glanced down, not wanting Gabriel to detect even a glimmer of the painful memories traveling through her mind.

"The cabin will warm quickly." His words were tense. "Do you want the bath in front of the fire?"

"That would be nice. Thank you."

She stayed where she was, standing behind the sofa with the kitchen table just behind her, as he brought out a large copper tub from a corner of the room and set it on the rug in front of the fire. There was just enough room for it between the hearth and the sofa. Then he went outside and started bringing in buckets of water. First, he filled two large pots and set them on the stove where he lit a fire to heat the water. Then he went about filling the tub with more buckets, two at a time.

He would be gone several minutes each time he stepped out of the cabin, and Eve wondered where he fetched the water from, but she didn't ask. She felt so awkward standing there while he got her bath ready. Back home, she'd never thought twice about the work servants did. But this was so very different.

Because no one could possibly mistake Gabriel for anything as domestic as a household servant. And because here, with just the two of them in this little cabin tucked into the woods, the act felt oddly personal. Intimate, even though he seemed to practically ignore her presence.

As he crossed the room with yet another bucket of water, Eve realized she did not want to be ignored. Words rose to her lips before she thought to stop them. "This cabin is very comfortable for the fact that no one lives here."

He slid her a quick glance, but otherwise revealed no reaction to what was surely the unexpected start of conversation.

"Luke's sister and her family use it when they come to visit. But we also use it for people passing through and need a place to stay for a while."

"People who need to hide?" Eve asked quietly.

He turned to face her. "It's a safe place."

Eve heard the words but felt them more.

A safe place.

Amongst robbers and kidnappers.

"I don't think I belong here," she replied softly. The

words caused a hollow ache in her chest. The truth was that she wasn't sure she belonged anywhere.

The confession seemed to cause a shift in him. His expression remained unchanged, his eyes deepened with some emotion that reached out and swirled thick and heavy through Eve's center. He gave a short nod and crossed the room toward the kitchen behind her.

He made an obvious effort not to get too close as he moved around her in the small space. For some reason, that small thing—that nearly inconsequential consideration—made her feel grateful and frustrated at the same time.

She understood her gratitude for his hypervigilance in making sure she did not feel threatened by him.

It was the frustration that confused her. And worried her.

Did she *want* him to come closer?

Setting the buckets aside, he went to the stove and hefted one of the large pots of steaming water. The muscles of his forearms strained as he carried it to the tub and poured it in. Only pouring about half of the second pot, he tested the water and set the half-full pot beside the tub.

"Once it cools, you can use it to rinse your hair," he said.

The cabin was dimly lit under the shadow of the pines. The light from the fire flickered inconsistently over the room, and the two of them stood staring at each other in the quiet space.

Eve was suddenly struck by the warmth of the room.

No. Not the room. The warmth came from within, like a rolling flame expanding from her center.

In the next moments, she was expected to strip down

and sit in the water, completely vulnerable, while he stood just outside. Her current circumstances would have been incomprehensible to her a week ago.

But now, despite the strange tension that always seemed to settle between them, she realized that she wasn't frightened by the stark vulnerability of her situation. How was it possible that she could feel almost exhilarated by it?

"Are you all right?" he asked in a rough voice that sent a tingle of awareness down Eve's arms.

"Yes," she replied softly, wondering why she felt so tightly drawn inside, as though her body was bracing for something.

He nodded and crossed the cabin to dig something out of a small chest of drawers in the corner. Returning to the tub, he set a folded towel on the floor and a cake of soap on top of that. He seemed to know his way around the place quite well.

Gabriel crossed to the door. "You should get started before the water cools. The key is in the lock. I'll be outside."

Then he stepped outside, making sure to secure the door behind him.

Releasing a heavy breath, she approached the closed door and turned the key in the lock before removing it and placing it on the kitchen table.

A gentle waft of steam rose from the tub as she approached. With another quick glance around, she started to release the buttons of her borrowed dress. Setting everything carefully on the armchair as she undressed, she allowed the quiet comfort of the little cabin to surround her.

The locked door helped, but it was more Gabriel's presence that made her feel safe enough to strip down. She knew he wouldn't disturb her and would prevent anyone else who might think to do so.

She washed quickly before the water fully cooled, using the now-warm water from the pot to rinse her twice-washed hair. After dressing again, she sat in front of the fireplace, working her fingers through her hair to free the tangles and encourage it to dry faster.

Though she was almost curious enough to explore the rooms beyond, she stayed where she was. Looking around, she noted that the cabin really was quite a lovely home. A vase of long-dried-out flowers sat on a windowsill. Some heavy snow boots were propped beside the front door, and a basket filled with toys sat in a corner of the room.

Eve stood and wandered to the basket, intrigued by the idea of a child living in this valley alongside a bunch of outlaws, but Gabriel had mentioned that Luke's sister had a family. In this case, that appeared to include children.

Lowering to her knees, she picked up a rag doll and noted its painted smile and bright-blue eyes, partially worn away, and its faded dress with a frayed hem. The doll had obviously been the object of many hours of loving play. Setting it back in the basket, she caught sight of a bright-red ball. It looked practically new and strangely familiar, though she had no idea where she might have come across such an object.

None of her friends had children yet. And her brother—

Of course. She knew exactly where she'd last seen a ball like this.

Eve had never been very close to Warren, who was twelve years older than her. He had left Boston to study medicine in Philadelphia when Eve had still been a child. But he'd fallen in love with the western territories during a summer he'd spent with their uncle before starting medical school. About four years ago, he moved from Philadelphia to a small town in the Wyoming Territory to take over a medical practice.

He was now married with a daughter and son. Eve recalled the last Christmas package she and her mother had prepared for Warren's family. It had included a ball just like this one.

It was an odd coincidence, and it had her wondering how far Warren lived from where she was now. She had known that her train ride would take her through the southern part of Wyoming but felt confident it was far enough from Chester Springs that she had no fear of encountering her brother along the journey.

Gabriel had taken her some distance from the railway. She had no idea where she was now, what direction they'd traveled into the mountains, or if she was even still in Wyoming.

Just being reminded of Warren's possible proximity made her anxious, but she reminded herself that she was deep in the mountains with a group of men who knew how to keep hidden. There was no reason to think she'd cross paths with her brother.

Twenty-Two

Gabriel heard the cabin door open behind him, then quiet footsteps on the wooden porch as Eve stepped outside. He remained where he was—leaning against a post, looking out through the tall pines toward the valley. He needed a moment. A moment to steel himself against the way his body and spirit reacted to her presence.

It didn't help.

As soon as he turned toward her, the sight of her sent a sharp spear of heat down through his center. She had dressed again in the blue dress that was a near-perfect match to her eyes. Her hair was parted in the center and fell free down her back. The pale tresses were damp from her bath, but still created a golden veil around her face and shoulders.

He liked her hair that way.

She appeared more relaxed after her bath, though her gaze was still shrouded. Soft. Beautiful.

The muscles that bound his ribs contracted, stealing his breath. Something inside him ached—deep inside, where words were replaced by instinct.

He couldn't allow such feelings to take root.

But they dug deeper with every encounter.

As he looked into her eyes and saw evidence of her secrets carefully secured in the depths, Gabriel felt an intense urge to draw her close, into the circle of his arms where he could be the walls that kept her safe.

She made a small gesture toward the interior of the cabin. "The bath will need to be emptied." Her voice was hesitant and uncertain.

She had likely never concerned herself with such things before. On the night of her capture, her clothing had denoted her status as a person of wealth and privilege. And in the days since, her manner and poise had supported that assumption.

He needed the reminder of how far apart their worlds were.

"I'll do it later."

Her soft gaze found his. "Thank you." Her words seemed to speak to more than the bath, but Gabriel had no idea what else she had to thank him for.

"We should head back."

Gabriel stepped to the side, nodding for her to precede him down the steps. Her step was regal as she passed by him, her gaze level, but just as she was even with him, her lips parted as she drew a swift breath.

He wanted to believe her reaction to his nearness was not due to fear, but he suspected that was the case. From what he had seen, she had reason to be wary. He just wished she knew there was no cause to fear him.

When they reached the valley and stepped free of the shadows cast by the tall pines, she tipped her face up toward the sun. A soft sigh slid from her lips. The sound of it made his stomach clench.

"Gabriel?" She spoke his name softly before turning to

glance at him over her shoulder. "Could we walk for a bit before going back?"

He furrowed his brow in a questioning look.

"It's a lovely day," she added as she stopped and turned to face him more fully.

A gentle wind teased wisps of her hair, lifting them in a dance of golden light. Silken strands swept across her cheek and her lips until she lifted her hand to tuck them behind her ear.

There was no reason to return right away. A walk seemed like a small indulgence.

"For a little while," he finally replied.

Her eyes brightened. The change was small, but it had an effect like a lightning bolt striking deep in his core.

He altered direction and started walking. She fell into step beside him.

The birds announced their presence as they passed, squirrels chattered from nearby trees, and the grass whispered with every step, but no words were spoken.

Gabriel was accustomed to a lack of conversation, even when in the company of others.

Such had not been the case when he was young. As many young boys do, he had enjoyed spending his days shouting and running with his friends.

After he was taken in by the missionaries, he learned quickly that a child did not speak unless being directly questioned by an adult. There was little opportunity for laughter and no time for song.

He'd hated it, but after many failed attempts at escape that ended in beatings and food deprivation, he came to accept it. And then hated himself for his acceptance and vowed he would free himself at the first opportunity. Along the way, he had learned to appreciate the benefits of keeping his thoughts to himself.

The woman walking beside understood what it was to keep silent.

Perhaps that was why the sound of her voice held so much weight when she spoke. "May I ask you something?"

He kept his gaze forward. "You may."

"How did you become an outlaw?"

Gabriel wasn't sure how to answer that. Sometimes, he didn't even think of himself as an outlaw. Of course, he was aware that his actions under Luke's direction often required that he break a law or two, but the West was a lawless place. Even those upholding the law often saw fit to break it toward their own ends.

And from the day he'd joined up with Luke, he'd seen that although the other man's methods required a certain disregard for the laws of the land, his motivation was based on a kind of honor Gabriel respected.

"Several years ago, the residents of a small town to the south took exception to me passing through. Luke stepped in when the townsfolk thought it'd be easier to shoot me than run me out of town." She gasped, and the quiet sound told him as much as anything how little she was aware of the world he lived in. "We traveled together for a couple of days. I was able to repay the debt when a couple of cowboys discovered Luke cheated them out of their monthly pay in a poker game."

He wasn't sure if his reply satisfied her curiosity, but it was the only one he had.

He and Luke had saved each other's hides more than

once since then. In those days, Luke had been young, reckless, impassioned, and angry. He and Honey had left their childhood home in search of a new beginning. Luke's responsibility to his sister and her daughter might have been the only thing he took seriously. Gabriel didn't know exactly how Luke started on the path of an outlaw, but he had a way of inspiring confidence and loyalty despite his youth.

"And you've stayed with him since?"

Gabriel nodded.

She said nothing more for a little while, and Gabriel could practically feel her trying to understand his choice to live as an outlaw.

"Sometimes breaking the law is the right thing to do." As further explanation, the remark was vague. But it was all he could say without betraying the gang and those they've helped.

"How was Sarah Cummings's abduction and ransom the right thing to do?"

Gabriel frowned. She would ask about that—one of the few jobs that was connected to a personal vendetta. He slid a glance toward her without turning his head. She walked beside him, her posture as sure and proud as always, her chin level, and her gaze thoughtful as she looked out over the valley spread before them.

"You'd have to ask Luke about that."

"Would she have been hurt?"

"No." That, at least, he could say with conviction. "Women and children are never harmed by our hands. Only men who deserve it."

"And who decides if they deserve it?" she asked, her voice lowering.

"Those they've committed crimes against."

She gave a barely perceptible nod, apparently satisfied with his answer. As he watched her from the corner of his eye, she took a deep breath, filling her lungs with mountain air as she closed her eyes and tipped her face toward the sun. The beginnings of a smile teased at the corner of her mouth but couldn't quite come into fruition.

Gabriel ached to touch his tongue to the crease of her lips. He wondered what her reluctant smile would taste like. Sunshine and honey, he imagined. Sweet and warm.

Opening her eyes, she took another breath, this one more fortifying, and the almost-smile slipped away.

"Luke said I could stay here in the valley for a while," she said.

Her soft gaze slid to meet his. The depth of her vulnerability was difficult to witness. He wondered how she managed to carry it inside her. "You told him...what you saw?" she asked. The words were raw and exposed, rising barely above a whisper.

The guilt of feeling as though he'd betrayed her was like a rock in his chest. "It's important for him to know the circumstances."

She nodded and averted her gaze, staring off across the valley. There was vulnerability in her eyes, but also so much pride. In her bearing, in her silence, in her determination and courage. But there was also something else. Something Gabriel recognized and could not stand for.

He stopped walking and she stopped as well, turning to face him with a question in her eyes. He lowered his chin and met her gaze with steady insistence. "There is no shame in what you've endured."

Her lips parted on his words, and something flickered in her gaze before it was closed off. "I know that now. But knowing and feeling are two different things."

Gabriel's stomach tightened at the truth in her words. Being taken away from his tribe as a boy was not his choice or his fault, but it didn't stop him from feeling guilt over his absence. Just as when he'd returned to his people as a young man and realized he couldn't stay, it hadn't prevented the sense of loss that followed that decision.

"It took courage to come west on your own."

She shook her head. "Not courage. Desperation."

The uncertainty in her voice struck him with a forceful blow. How could she not see her own strength? It astounded him. Her bravery and fierce determination were evident in her watchful gaze and steady refusal to return to a life that mistreated her. He wished she could see herself as he saw her.

"Our lives do not always travel the path we imagined," he said. "The results of our choices cannot be foreseen. All you can do is choose what steps you take next."

She tilted her head as she looked up at him. "Do you think I should stay here?"

Gabriel shrugged. The gesture was casual while he felt anything but. "It's not my choice to make."

Eve was disappointed by his answer, but she should have expected it. She wasn't sure why she wanted to know what he thought. He'd brought her here, but only as a duty to his gang. Not because he had any personal investment in her well-being.

She took a breath and looked back over her shoulder toward the bunkhouse and the barn. The idea of staying in this valley, even for a short while, filled her with hope and dread. She did not want to hide for the rest of her life.

Could she be comfortable in a valley full of outlaws?

Could she risk leaving?

She returned her gaze to Gabriel's patient stare. "You trust Luke a great deal," she noted quietly.

"There are few people I trust," he replied. "Luke is one."

She had a swift and sudden desire to be one of the few herself. How would it feel for a man like this—a man who needed no one, who asked for nothing from the world—to believe in her?

She noted the seriousness of his features. He was always so stoic and emotionless. Detached. Yet he possessed an undeniable strength—a calm, steady certainty—in everything he did. He did not need to rely on anyone else.

She dreamed of being so self-sufficient.

"*You* could trust him," he suggested.

She shook her head slowly.

"You could trust me." He spoke in a lowered tone, as though they shared a private conversation, even though there was no one else around to hear them.

Looking into his eyes, his words hovering between them, Eve felt a blast of sensation travel through her body. It was a mix of heat and fear and something else unnameable. A force deep within her wanted to step into him, to step into his strength and warmth and confidence. Would he keep her safe from all she'd left behind? From all she still faced in her uncertain future?

"I wish I could," she whispered, the confession slipping

free before she could stop it, before she could keep the longing from filtering into the words.

"You are stronger than you know."

Eve wanted to believe him. For a second, his dark gaze and firm words almost convinced her they were truth. But she was far too aware of the trembling she felt inside. The uncertainty and the fear she was getting too weary to hide. How could he see strength in her when she felt as if she could fall apart at any moment?

A frown pulled at his black brows, as though he saw something unusual in her eyes. His wide, full lips parted to say something, and he lifted a hand toward her. But she would not know what he intended to say, because before she could even assess his intention, she flinched in anticipation of his touch.

It was a subtle movement, no more than a flicker of her gaze and a tip of her chin, triggered by an instinct to protect herself at a moment when she felt nearly overwhelmed by her vulnerability.

However subtle her reaction might have been, Gabriel saw it.

He stiffened and lowered his hand back to his side. "You have no need to fear me," he said firmly, though his voice remained in that low tone.

She did not need to respond. She could have let the declaration settle between them, but something in her would not allow it. "I don't know what it is you make me feel, Gabriel. Perhaps it's fear, though it doesn't feel like any fear I've known before."

"I would not hurt you."

"I know."

He was quiet for a long moment, his dark eyes searching and silent. “I won’t try to touch you again.”

Regret twisted through her belly. She wanted to tell him not to make such a promise. For a sudden desperate moment, she wanted nothing more than to know how it would feel for his fingers to drift over her skin in a touch that was as intimate and quiet as his voice. But how could she explain that it wasn’t his touch she feared so much as her own reaction to it? Her near-craving for it.

As he stared hard into her eyes, she nearly glanced away, dreading what he’d see, desperate to keep her secrets. But she didn’t want to hide the truth from him. Something inside her wished he could see...everything.

For a moment, it seemed that maybe he did.

But then his features tensed, and he lifted his gaze to peer over her head toward the mountains that rose in the near-distance. “We should head back.”

“Not yet.” Eve spoke without thinking. She wasn’t ready to return to the bunkhouse and the watchful, curious gazes of the other outlaws. She wasn’t ready to decide if she should stay in the valley or take her chances that Matthew had discovered her abduction from the train. For a little longer, she needed to breathe free.

“You didn’t stay in the bunkhouse last night,” she said, latching onto the first excuse that came to mind that would extend their outing.

He looked down at her with a question in his eyes.

She almost blushed as she realized that her words made it sound as though she missed his presence. “Do you have a cabin like the one we just left?”

His brows lowered. “Somewhat.”

Eve glanced back at the bunkhouse then returned her gaze to Gabriel's. "Will you show me?"

At first, she felt certain he would refuse. The resistance in his stance and in his dark eyes was plain to see. But then something changed. Resistance slid into acceptance and then…anticipation. Eve felt the change more than she saw it. A gentle wave of excitement flowed through her when he gave a short nod and said, "This way."

Twenty-Three

After only a few minutes, they came up alongside a winding river with a narrow, rocky shore. They followed it upstream, leaving the barn and bunkhouse and the little forest cabin behind them. The farther they went, the more Eve found herself relaxing. The sun was warm, the air was fresh, the river flowed in a gentle rhythm, and the man beside her made no demands on her attention—though he had it anyway.

They soon reached a spot where the river curved around a cluster of trees that had spread down from the mountainside into the valley. Past the trees, the landscape widened to reveal an open meadow of green grass dotted with wildflowers, and in the center of the field stood a little cabin that was even smaller than the one where Eve had bathed. The dwelling sat gently on the earth with wildflowers growing around its base and no porch or stairs leading to the front door.

Eve noted a permanent campfire off to one side, and behind that stood a tall, standing frame structured from raw wooden poles that she imagined might be used for dressing large game. Gabriel's riding blanket had been tossed over the pole that spanned the top of the frame and danced playfully in the wind.

They continued along the edge of the riverbank, and Eve noticed that although the little cabin was on the opposite side of the river, there was no bridge in sight. She was about to ask Gabriel how they would get across when they reached a spot where the water ran swift and shallow over the riverbed, winding between large boulders that rose above the water and spanning the distance to the opposite bank.

Gabriel stepped onto the first big rock and turned to offer a hand.

His expression was carefully controlled—a direct contradiction to the anticipation she felt in the air. She didn't believe the exhilarating sense of expectation belonged only to her.

With a shallow breath, she placed her hand in his and executed a short leap to join him. The surface of the rock was uneven and just barely big enough to fit them both. Her balance wavered a bit at first, but his grip was sure. One by one they crossed the creek. Gabriel first, creating a solid foundation for Eve to leap to. It reminded her of the days before she was considered too old for games, and she and her brother used to play tag and leapfrog and run about the lawns of their estate. That had been so long ago, she'd forgotten what it felt like.

Something of her sense of joy must have shown in her face, because Gabriel's hand tightened around hers, and she looked up at him to see a fleeting smile cross his lips. It was there and gone in an instant, but Eve felt its effect in the sudden rushing of her blood and the swift beat of her heart.

For a moment, she couldn't look away from his wide mouth as she silently, fervently wished for another smile.

She slid her gaze over his broad, handsome features to look into his eyes.

She didn't know what she expected to find there, since he was so adept at shielding his thoughts. She certainly couldn't have anticipated the hunger. The soul-deep longing.

And then it was gone. As though it had never been.

Eve was left breathless as his expression shuttered and his gaze became flat and silent.

He released her hand and gestured with a lift of his chin up the bank toward the cabin. Eve ignored her disappointment at the swift return of his careful control and turned to start up the gentle slope to where the land leveled and the grass grew soft and thick. She had expected to find some sort of path, but the grass and flowers looked almost completely undisturbed, as though no one had crossed the field in a long time.

The lack of a well-worn path struck her delicately.

For Gabriel's passage to and from his home to leave no mark had to have taken conscious effort. The idea that he would choose to disturb as little of his environment as possible was not surprising. But it made her wonder if he saw this place as his home or a temporary camp like the ones they'd made through the mountains.

The question lingered in her mind as she drew nearer to the cabin.

Gabriel had remained a couple of paces behind her after they left the bank of the river, but as they approached the dwelling, he came up beside her.

She looked at him, wondering if he was aware of the excitement rising quietly within her.

But he kept his expression stern and his gaze forward, almost as though he didn't want to see what she might be thinking. Reaching for the door, he drew it open, then stood to the side so she could enter.

Eve kept her gaze lowered. Her fingers and toes tingled with anticipation as she crossed the threshold.

She'd expected it to be dark inside, but filtered sunlight reached in through the windows, casting the interior in a dreamy sort of half-light that smelled faintly of dried herbs and rich earth.

The floor of the single room was covered by woolen rugs—brightly colored and tightly woven—and Eve would guess that beneath them lay bare earth. A fireplace framed in fieldstone took up the wall to her left and various furs were spread carelessly on the floor before it. To the right, directly across from the fireplace was a wide dais. It was built low to the ground and was covered in colorful blankets and more soft furs. His bed.

A flush of warmth had Eve shifting her gaze to note the various cooking utensils and other curious tools that were neatly hung from hooks around the fireplace. The wall directly in front of her contained a large window that provided a view of the meadow where his horse grazed and beyond to the pines shading the rocky mountainside. A large wooden chest and several baskets that he appeared to use for storage were kept along the wall away from the fire.

The dwelling was unlike anything she'd ever seen.

Simple, serene, safe.

Those were the words that came to mind as she wandered around in Gabriel's private space.

She didn't realize she had wandered so far inside until she turned to see him still standing beside the open doorway with his feet braced wide and his arms crossed over his chest. He looked tense and wary.

Eve cast another glance around her. "It is wonderful," she said, her voice breathy and low. "Did you build it yourself?"

He nodded.

Feeling inordinately brave in the tranquil setting, Eve asked the question burning in her mind. "Why build it so far from the others? Why not stay in the bunkhouse?"

At first it seemed like he wouldn't answer. He remained tall and stoic as he stared back at her through the hazy sunlight. Then he uncrossed his arms. As he did so, he paused briefly, exposing his palms as though waiting to hold something before lowering his hands to his sides.

"It is best for me to keep apart from others."

The words—low and heavy—pressed against Eve's heart. "Why?" she asked.

He made a sound in his throat that suggested he didn't want to answer. Disappointment flooded her chest. She had no idea why she wanted so badly to understand this man, but there was no denying it was true.

Then, in a flat tone that revealed no emotion, he replied, "There's a risk in getting close."

Eve searched his dark gaze, feeling rather than seeing what went unsaid. Awareness and longing and loss swept through her. There was much to be inferred by his words, but she couldn't help but wish he would reveal more to her. Openly and freely. What would it be like to have this man look into her eyes and offer the true depths of himself?

Glorious. Humbling.

Her throat tightened as she imagined how it might feel to have Gabriel's trust and...devotion.

The thought was swiftly followed by the sobering truth—in order to earn that much from him, she would have to offer the same.

She lowered her gaze as reality cleared away the clutch of yearning that had claimed her. She was not free to wonder such things...and certainly had no right to long for them.

"We should return."

Eve nodded, but her steps were reluctant as she crossed back to Gabriel's side. Before she stepped out into the full sunlight, she paused and looked up at him.

He turned his head to meet her gaze, though he kept the rest of himself angled away.

"Thank you for bringing me here."

He gave a short nod of acknowledgment, which should have been enough for Eve, but something inside her kept her from moving.

As they stood there, shoulder to shoulder, she felt a draw so fierce and strong it nearly startled her. She experienced a sudden urge to turn toward him, reach for him, feel his hands grasp her hips as she rested her palm against his chest.

It left her trembling with an emotional hunger unlike anything she'd ever felt before. And as she looked into Gabriel's dark gaze, she saw the same deep craving reflected there.

Her lips parted on a swift inhale. Her belly fluttered with wild sensations. Heat flowed through her blood. Everything inside her wanted to reach for him, touch him, embrace him. The shock of physical desire startled her from the strange reverie.

With a harsh exhale, she ducked her head and stepped

out into the sunlight, effectively breaking whatever spell she'd fallen under.

The walk back along the river to the bunkhouse was a silent one. Both of them, it seemed, were caught up in their own thoughts.

But Eve was not so distracted that she didn't notice the moment Gabriel's focus became suddenly intent as he stared straight forward. She followed his gaze to the far end of the valley where three riders had emerged from a narrow, rocky pass and were heading toward the main house.

Her body froze with a wave of fear.

Gabriel looked down at her as he noted calmly, "They are friends."

The chill slid from her blood, replaced by a flush of embarrassment that he could so easily detect her weakness.

Would there ever come a day when she didn't expect Matthew to appear from nowhere to drag her back to the hell she'd escaped?

"You're safe here."

The assurance in his tone and the flicker of concern in his gaze only increased her discomfort. "You must think me ridiculous," she muttered.

His brows furrowed subtly as he dipped his chin to an intimate angle. "There are many things I think of you, Eve. Ridiculous is not one."

The words—spoken in his smooth, dark voice—sent another flush of heat through her body, but this one had nothing to do with embarrassment. It was on the tip of her tongue to ask what he *did* think of her.

She held the question behind her teeth.

They continued toward the bunkhouse, entering through

the back door after coming around the barn and passing Ramsey on the way. The young man was grumbling under his breath as he led the newcomers' horses into the barn.

Stepping into the bunkhouse, Eve immediately heard a cacophony of voices talking and laughing at once. The noise made her anxious.

Even the crowded ballrooms back home did not boast such boisterous activity. She had to remind herself that these men were not cut from the same cloth as anyone with whom she had previously associated. In Boston, she knew all the rules and how to follow them to perfection.

She did not know how to be amongst these rough men who made their lives outside the laws of society. Traveling with Gabriel had been different. She hadn't felt any expectations on her behavior. But this morning, around Luke and Johnny, she'd felt like an oddity—as though she was on display. She could only imagine that what faced her in the room beyond would be so much worse.

Gabriel came up behind her but could not pass her in the narrow hall. The strength of his presence formed a protective wall at her back as he waited, ever patient.

She turned toward him, tempted to reveal her cowardice and suggest they go back outside for just a little longer, but he was closer than she'd expected, and the words died in her throat.

She took a breath to steady the sudden jump in her pulse and was instantly overwhelmed by his scent—cool pine and warm wool.

Trembling erupted in her belly, and the deep breath she'd taken expelled on a weighted sigh.

He lowered his head toward her. His voice was a low rumble. "You are braver than you think."

Her gaze lifted to his, so close she could see black striations through the rich brown. His expression was so stern. She wished he would reveal something more of himself than hard lines and angled shadows.

She was terrified. She had been locked in a perpetual state of fear for what felt like forever.

Yet he called her brave.

She wanted him to be right.

He gave a short nod of assurance, of encouragement.

The movement drew her gaze to his mouth. His full lips were unsmiling, but their softness could not be disguised by the harshness of his jaw. Not even when he pressed them firmly together and raised his chin to gaze straight over her head.

Warmth flowed through her center, distracting her from her anxiety as she wondered at the softness and heat that claimed her body when she stared at his mouth.

"Go," he said. One word, muttered quietly.

Though she would have preferred to stay in that hallway with him alone, she turned in place and continued into the main room.

Twenty-Four

The large red-haired British man still sat at the table, though his food had been cleared away. The older man with the gray beard, who Eve recalled from that first night, sat beside him. The older man was telling what appeared to be a rousing tale of some sort. The Brit suddenly leaned back and slapped his thigh as his great thundering laugh filled the room.

Johnny sat in one of the big armchairs with a book held close under his nose, though how he could read with so much distraction was a wonder. Not only because of the noise, but also because the outlaw she remembered as Eli with the pretty blue eyes kept flipping the pages of Johnny's book every time he passed by. Eli was clearly having a lot more fun with the teasing than Johnny, who was getting a bit red in the face.

"Christ, Eli, leave the kid alone for once," someone suggested in a calm and even cadence.

Eve turned her head to see the last of the members she remembered from that first night standing against the kitchen counter with a coffee cup in hand. His skin was a dark, warm brown in the daylight, and his eyes were just a touch lighter than Gabriel's. He still wore his hat, but Eve could see that his black, curly hair was shorn close to his skull. His expression as he looked over the rim of his mug seemed to reveal a hint of amusement at Eli's antics despite his admonishment.

"Listen to Jackson," Johnny asserted in a grumble.

"Aww, but it's just so easy to get your temper up," Eli argued, taking another swipe at the book.

Johnny avoided him this time by pulling the book aside at the last minute and shooting his leg out to give Eli a sharp kick in the shin.

Eli gave a yowl and hopped away on one foot to fall into the corner of the sofa where he sat rubbing his shin with a comical expression of hurt and accusation. "Jesus, Johnny, you didn't have to aim with the point of your boot, did ya?"

"It's the only way to get you to stop houndin' me," Johnny replied, unapologetic.

"But it's so damn fun to get you riled up," Eli argued with a wide grin. "And I'm bored."

"You're always bored," Johnny retorted. "You know I gotta practice if I wanna get any better at reading."

To Eve's surprise, Eli's expression shifted to one that was almost repentant. "I know, kid. Sorry."

Johnny snorted his acceptance of the apology as he slumped down farther into the chair and buried his nose in the book. Which left Eli with no further distraction...until he noticed Eve and Gabriel standing at the back of the room.

"Hey there, Gabe," he said before he gave an elegant sweep of his arm followed by an exaggerated bow. "Miss Eve. So nice to see you again." Then he straightened and gave her a wide wink, destroying the effect of his dramatic greeting.

She almost smiled at his antics, but then realized everyone in the place had turned to look at her. Her gaze bounced from Eli's bright-blue eyes to Johnny's curious side glance, over to Jackson's calm curiosity, and then to the table, where the Brit and the old man had stopped their conversation.

"Let her be, Eli," Luke interjected as he emerged from the hallway. Luke's gaze swung to Gabriel, and a silent message seemed to pass between them before Luke continued into the room.

Just then, the door behind Eve and Gabriel opened, and Ramsey came stomping in.

Eve quickly stepped to the side for the youngest outlaw to pass by.

"Well, the stalls are clean, the horses watered and fed," Ramsey declared in an annoyed tone. "Now can I eat?"

Luke's gaze was hard. "You know where the kitchen is." He watched as Ramsey strode past him, and then he slid a studied glance over the room and its occupants. "Since we're all here, I may as well remind everyone"—Luke's gaze narrowed on Ramsey—"how we treat guests in this valley."

Ramsey's expression grew pinched at being singled out, but he nodded anyway.

"Miss Eve will remain in the bunkhouse for now. If she decides to stay awhile, we'll move her out to the cabin where she'll be more comfortable."

Luke slid his light-dark gaze to Eve's. "There are only two safe ways out of this valley, and they are difficult even for someone familiar with the terrain. You wanna go anywhere, you let one of the boys know. Leaving the valley on your own is not likely to end well. Understand?"

Eve returned his steady stare.

"That's not a threat," he clarified. "It's just a comment on how dangerous the mountains could be for someone who's unfamiliar with them."

"I am well aware of the danger," she replied.

His mouth tilted into a half smile, though his eyes remained unmoved. For a moment, it looked as though he intended to say something else. Eventually, he glanced away again, then strode toward the two men at the dining table. "You wanna deal me in or what?" he asked.

"Me too," Ramsey piped up from the kitchen.

As everyone slowly turned their focus back to whatever they were doing, Eve released a heavy breath. She looked over her shoulder to where Gabriel stood in his usual pose, tall and unmoving against the wall, his arms thick across his chest, his jaw firm.

It struck her how different he'd looked earlier when it had just been the two of them. It wasn't a great and noticeable difference, but more something she felt.

Now that they were back amongst the others, he'd closed himself off. Efficiently and completely.

His gaze flickered to meet hers, and she wished for a return of that depth. But it was thoroughly concealed.

She tried not to feel disappointed. He didn't owe her anything. "If there is something you need to do," she said, "I'm sure I'll be fine here."

He seemed to study her for a moment, then gave a short nod. Pushing away from the wall, he unfolded his arms and strode to the front door, leaving without a reply.

Eve stared at the door for a while after it closed behind him.

"It's not you. He's always like that."

Eve turned to see Johnny peeking at her over the top of his book. She had forgotten the outlaw was so close. She glanced across the room to see the others fully engaged in a card game. "Excuse me?"

"Gabe," Johnny said, then waved his hand toward the door. "All silent and...mean-looking. He's that way with everyone, so don't let it bother you."

"His silence doesn't bother me," Eve replied.

Johnny eyebrows lifted at that. "Really? For the first few years after I joined up with him and Luke, I thought he couldn't stand me. Until I realized he doesn't care much for people in general."

"Why is that?" Eve asked, unable to contain her curiosity now that she had someone who seemed quite willing to share.

Johnny's eyebrows dipped low in the center, and his lips curled with a hint of disgust. "You can imagine he's not always treated well by people. Not only on account of him being Cheyenne and all, but also because he's such a big, scary-looking fella. People just assume the worst about him. Then there are the females who like to treat him like some sort of novelty."

Eve's stomach tightened with a slightly ill feeling. "I don't understand."

"You know...women who get excited by danger and wanna see if they can handle a night in bed with a savage," Johnny answered bluntly.

"That's awful," she murmured.

"Yeah, well, Gabe's dealt with worse."

Worse? No wonder he held himself apart from everyone. "Have you known him long?" she asked.

Johnny flicked his attention back to the book in his hands. “I’m not sure *anyone* knows him,” he admitted coolly.

Eve sat with that for a bit. Maddy had said close to the same thing.

Gabriel was obviously a respected member of the gang. Yet he avoided sitting down with them and rarely spoke. The others apparently accepted his distance, but Eve couldn’t help wondering why someone would choose such a solitary existence.

Twenty-Five

Gabriel left the bunkhouse and headed back toward his cabin. He didn't have any reason to go there, but he had no reason to go anywhere else either.

He'd built the separate dwelling so he could claim solitude when he started to feel the need for his own space.

But right now, he didn't want solitude.

His body craved Eve's presence. His skin yearned to discover the texture of hers. Her spirit called to him. It was odd to feel the power of such a lure. Gabriel had never experienced anything similar before.

It didn't matter.

Wanting her did not make it possible to have her. It was best for him to stay away. Maybe he should leave the valley. The nearest town was at the base of the mountains, about a three-hour ride away. It had started as a mining base but never grew beyond a thousand people or so before the mine closed. Some residents chose to stick around, but not many.

But Luke insisted that his men only go to town on the rarest occasions. It wasn't good for locals to become too familiar with their faces.

Maybe he should talk to Luke and see if there was anything he needed Gabriel to do. Something that would keep him away for a while—long enough for the woman to be gone by the time he returned. Even as he considered it, his stomach muscles clenched in resistance.

Leaving her would be difficult. Not because he didn't trust the others in the gang to treat her well but because he just couldn't keep from feeling that it was *his responsibility*.

Eve passed the rest of the day in a mixed state of wariness and boredom. It was not completely unlike spending a lazy day in the drawing room back home, except for the company. The card game continued for a couple of hours, and for a while it was interesting enough to watch their interplay and muse at the challenging and often rudely insulting way they spoke to each other.

Eventually, Johnny offered to lend her a book from his spare collection made up mainly of dime novels.

She selected a rather tattered volume about a frontier man named Seth Jones. The story was full of sensational, unbelievable occurrences, but at least it gave Eve something to do for a while. When she reached the end of the thin novel, Johnny glanced up with an expression caught between disbelief and annoyance.

"You read that whole thing already?"

Eve gave a light nod. "It was an interesting story. If you can believe any of it actually happened."

"But how'd you get through it so fast?"

Seeing the young man's frustration, she explained, "I

read quite a bit when I was young. It just takes some practice, I suppose."

Johnny mumbled something under his breath as he rose to his feet and tossed his own book onto the chair. "I'm going for a ride." He stalked out the back door of the bunkhouse.

In the wake of Johnny's exit, Eve didn't notice Luke's approach until he swept the discarded novel up in his hand and lowered himself into the chair Johnny had vacated.

Eve shifted her attention to the leader of the outlaws.

Though he lounged casually in the overstuffed chair with one foot planted firmly on the floor and the other extended straight in front of him, there was an alertness about him.

"I meant what I said before about this valley being a safe place to hide out for a while."

Eve studied him for a moment. An essence of danger hovered about him and sparked in his eyes, but she realized she was not particularly afraid of him. In fact, aside from that first night when she'd suspected the men of working for Matthew, she couldn't say any of them had inspired true fear in her. They were all a little—or a lot—rough around the edges. Their manners and way of speaking were far more bold than what she was accustomed to, but she was surprised to acknowledge that she was not afraid of them.

Meeting Luke's watchful gaze, she said, "I have decided to stay. For a short time, anyway, until I can figure out how best to continue my travels."

Luke nodded, showing no indication of pleasure or otherwise at her decision. "We could help with some of that too, but you'd have to fill me in on what kind of trouble you're facing."

She considered telling him. For just a second. But then she realized he couldn't keep her safe from Matthew. As her husband, Matthew had every right to hunt her down and claim her.

Luke's gaze narrowed when she said nothing more, the golden flecks sparking with something akin to anger. Then he spoke in a low tone. "Take it from me, darlin', running isn't all it's cracked up to be. At some point, you might have to turn and face whatever demon is chasing you."

Eve shivered at the thought of squaring off against Matthew. It took all of her willpower not to start shaking her head in fierce denial. Her only option was to disappear. And though she could see the benefit of staying here for a short time, she couldn't stay forever.

That night, as dusk started to gather in the valley, the energy of the bunkhouse shifted. Luke had gone back into his office some time before. Jackson and Eli assembled in the kitchen where they started banging around with the apparent intention of preparing the evening meal. Johnny eventually came back, looking wet and bedraggled, as though he'd jumped into the creek, clothes and all. He went straight to his room down the hall and didn't return until dinner was nearly ready.

Meanwhile, the red-haired Brit went about hauling in more wood to stack beside the fire, and Pete, the oldest member of the gang, pulled out a fiddle and started playing quietly in the corner.

Eve almost offered to help in the kitchen, but Jackson and Eli seemed to have things well in hand. She wouldn't know what to do anyway.

Besides, she was way too busy glancing toward the door every few minutes, waiting for Gabriel to appear. By the time Eli and Jackson had the dining table covered with steaming bowls of food, she realized Gabriel wasn't coming.

He didn't come the next day.

Or the next night.

Or the next.

Eve discovered almost by accident that Gabriel had not just been avoiding the bunkhouse, he'd actually left the valley altogether.

She tried not to acknowledge the pang of disappointment she felt in the fact that he hadn't told her he was leaving. But it was there all the same. And as more days passed without his return, the pang grew to a subtle, pervading ache of disquiet.

She considered asking about moving to the little cabin in the woods but decided against it. It just seemed a little too isolated and distant. Besides, once she managed to settle in at the bunkhouse, she realized she rather enjoyed being around the others. She eased into a sort of rhythm that suited her. Most of her direct interaction was with Johnny, who she was coming to see as a friend. The others maintained a respectful distance, but she could imagine even that eventually easing if given more time.

In her observations, she saw that although Ramsey was young and careless, he held Luke in high regard and truly wished to please him. Eli was clearly the jokester of the group, but Eve suspected the man had more going on his mind than he often let on. Gentleman George was just that, a true gentleman in bearing and demeanor who was also capable of a bellowing laugh that often filled the great room. Jackson was the most reserved and mellow of the men. He seemed to fill the role of mediator and voice of reason more often than not. Lastly, there was Old Pete, who seemed most content when simply enjoying the casual company of his friends. Eve got the sense his life had not been an easy one.

In truth, she got that sense from all of them. Each of them, in their own way, seemed to keep an aspect of themselves tucked out of sight.

And then there was Luke. He kept to himself the greater part of every day, though the men appeared to have no problem seeking him out in his office if need be. He didn't bother broaching the subject of her past again, and Eve certainly had no intention of doing so.

For the most part, she was left to herself.

Which allowed her to find her bearings in this new environment, but it did nothing to ease the increasing sense of restlessness inside her.

In the late afternoon on her fifth full day in the valley, Eve found herself struggling to keep her inner disquiet under control.

Just the day before, Old Pete, Jackson, Eli, and Ramsey had ridden out with saddle packs full and determination on their faces. They had provided no explanation of their destination or purpose. Considering the discussions she had overheard about how much ammunition and gunpowder they'd need, Eve didn't ask for one. Even Luke was planning to leave in a few days, which would soon leave only Johnny and Gentleman George to keep her company.

Luke was back in his office as usual, and Johnny and George had started up a game of cards. They had offered her a seat if she'd wanted to join them, but she'd declined. Instead, she'd sat with another of Johnny's dime novels for a bit, but the words couldn't hold her attention.

Something in her wanted to move. There was a jittery energy in her limbs, a dissatisfaction in the confining walls of the room as she started to wander about the space.

Stopping at a window, she looked outside and noticed that the sun was making its descent toward the mountaintops. Another hour or so, and it would be dark.

Something about the shifting shades of day transforming into night called to her.

She passed by the table where Johnny and George were arguing over a detail in Johnny's card play on her way to the front door. "I'm just going to go for a little walk before retiring for the night."

"Okay, sure," Johnny replied with a distracted wave before directing his next words back at George. "How the hell can you call that play a cheat? It's well within the rules of the game."

"*Your* rules," George countered as Eve stepped out on the porch and took a deep breath of the fresh evening air.

The sky was just starting to reveal the muted shades of dusk. Bright blue slid into gold and pink as the sun's rays stretched across the tops of the mountains, casting an almost magical glow on the highest peaks.

It was stunning.

Soon the blue would fade to lavender, and after that, the stars would start to appear.

Luke had advised that the valley was safe enough as long as she didn't venture into the forest, so she directed her steps through the tall grass where wildflowers were blooming in various colors.

As she walked, she did a quick count of the days and realized it was well into June. It had been more than a month since she'd left Boston. Surely by now someone beyond her husband had noticed her prolonged absence from society!

What story had Matthew told about her whereabouts?

Was her mother worried?

She hoped not, but eventually Matthew would have to give a more permanent explanation for Eve's disappearance. It broke her heart to think that her mother and her dear friends would never know the truth of what had happened to her.

The last few days that she'd spent in the valley had lulled her into an uncertain sense of security. Late at night, as she fell asleep in her narrow little bedroom, she often wondered what it might be like if she just stayed there indefinitely.

Would it be so bad?

On the day she'd decided to leave Boston, she'd declared that never again would anyone else have power over her life. It was important to her that she learn how to feel strong and capable of taking care of herself. She wanted to feel free to make her own decisions, direct her own fate.

When she was kidnapped from the train, she had despaired that once again she'd fallen under someone else's control. But perhaps fate had simply been redirecting her path.

Coming to this valley had not exactly been her choice. But it *had* been her decision to stay.

Surrounded by the imposing mountainous terrain and men with guns, she felt safer than she had in a long while. But was she choosing to stay out of fear of what she'd encounter beyond the valley?

Had she truly taken her life back if she continued to hide?

Her train of thought troubled her, and she couldn't help but wish she could discuss her concerns with Gabriel.

As his name filtered through her mind, she happened to glance up and suddenly realized she had been following the river upstream and was nearly to the bend that flowed past his meadow. Her steps faltered with a jolt of anticipation before she recalled that he wasn't there.

Still...thinking of him gave rise to another track of emotional pondering.

She had missed him over the last few days. The loss of his steady presence had been like a constant hum of discontent originating in the deepest, quietest part of her.

Coming around the trees, she gazed out over the meadow beyond and drew a long breath. She soaked in the quiet beauty of his home nestled in the approaching shadows of dusk. It was so peaceful and simple and perfect.

So perfect that she almost failed to notice the front door was open and a thin thread of smoke drifted gently from the chimney.

Her heart stuttered as she felt compelled to continue along the riverbank. Several steps later, she caught sight of Gabriel's large mustang grazing behind the cabin.

He had returned.

Eve came to a stop at the edge of the river where the stepping-stones could take her across to Gabriel's meadow. She stood there in a sort of breathless reverie. The urge to go to him—to look into his eyes and hear his voice—ran deep in her blood, but she resisted.

Gabriel's privacy and solitude were sacred to him. She would not intrude upon that.

If he had wanted to see her, he would have come to the bunkhouse.

As she stood there—surrounded by the call of night birds and the scent of wildflowers swirling on a breeze that lifted the long strands of her hair and sighed through the tall grass—Gabriel stepped through the doorway.

His hair was free down his back, his feet were bare, and he wore a buckskin tunic over his denims. His gaze found her immediately.

The connection she'd been pondering flared to full life.

Eve's heart leapt to a furious pace. It was as though with his return, he brought life and warmth and hope back into her existence. That and something else, she realized, as heat and heaviness spiraled outward from her core in a delicious dance of physical yearning.

He walked slowly down the slight slope to the bank of the river, his movements graceful and strong. Then he lifted his hand toward her. "Come."

He'd spoken the single word to her many times, in command or instruction. But something in the way he said it this time felt different. Richer, more intimate, and slightly uncertain.

As though he'd been waiting for her.

Twenty-Six

The earth seemed to hold its breath as Gabriel waited for Eve to cross the stepping-stones. The sight of her—so serene and fierce at the same time, with her long, pale hair flowing unconstrained down her back—made the flow of his blood feel thick and heavy.

He almost crossed the river himself to fetch her but did not. She needed to come to him freely.

And seeing her leap over the winding waterway with her skirts lifted in one hand was beautiful to behold. As was the sparkle in her eyes when she reached his grassy shore and slid her fingers into his.

As their palms met, she exhaled in a long sigh. The soft sound soaked through his skin to twist through his insides. He felt the rightness of linking hands with this woman. An aspect of his nature understood and accepted that they were already joined. But the part of him that knew something of the world she came from understood that life was not so simple.

Gabriel searched her face. At least now, in this moment, she showed no fear. Only the unique sort of quiet strength he had become familiar with in the set of her smooth jaw and the directness of her gaze. Something compelled him to close the distance that remained between them. He almost did it—his body swaying toward her—but he stopped himself, remembering the way she had reacted to his touch.

But she had seen his intention. For a second, her lips parted as though in anticipation and her gaze flickered to his lips. "I didn't know you were back," she murmured.

Gabriel lifted a brow, and her cheeks flushed a soft and pretty pink as she glanced toward his cabin. "I felt like a walk this evening, and…my feet just brought me here," she answered as though she'd heard the question in his mind.

"I'm glad they did," he replied. Lowering his chin, he asked, "Would you come inside?"

Light flickered in her gaze, and Gabriel's chest tightened to a point of near pain. But the feeling was good. It felt right.

"I'd love to."

They turned to walk up the slope to his home, their hands sliding apart as they kept pace beside each other, until Gabriel paused to allow Eve to walk ahead of him through the open doorway.

Just as the last time she'd been there, it felt as though the dim, quiet place breathed with new life in response to her presence. Where there were usually shadows, he now saw glimpses of sunlight.

She took only a few steps before turning to face him, a question in her eyes.

Gabriel gestured to the fur-covered dais he used as a bed with a lift of his chin. "Please. Sit."

As she did so, he crouched before the fire. The flames had been reduced to a bed of hot, glowing coals below the grouse roasting on the spit. The coffee he'd set to heat was steaming, and he poured her a cup.

After getting some coffee for himself, he sat on his rug-covered floor with his legs crossed and rested his back against the stone hearth. He openly soaked in the sight of Eve as she sat straight and proper across from him.

Staying away from the valley the last several days had been pointless.

The feelings rushing through him remained as strong as ever. The thoughts in his head were no less focused.

He still wanted her.

Her eyes met his over the rim of her mug, and his belly clenched with the need inside him. It took a great deal of willpower to contain his hunger for her. If she caught even a glimpse of what he was feeling…

"Where did you go?" she asked into the lengthening silence.

A safe topic. "Hunting."

Confusion flickered in her eyes. "I did not see any kills. Were you successful?"

Gabriel nodded. "There are people in these mountains who sometimes welcome the extra meat."

"You gave it away?" she asked, her eyes wide.

He nodded again. The bunkhouse had plenty to feed the gang for the summer. Come fall, Gabriel would hunt again to restock their stores for the winter.

"You've been well?" he asked.

She lifted her shoulders in a subtle shrug. "I've settled in, I suppose."

He could see what she didn't say. "You are not happy here," he murmured.

"I don't know." Even in the dim light of the cabin he could see the uncertainty and indecision in her eyes. "When I'd decided to"—she hesitated—"come west, I'd planned to establish a new life in the anonymity of a big city. To be honest, I feel rather adrift here in the valley."

"You wish to put down roots."

She met his gaze, and he thought he saw something there, something soft and quiet—vulnerable yet strong and determined. "Yes. I suppose I do." Her voice dropped to a whisper. "I worry that in staying here, I am being guided by my fear."

Gabriel understood. He had faced something similar, many years ago.

He had never told anyone the full story of his path to manhood. Those years had been a struggle to find his true direction, to fulfill a purpose he could not identify. Inner peace remained out of reach until he finally accepted a simple unavoidable truth.

Taking a long and steady breath, he set his mug aside and looked into the flickering glow of red coals. Most times, the past was like a distant dream, but as he focused on the memories, they became fresh and real again.

"My father was killed in one of the many battles between our people and the rush of settlers who came to stake claim on our land when I was still an infant," he began. "My mother died only a few years later. But my sister and I were never orphans among our people. All are family." Those earliest memories of his life on this earth filtered through his mind, carrying with them gratitude and a thin layer of grief.

Eve did not speak. As the silence lengthened, she eased from the short dais to sit on the floor as he did, folding her legs beneath her skirt and setting aside her mug to link her hands in her lap.

Gabriel looked at her hands, wishing he could hold them in his as he continued his story.

"One day," he started again, "I followed a hunting party away from camp. I was too young to join them, but I was eager to learn." He clenched his teeth and forced his next words to come swiftly. "The hunting party was attacked by a small band of General Custer's men. By the time I reached the battle, the hunting party had all been killed. I was taken and later handed over to a missionary couple to raise. They tried to mold me into something I refused to be. I thought myself a man when I finally reclaimed my freedom and struck out on my own, but at thirteen, I was still just a boy. The tribe had been forced to move several times during my long absence. It took more than two years to find them again."

Eve studied the hard angles of his face, feeling a squeezing pain through her center at the sorrow and anger he fought to keep from his voice.

"My sister is older by a few years," he continued after a moment. "By the time I'd returned, she held the honored position of wife to the chief's son. She welcomed my return, but her husband was wary. He worried that I had spent too much time among the enemy. Some people in the tribe agreed with his concerns. The elders decided I could stay and prove myself." His breath lengthened and his voice lowered, originating from a place deep in his chest as he said, "I soon realized my spirit was as divided as my tribe. I thought my return would feel like coming home. I thought I would have a family again. But I *was* different. I could not stay."

"I'm sorry," Eve whispered past the ache in her heart, yet the words felt ridiculously inadequate. He had lived through so much loss.

He lifted his eyes to meet hers. In the silence that followed, she felt as though he reached out to her—not in any physical way, but with that intangible force that had seemed to exist between them from that first time their eyes had met. Even from across the fire, she felt his indelible strength and the balanced calm he seemed to so naturally possess.

It amazed her. And it inspired her.

"Do you still wish you could go back?" she asked to keep herself from thinking things she shouldn't.

"No." His ready answer was unexpected. "For a time, I wondered what life would be like if I'd never been separated from my people. But that is not what was intended for me. I've accepted that my path has led in another direction."

And she could see that he did. Yes, there was loss in him, but no regret filtered through his words.

"It is painful to yearn for something that cannot be," he added in a lowered voice.

Though his words followed their conversation, she suspected they referenced something else. The yearning he spoke of was evident in his eyes. "Yes," she replied softly. "It is."

There was a brief moment of silence, then Gabriel gave a slow nod. "You too find yourself on a path you hadn't expected to travel."

"How do I know where to go from here?" she asked quietly.

He shrugged, but it was not a dismissive gesture. "When it is time, you will know," he said simply, and then he leaned forward to turn the spit. "Are you hungry?"

"I am," Eve answered.

He made a sound of acknowledgment and rose to his feet to fetch some metal dishes from a small trunk set to one side.

They both sat on the floor in front of the fire as they ate. It reminded Eve of those first days after the train. Her feelings toward the man across from her were no less intense and intimidating, but it was in an entirely different way.

When they finished, Gabriel stood again and collected their dishes. "I'll go wash these in the river," he said. "I'll be back."

Eve nodded.

She sat in the silence of the cabin for a while after he left, breathing in the peace and comfort of the place. It was so like him. His home. His sanctuary.

When he returned, his expression was stern. "Night has fallen. I should take you back."

His words caused an instant tightening in her chest and a rebellious twist in her belly, but she rose to her feet. As he placed the dishes back in the trunk, she didn't move, and when he turned back to face her, she knew she wouldn't.

The fire had burned down to coals, casting an uncertain light that flickered in a familiar pattern across his features. She didn't want to leave him. Didn't want to return to her narrow little room in the bunkhouse. Alone and lonely.

"Can I stay?" The question was uncertain, leaving her lips before she could consider what it implied.

His dark eyes searched hers. She waited with her breath held. Her insides trembling with anticipation and embarrassment that he might have heard the depth of longing hidden in her voice.

Then he made a quiet sound in his throat, a rich rumble of acceptance, and he crouched beside the fire. Using a stick, he stirred the coals back to life, then added more wood from a stack in the corner. Flames leapt, casting long shadows on the walls as heat billowed outward, bathing Eve in warmth and a sense of belonging.

It didn't seem odd that she would feel so comfortable in this simple dwelling, but she wondered if it was the place or the man himself that triggered such rightness of being inside her.

"You can rest here," he said, gesturing to the bed behind him.

Eve turned and settled amongst the soft pelts as Gabriel went about setting a few things in order around the cabin. Eve couldn't tell if they were truly things that needed to be done, or if he was trying to distract himself.

When he finally seemed satisfied with his tasks, he made as if to settle on the floor before the fire.

"Gabriel?"

He straightened again but did not look at her. The tension in his body was evident in his wide shoulders.

Eve felt the moment like a promise tethered in the dark, crouched in anticipation.

"Will you lie beside me?" she asked, trembling deep in her center.

His chest expanded with a heavy breath that expelled in a rush. Then he lowered his chin and took long strides around the fire. Eve brought her legs up onto the bed and scooted back toward the shadows. Without a word, he sat on the edge, his broad back blocking much of the firelight before he turned and stretched out on his back. Not so close that he touched her, but close enough that she felt his warmth.

The trembling inside her increased to a steady hum, a heightened vibration of awareness that should have made her tense and unable to relax. Instead, it made her feel safe in a way she had started to accept was directly linked to this man. She lay on her side and closed her eyes, soaking up his nearness, trying not to imagine how it would feel if he eased the hard, solid length of his body into contact with hers.

She hadn't wanted the touch of another person for so long. It felt strange and confusing to want something that still terrified her. But she allowed it. She sank into that wanting, letting it flow through her, letting it change her in tiny ways. She was able to do it because she trusted implicitly in the fact that he would never hurt her.

And he wouldn't touch her unless she asked him to.

Twenty-Seven

The Eastern woman had completely disappeared.

Whoever had taken her off that train didn't want to be found.

Frustration over his inability to track any farther than the base of the Absaroka Range kept him there longer than he should have been. By the time he returned to town and received the telegrams that were waiting there for him, several days had been lost in futility.

At least one of the telegrams had some news.

It wasn't anything to help him in finding the woman's current location, but it was something he could work with.

The other telegram had him gritting his teeth. He should have known he wouldn't be allowed to manage this task on his own. He'd have to ride hard to make it to Chester Springs in the next couple of days if he hoped to meet up with his partner before she decided to go and do something reckless.

Twenty-Eight

Eve moaned softly in resistance as she felt the pull of consciousness tugging at her slowly stirring awareness. Cool air touched her cheeks, but the rest of her was warm and cozy. She didn't want to face the cold just yet. Not when her sleep had been so deep and dreamless.

In an effort to hold the morning at bay, she snuggled into the warmth, sighing as strong arms tightened around her and a slow exhale bathed her temple.

Gabriel's breath.

Gabriel's arms.

And his heartbeat, thudding against her chest. His thighs and belly pressing against hers. His shoulders blocking the chill in the air. His steady gaze meeting hers when she opened her eyes.

Still sleepy and disoriented, she easily became trapped by those eyes. Seeing in them a place of comfort, security, and something more.

The something more should have made her uneasy. Instead, it matched the feelings coursing through her. Feelings that didn't have a chance to be masked by a fear that had been planted by another man far away. Feelings that made her breathless and…wanting.

She should pull away. But she didn't want to. It felt right to be there—in his arms, chest to chest, face to face, one of her hands tucked between them, the other resting on his side, feeling the rise and fall of his steady breath.

"Who hurt you?" he asked in a tone cloaked in dark emotions and quiet danger.

She hated the old feelings that rose up at the thought of Matthew. "My husband," she replied on an exhale and was surprised at the ease of the admission.

Gabriel's expression did not change, but there was a shift in his eyes, a subtle darkening. A silent acknowledgment.

They said nothing for another long moment. Neither of them moved.

"Would he come after you?"

"I did my best to leave nothing for him to follow," she replied softly, lowering her gaze. "But he is resourceful and…likely did not take well to my disappearance. He… There is a chance."

"He won't hurt you again," Gabriel said, the words sounding like a vow.

She returned his confident stare. "No. He won't."

Eve allowed herself to feel the solid muscle of Gabriel's upper arm beneath her head and his large hand cupping her shoulder, keeping her close. She noted the weight of his other arm around her waist and how it made her feel. She looked deep into his eyes, letting him see the uncertainty and the need.

He remained unflinching, strong, accepting.

In a low murmur, she asked, "Have you always been known as Gabriel?"

There was a slight pause. "No."

"What did your family call you?"

There was a flicker deep in his eyes. "Kuckunniwi," he replied in a gravelly whisper. "Little Wolf."

She wished she could sweep away the loss in his tone, but it was a part of him, just as her past was part of her.

"Little Wolf," she murmured, then smiled. "Not so little anymore."

His brows furrowed over his gaze. "This is the first time I have seen you smile."

The smile faded. "I'm sorry."

"For what?" His confusion was clear in the deepening frown. "You have a right to your sorrow. And your smiles."

She lowered her gaze, settling her attention on the full curve of his mouth.

His arms loosened from around her, and though she had no wish to, she moved away from him as he rolled to his feet. "Morning has come," he said.

Kneeling in front of the fire, he stirred the dying coals and blew life back into the last flickering flames. Then he sat back on his heels and tipped his face upward as he combed his fingers back through his hair. After he nimbly plaited the length into a single braid down his back, he gave Eve a sideways glance.

She didn't realize she had been openly staring until he caught her.

For a second it looked like he might tease her for it, but then he said, "Would you ride with me today?"

Eve sat up, her stomach tightening with apprehension. "Beyond the valley?"

"I'll assure your safety."

His tone dropped with the assurance, and Eve felt the sentiment in a way that went beyond what he'd likely intended. If anyone in the world could keep her safe, it would be him. Though he had never given any indication of violence or aggression, she knew intuitively that he would not back away from danger, whether it be in the form of a wild animal or humanity in its evilest form.

Was that why she trusted him? Because she knew he could protect her?

It felt like more than that. Her trust went beyond the knowing that he wouldn't hurt her, beyond his obvious physical capabilities—far deeper than the darkness of his gaze.

It had grown slowly but now felt like an indelible part of her. She trusted him with everything she was.

It was a heady realization.

And the idea of seeing more of the mountainous terrain filled her with excitement. She hadn't realized she'd gotten so tired of the bunkhouse until she had the opportunity to leave it. "Yes. I would enjoy that."

Gabriel nodded. "Can you start coffee while I check on Twig?"

Eve's doubt over being able to make coffee didn't have time to solidify. "Twig?"

"My mustang," Gabriel explained with a beautiful curving of his lips. "He was all skin and bones as a foal. The name suited him then."

Eve thought of the giant beast outside and smiled. "I like it."

After he left, she sat for a moment with the metal coffeepot in her hands—the completely empty pot—biting her lip as she tried to recall the steps she'd watched him perform on more than one occasion.

Water. She needed water. Looking around, she did not spot even a glimmer of the stuff.

The river. She brightened with inspiration as she stepped from the cabin and strolled down to the river with the coffeepot in hand. She could hear Gabriel speaking to his horse in low, murmured tones, but she refused to glance his way.

He had entrusted her with this small, inconsequential task. She could figure it out.

After filling the pot about halfway, she returned to the cabin, taking a moment to breathe deeply of the faint herbal smell that filled the space. Then she went about searching for the canister of ground coffee beans Gabriel had carried with him on their ascent into the mountains. She found a variety of similar containers and started opening them one by one until on her fourth try, she found what she was looking for.

Now...how much?

The coffee Gabriel made was always rich and dark, so she added a couple of big scoops to the water and set it over the coals as she seen him do many times. Then she sat on the floor and waited for it to heat up.

After a while, she checked the coffee. It was quite hot, but the liquid looked far too light. It was more golden than dark brown. So, she added three more scoops of the coffee grounds and set it back on the coals. Hoping it would only need a bit longer to brew, she decided to step outside and let Gabriel know the coffee would be ready soon.

As she made her way around the outside of the cabin to where he was brushing down the large gray mustang, Twig lifted his head and gave a big snort as he peered in Eve's direction.

"He's missed you," Gabriel said.

Eve cast him a dubious look, thinking he might be teasing her, but his expression was earnest. She approached slowly until she stood at Gabriel's side, with the great beast's head looming over her.

Twig made another heavy sound, expelling breath swiftly through his nostrils, before he lowered his head over Eve's shoulder. She gave a soft laugh and ran her hands along his strong neck as she murmured, "I've missed you too."

After a moment, the horse lifted his head again. As Eve stepped back, she caught Gabriel's eye and shivered at the depth of emotion she saw there. But then he made a short sound and glanced toward the cabin. "Is the coffee ready?"

"I believe so, yes. At least, I think it should be."

His lips twitched. "Let's see."

He led Twig around to the front of the cabin and then followed Eve inside.

She sat on the bed and waited while he filled both cups. From what she could see, the brew was nice and steamy and certainly looked darker than it had earlier. Gabriel sat across from her on the hearth and lifted his mug for a sip.

Eve did the same.

Their gazes locked at the same time—Eve's wide with shock, Gabriel's sparkling with amusement.

Not knowing what else to do, she spit what was in her mouth back into her cup. "That is dreadful."

Gabriel audibly swallowed what was in his mouth, then took another sip as Eve stared in disbelief.

"It's not bad," he said evenly, "if you wish to poison someone."

Eve choked on a short laugh and shook her head. "Please, dump it out. It's awful."

"For a first attempt, it is..." He paused to find the right word.

"Disgusting? Disgraceful? Alarming?" Eve offered.

He smiled. "Admirable."

She murmured a denial and reached forward to take the offensive brew out of his hand. "You are too good to me."

"No."

The tension in his voice stopped her in midmovement, and his dark, serious eyes locked on hers, effectively holding her in place. "You must stop seeing yourself as he saw you. You are worthy of kindness and respect and deserve every drop of happiness the world can offer. It is time you claim that truth as your own."

A tumult of sensations tripped over themselves inside her. His nearness and the intensity of his gaze made her feel weak and shaky, but the strength in his words and the force of his conviction stirred a flame of confidence in the depths of her soul.

"I'm trying," she whispered.

After a moment, he gave a short nod.

Then he rose to his feet and took her mug. Setting the offending brews aside, he removed the pot from the coals and spread out the remaining embers. Then he poured what was left of the coffee on top, sending a pungent plume of smoke up the chimney.

"The smell should keep wild animals away for a month or two," he said, before he gave her a sideways look, followed by a brief heart-stopping grin.

Her entire body warmed in response to his teasing, and for the first time in a very long while, the happiness he'd spoken of seemed frighteningly within reach.

TWENTY-NINE

GABRIEL AND EVE SPENT MUCH OF THE DAY RIDING along scenic passes and dramatic overlooks. They kept to well-worn trails, which should have made it a calm and relaxing trek, if not for the fact that Eve remained in an acute and near-constant state of anticipation.

Sharing a horse with him was so very different this time around.

She didn't try so hard to limit the contact of her body with his. She didn't force herself to sit so stiff and straight between his spread thighs, allowing her back to curve against his sturdy chest. She didn't flinch when his arm occasionally brushed hers or when his breath stirred the hair at her temple as he spoke of various animals or scenic wonders they saw along the way.

It was…nice.

More than nice.

And it was a little bit terrifying.

Because while her body managed to soften and accept his nearness, her insides had gone into a secret little riot the moment he leapt up behind her on the saddleless horse. A riot that continued to clamor and expand inside her until she breathlessly anticipated every extra moment of contact.

She knew he didn't intend to stir such contradiction inside her; knew that he likely would have regretted any discomfort he inadvertently caused. But that was exactly what she wondered at most—she liked the discomfort. She reveled in it.

It was real. It made her feel alive and hopeful as they made their way through the gorgeous and rugged mountain passes.

But eventually they had to turn back. After entering the valley through the steep and narrow ravine, he turned his horse away from the bunkhouse, continuing along the river toward his cabin.

Crossing the river on horseback, he dismounted on the other side but didn't reach up to help her down. "Wait here. I'll be right back."

Eve looked down at him in question. "We aren't staying?"

"Just wait here."

She watched as he disappeared into the cabin and came back out a moment later, carrying what appeared to be a handmade fishing pole.

The hint of a smile pulled at his lips when he handed her the pole so he could leap onto the horse behind her. "I'm hungry," he said in a low voice that warmed the back of her neck. Earlier in the day, they'd snacked on some fresh bread he had packed before leaving that morning—a gift he'd received in trade for some of the fresh meat he'd given away on his hunting trek. And they'd enjoyed some berries they'd come upon while riding, but other than that, neither of them had eaten much and it was well past midday.

Not far beyond the cabin, the river began to widen and deepen. Soon after, they reached a curve where the water slowed and lapped gently at its banks. Eve realized this was likely the spot Johnny had mentioned that they used for swimming and bathing.

Eve could see the appeal. The water was clear and refreshing. Sheltering trees and thick bushes extended along both sides of the river, providing privacy from anyone riding past.

Twig was left to graze at his leisure on the lush grasses, while Gabriel and Eve found a spot along the shore where he promised they'd have excellent luck. Though Gabriel offered to let her give fishing a try, she preferred watching his expert skill, and it wasn't long before he pulled in two good-sized fish.

A short time later, they returned to his cabin. The fish were cleaned and set to fry in a pan over the fire as Gabriel talked Eve through the steps of making a pot of coffee.

Stopping in the midst of his instruction, Gabriel lifted his head as though listening.

Eve looked up and waited. Then she heard it as well. Someone was yelling.

He rose smoothly and quickly to his feet, then crossed to open the door while Eve kept to the shadows a few steps behind him, fear running swift through her veins.

Past Gabriel's shoulder, she saw Johnny riding across the river on his black gelding. He didn't slow his approach until he was right in front of the cabin and didn't even bother to dismount as he spoke in a voice that was slightly out of breath. "Gabe, thank God you're here."

"What is it?" Gabriel asked. A calm but alert readiness emanated from him.

"No one's seen Eve all day. I've been all over looking for her. She went for a walk late yesterday, and we don't know if she ever came back."

Gabriel hesitated only a moment—probably not long enough for Johnny to notice, but Eve saw it. She tensed as he stepped to the side so Johnny could see past him.

Johnny's eyes grew round with shock as he glanced back and forth from Eve to Gabriel, then back again. Finally, settling his focus on Eve, he asked, "Are you okay? We were worried."

Gabriel didn't turn to look at her.

"I'm sorry," she replied, taking a step forward. "I'm fine."

Johnny studied her for a moment, then nodded. "All right then. I'll let the others know you're okay and that you're here with Gabe." There was a hint of question in his words.

Eve nodded. "Thank you."

Johnny gave a nod, then directed his next words to Gabriel. "Luke's heading north in two days. He needs you to come by the bunkhouse before he leaves."

Gabriel acknowledged the order with a dip of his chin.

With another glance at Eve, Johnny turned his horse and rode back across the river.

An odd tension settled between them after that. As though the intrusion of the outside world had set them off-kilter and they weren't exactly sure how to set it right again.

Finally, as the night started to gather closer around them, Eve realized she couldn't let it be. "Did you want me to go back with Johnny?"

They were both sitting on the floor in front of the fire. Gabriel's legs were crossed, while Eve's legs were swept to one side as she leaned on a hand. He had been staring rather intently into the fire but turned to look at her when she spoke.

"I want you to do what pleases you," he replied in a tone that rolled through her center like a gentle fire.

"It pleases me to stay here," she replied. "With you."

His intent focus remained on her face. Though his expression didn't change, she felt a difference in his regard. His studied gaze reached deeper, explored further, questioned and searched.

"What pleases you, Gabriel?" she asked, her voice lowered to an uncertain whisper.

"You."

His answer was a rough murmur, and at the sound of it, something broke free inside her. It unwound throughout her body, loosening the tightness in her chest, swirling through her belly, lightening her limbs. It was a truth she couldn't deny any more than she was prepared to name it.

She thought of that morning, when she had awakened in his arms. The feeling of rightness—of peace and comfort—that had filled her at the time. What she felt now was nothing of the sort. There was no peace, just yearning. Deep, heavy, and undeniable.

Before thinking too much more about it, she rose to her feet.

He remained seated, still as stone. The breaths he took were long and deep, but he stared boldly back at her, the black depths of his eyes reflecting the flickering light of the fire.

"Lie with me?"

Her question seemed to spark a brighter light in his gaze before he rose to his feet and approached the bed. Lying down, he shifted back to make room for her between his body and the fire. No more words were spoken as she lowered herself beside him, lying on her side to face him. He had bent one arm beneath his head. With his other hand, he carefully pulled the fur up over her shoulders. Her gaze never left his face.

He was so accepting. So willing to just be beside her, though she could feel something more like a vibration of need coming from him. She had felt it from the beginning but had been too afraid to recognize it. But now, she saw it all and finally acknowledged the swirling fire in her belly for what it was.

Once he had the furs as he wanted, he rested his hand in the space between them. He was so careful not to touch her. Staring into his dark, silent eyes, she knew that she would have to be the one to do it.

Could she?

She wanted to. So badly.

She wanted to feel the comfort and strength of his hands on her, knowing down to her soul that his touch would never cause pain or shame or degradation. She wanted to show him the things he made her feel—the things she couldn't put into words. The things she'd never felt before.

Perhaps he would not want such an admission from her. She thought of what Johnny had told her; of how Gabriel was often treated by women like her—women of privilege and pride. Would he think she was the same as them?

The thought made her sad and slightly ill.

Something of her thoughts must have shown in her eyes because his expression shifted to one of concern. His straight brows furrowed, and his jaw tightened. "Sleep," he said, his tone rough and intimate. "You are safe."

"I know," she whispered. "I trust you, Gabriel." She saw the spark in his gaze just before she closed her eyes.

Listening to the steady flow of his breath as it mingled with the sound of the quietly flowing river, she fell asleep.

Gabriel lifted his hand. For a moment, he allowed it to hover over the curve of her cheek. He wouldn't touch her, but he wanted to imagine what it might feel like if he did.

Silk and sadness.

Freedom and fear.

Longing and the strength of a woman whose spirit had been too long trapped in shadows.

His hand curled into a tight fist as he thought of the man who had caged her in that darkness.

He did not need to set eyes on this man to know his nature. Gabriel had known such people. They existed everywhere. Some people could not stand to be in contact with something so beautiful without desiring to possess it. And destroy it.

But she had not been destroyed. He could see her coming out of the darkness little by little, and soon she would stand in the light again.

Gabriel didn't doubt it.

His stomach clenched with the depths of his longing.

He would sacrifice much to be so fortunate as to stand beside her.

The delicate fan of her eyelashes fluttered against her pale skin, and a tiny sound slipped from her throat as she dreamed.

Heaviness wound through Gabriel's blood, like roots sinking into the soil. Grounding and comforting.

Thirty

Eve knew without opening her eyes that she had awoken alone.

But she could still feel the lingering essence Gabriel had left behind. She sighed and reached her hand to smooth over the spot where he'd lain with her through the night, offering warmth and assurance.

Since meeting him, she felt stronger and braver. She had also become more accepting of her personal yearning for companionship and understanding. Her desire to be appreciated and loved.

A similar yearning had lured her into the nightmare her life had been with Matthew.

But Gabriel was not the same man her husband was.

Gabriel would never tear her down or make her feel small. He had only tried to convince her of her power and courage.

She trusted him. And she had finally accepted that she desired him. So why was she still holding back?

Last night she could have reached for him, and he would have accepted her. She could have curled her body into his warmth, and he would have drawn her closer.

With a frustrated sound, she opened her eyes and pushed to a seated position.

The fire had not yet been stirred to new life, and the coffeepot sat off to the side, cold.

Eve left the cabin and stood for a moment under the warmth of a bright sun and cloudless sky. The gentle breeze awakened her more fully, filling her with a strange sense of purpose. She saw Twig down at the river, sipping from the shallow shore.

Gabriel wasn't with him.

She didn't see him anywhere.

But that didn't alarm her. He wouldn't have gone far.

The beauty of the early-summer morning had her strolling down to the river. After greeting the large mustang with a quiet word, she turned upstream. As she walked along, she used her fingers to comb through the tangle of her hair, and she hummed a song she hadn't recalled in years.

It was a short walk to the spot where the river widened. As she drew nearer, the soft sound of splashing water reached her ears. A spark lit inside her. Anticipation. Excitement. A touch of uncertainty laced with need.

She found the worn footpath through the trees. A moment later, she caught sight of the golden sunlight reflecting off the water.

And then she stepped free of the foliage and saw him.

He was turned away from her, hip deep in the calm flow of the river several yards from the shore. Water glistened on his bronzed skin and rippled in tiny waves as he moved.

She stood on the sun-dappled shore, unashamedly claiming the opportunity to observe him.

Muscles rolled beneath the skin of his back and bulged

in his arms as he worked his fingers through his braid until the length of his black hair fell straight down his back. Then he made a quick dip down into the water, submerging his entire body before standing again.

Water slid from his shoulders, down his back and arms in a tantalizing stream.

Eve was mesmerized.

What should have been a vulnerable moment—a man standing naked at his bath in the middle of the wilderness—instead demonstrated how beautiful he was in his stark masculinity.

An ultimate example of manhood. Perfection.

Not because he could hold the attention of everyone at a dinner party with witty stories and charming nuance. Not because he had the finest house, the grandest carriage, and the most well-behaved and elegant wife.

It was his quiet consideration. His capacity for understanding and compassion. His endless patience and the way he sought to ensure her comfort. It was in the way he never made her feel pitied or shamed for what she'd lived through.

Even though she could feel his attraction to her nearly as strongly as she felt her own to him, she knew he would never initiate anything between them. He would respect her boundaries and wait forever, perhaps, for her to make the decision that would set them along the path that had been before them from the beginning.

Gabriel lathered up with soap, spreading the suds over his arms and chest and shoulders before plunging his hands back through his hair. He gave no indication that he knew of Eve's presence. Not even when she removed her dress and laid it out on the grass so she could sit on it to remove her shoes and stockings.

After thoroughly soaping his body, he dunked beneath the water to rinse. By the time he emerged once again, Eve had stripped down to her underclothes.

She made it a few steps into the water before she stopped in surprise at how cold it was.

She wasn't sure if it was an involuntary gasp, the movement of the water around her legs, or something else that prompted him to turn around, but when he did, there wasn't a hint of surprise on his face. She realized with flush of foolishness that he had likely known she was there the whole time.

The moment of embarrassment was swept away as her gaze met his. The chill of the water lapping at her calves was forgotten, along with every ounce of uncertainty and self-doubt.

The hunger in his eyes swirled dark and deep. He wanted and resisted. His desire was clear in the taut line of his jaw and the firm press of his mouth. It was barely contained within his tense muscles as they flexed across his chest and tightened into hard ridges over his abdomen. So much strength and power held in check.

It should have frightened her—his obvious physical dominance—and it shocked her that it didn't. Instead, she felt a wealth of heat through her limbs, through her blood, between her legs.

And she felt empowered.

Because she trusted him.

Because she trusted herself. She wanted him. And she felt no shame in it. The rest of the world might consider it a betrayal of her marriage. But their vows had been voided long ago by the man who'd promised to honor and cherish her. Now, her only loyalty was to herself.

She continued toward Gabriel.

Eve was unsure of how far she could take it, had no idea when or if the fear might return.

She only knew that she wanted more and couldn't keep holding herself back from the things in life that might bring her peace…or pleasure. And right now, Gabriel stood so close, his body warm and his gaze hard. Eve couldn't keep her hungry focus from wandering intently over every inch of his muscled form, wondering what those lines and ridges would feel like beneath her hands.

"You shouldn't look at me like that." His voice was deep and weighted with tension.

Her eyes lifted to meet his, and a jolt of desire pierced her center like lightning. "Like what?" she asked in a quiet murmur.

His jaw tensed, and his eyes grew hooded. "Like you want to touch me."

Her breath caught in her throat. Only the truth could release it. "I do want to touch you."

She had never seen his eyes so dark. The tension in him was intimidating. Forcing courage into her limbs, she steadily approached him. Cold water slid up her legs, soaking her cotton underclothes, plastering them to her skin. She barely noticed. Her focus was on Gabriel as he stood unmoving, watching her.

She sucked a swift breath as her belly submerged, getting to within arm's reach of him before she stopped. Due to his greater height, he stood only waist deep while the water lapped against the undersides of her breasts, making the points of her nipples peak beneath the thin cotton of her chemise.

He looked down at her in tense silence, his gaze so dark and heavy, his expression stern, his hands at his sides.

A flash of uncertainty came and went. In that moment, Eve was more vulnerable than she had ever been in her life, yet she also felt stronger and braver than she'd thought possible.

After searching her gaze with his, he made a low sound in the back of his throat. The sound reverberated through her, stirring the coals of her longing. Then he held his hand to her palm up. Such a large, capable hand with blunt fingertips, fine scars, and callused ridges.

Without hesitation, she slid her hand into his. Warmth infused his touch. A rush of energy flowed through her. Need pooled low in her body.

She wanted more.

Slowly and deliberately, he lifted her hand to press her palm to the surface of his chest. She felt the hard muscle beneath warm skin that had been roughened by scars. He held her hand there for a moment, secure between the thud of his heartbeat and the weight of his palm. Then he lifted his hand and lowered it back to his side.

"Touch me," he said.

Her lips parted and her gaze flickered, falling from his eyes to where her hand pressed firmly to his warm skin.

She stirred the flow of water between them as she stepped closer and brought her other hand to join the first. The pads of her fingers traced the matching scars located above the flat disks of his nipples.

"What are these from?" she asked quietly as she gently caressed the puckered skin.

"A sacred ceremony called the sun dance." His reply was given in a rough tone, and she wasn't sure if it was the subject or the fact that she was touching him that affected him more.

She looked up into his face. "This was done intentionally?"

He nodded. "As a means of seeking greater understanding of oneself and one's purpose."

Sliding her hands away from the scars, she pressed her fingers into the firm muscle of his chest. Then she slowly slid her palms up to his shoulders. He sucked in a swift breath through his teeth at her bold exploration, but otherwise remained still and silent.

With her belly swirling in delicious anticipation, Eve kept her gaze on the path of her hands, knowing that looking into Gabriel's eyes right then might be more than she could manage. She watched as her hands moved up and over the crest of his shoulders, her thumbs briefly brushing over his collarbones and then the sides of his throat, before she smoothed her palms down his arms. She explored every bulge and rope of muscle, alternating between a light, trailing of fingertips and a firmer, more intentional exploration. The hard strength that formed beneath such soft, smooth skin was fascinating to her. His patience, even more so.

She heard the way Gabriel's breath hesitated at times and felt the moments when her touch made him tense. Yet he made no move to stop her or direct her touch to his preference.

He wanted her to feel in control. She knew it as well as she knew her own desires.

But she wasn't in control. The wanting inside her had

already surpassed that. She existed purely in a state of instinct. Touching him because she needed to feel his power and know that it would not be used against her.

And she did know that. She'd known it from the beginning.

Just as she had known, somewhere deep inside, that it would eventually come to this.

As her fingertips reached the pulse at his wrists, she shifted her hands to place them on his waist, curving her hands around the taut muscle there as she stepped toward him. Then she pressed herself against him, wrapping her arms around his back as she rested her head on his chest.

The thud of his heart was heavy beneath her ear, his skin warm under her cheek. She could feel the solid form of his thighs against hers and the hard press of his erection against her belly.

The evidence of his arousal should have scared her. Her prior experience with male physical desire had led to pain and shame.

But knowing Gabriel was not unaffected by her touch only fanned the flame of her own need. It also reminded her of how lost she was in terms of knowing how to proceed.

With a low sound vibrating in his chest, he brought his arms up around her, curving one around her shoulders to hold her closer and the other around her waist. His head dipped down until she felt his soft breath against her forehead. And he held her. Just like that. Making no further demands. Asking no questions.

Eve closed her eyes, soaking in the beauty of that moment. The beauty of the man who held her. The beauty of the feelings that coursed through her while she stood in his full embrace. Safe. Cherished. Desired.

But it wasn't enough.

Her stomach tightened as something unsettling swept through her. She did not want him to think she was like those women who had taken from him to please themselves. He must know it was not like that for her. But how could she explain the depth of what she felt? Words seemed so ineffectual in trying to describe the truth inside her.

But she wanted him to know. She needed him to know.

She tipped her chin up. His eyes were so dark, but they were filled with swirling heat. Physical need, emotional longing. Strength, fear. All of it was there for her to see. An exact reflection of everything she felt.

"I don't want..." she began, then stopped. Her chest was too tight. It had been an age since she'd been so vulnerably honest. In truth, she wasn't sure she'd ever bared her soul the way she wanted to now. She drew a heavy breath to gather her courage.

Her pause made Gabriel tense. His arms tightened briefly, then began to loosen around her. "I understand," he said. The resignation in his tone sent a spark of panic through Eve. "You are another man's wife."

"No," she asserted quickly, her hold firm around his waist. "The man I married was never a husband to me. He broke his vows long ago and deserves nothing from me. I belong to me."

She was surprised by how confident her words sounded. Every one of them rang with truth. She was bound to Matthew by a paper document, but she was not and had never been his wife. Her existence had been as a possession—an object to manipulate and torment—never as wife.

She owed nothing to a man who had given her only pain and degradation.

"I belong to me, Gabriel," she repeated, accepting the truth of the statement, feeling it down to her marrow. "And if I decide to share myself with you it is because I want to."

His expression barely changed as he swept his gaze over her face before staring into her eyes so intently she felt certain he could see to the bottom of her soul—past the indignities and pain she'd suffered, past the uncertainties and her desire to please, past the determination to be strong and brave. He saw through it all to the core of her, where she was just a woman wanting to be desired by a worthy, noble, honorable man.

His lips parted, and he released a slow, raw breath. A tingle of anticipation danced along Eve's spine.

Lifting her hand, she gingerly touched two fingers to his mouth. She'd been wanting to explore the sensual fullness of his lips, to know what they might feel like pressed to hers. Warm. Generous.

His breath was heavy and deep as it slid from his lips to bathe her fingers. Feeling bold, she smoothed the pad of her middle finger across the surface of his lower lip, the velvet texture sending shocks of pleasure through her belly. Pleasure that expanded to the peaks of her breasts and down between her thighs as his arms tightened around her.

A low growl rumbled in his chest as he bowed his head toward hers.

And then it was easy. All she had to do was rise up on her toes and lift her mouth to his.

The first contact of his lips was like lightning cutting through the black of night. Silent, bright, and almost frightening in his intensity. Every nerve came alive; every inch of her skin felt charged with sensation.

A guttural sound vibrated in his throat as he deepened the kiss. With a subtle tilt of his head, he fit his mouth more fully over hers, closing off her breath, sealing her quiet moan between them. She wrapped her arms around his neck. She needed to be closer. Desire swept like an undeniable force through her. Rather than scaring her, his crushing embrace made her feel powerful. In her need, she was equal to him in a way that went beyond the disparities of their physical strength.

It was a kiss unlike anything she'd know was possible. It was fire and light and pure hunger. But even in its ferocity, there was gentleness that came from the man himself. The way he could hold her so tight in his arms, yet not hurt her. He claimed her mouth with a passion and intensity that felt more reverent than possessive, giving rather than taking.

It stunned her. It enflamed and awakened her.

On instinct, she parted her lips beneath his to sweep the tip of her tongue across the seam of his lips.

The sound he made in response urged her to do it again.

The deeper intimacy felt natural and right. She darted her tongue forward once again, and this time, his was there to meet it. The velvety texture of his tongue, the heat, the decadent taste of him… She couldn't get enough.

The need coursing through her was terrifying and new. The way her body yearned for his was overwhelming, but so perfect it tightened her chest. Despite her wary anticipation, she wanted to open herself to him, take him into her until the hollowness inside her was filled.

With a low groan, he shifted his mouth from hers and dipped his head to press a hot kiss to the side of her throat.

His lips moved gently over her skin to the crest of her shoulder as he held her in a tight embrace.

It took a moment for the haze to clear from her mind before she could look up at him.

While she felt on the verge of flying off in a million pieces, he appeared to remain fiercely in control despite the fire burning deep in his eyes.

His arms tightened briefly around her before he released her. "Turn around," he urged gently, his voice rough and unsteady.

On shaky legs, she did as he said.

He gathered the length of her hair in his hands and urged her down into the water. She tipped her head back to dunk her hair and gazed at his broad form framed by the blue summer sky. When she rose again, he lathered soap into her wet tresses. The competent working of his fingers through her hair and against her scalp was calming and invigorating at the same time. Her limbs grew soft and heavy, her spine curved in relaxation, and her eyes drifted closed. But inside, her nerves felt more alive than ever, her blood flowed swiftly, pulsing with life and increasing desire.

After rinsing the soap from her hair, he assisted her in removing her undergarments and tossing them up onto the grassy shore. Then he swept her hair over her shoulder, exposing her bare back to his attentive view.

His touch was gentle and intentional across the marks of violence that crossed the length of her back and hips. He ran the flat of his thumb in a soothing stroke along the crest of one scar and then trailed his fingertips along another. From her nape to the upper curves of her buttocks, he caressed each and every inch of the pain and indignity Matthew had inflicted.

His touch transformed the scars into something that—although they would always be a part of her—would never again define her. The path of his caress left pleasure rather than pain in its wake. It made her feel beautiful and brave and all the things he saw in her.

She felt it not just on the surface of her skin, but in her soul where his tender regard brought a thickness to her throat.

Once he was confident he wouldn't hurt her, he smoothed the soap down the full length of her back, then gently pressed his thumbs into the muscles along her spine and kneaded the flare of her hips and upper buttocks.

His touch was steady and reverent—confident in its ability to soothe rather than hurt. His strength was tempered by his compassion. His only intention was to bring her pleasure.

Still standing behind her, he slowly swept his hands over her low belly. She sighed at the sensation and allowed her head to fall back against his shoulder. His breath flowed in a steady rhythm against the side of her neck as he eased his hands up along her lower rib cage. She wished he'd press his mouth to her skin, there below her ear where his breath tickled so delightfully. But he remained focused on his task.

Until he reached her breasts.

As his hands slipped over the soft mounds, weighted and sensitive with desire, a velvety groan issued from his throat, and he dipped his head alongside hers. Her nipples pebbled against his palms as she arched into his hands. He answered her silent plea with a firm squeeze followed by a circling caress that teased the peaks and made her moan. Turning her head, she sought his mouth.

But he drew back from her and scooped handfuls of

water to rinse the soap from her body in a breath-stealing shock of cold.

Then he palmed the soap in his hand and crouched down in the water to wash the lengths of her legs. His long fingers circled around her ankles and knees and massaged her thighs. And though she held her breath in near-fearful anticipation, he did not venture between her legs.

By the end of it all, she was shaken and breathless and half-mindless from everything swirling through her. It was then that he took her hand and led her to the grassy bank of the river. The morning sun had risen higher and warmed the earth, but the breeze that moved through the trees and over the tall grass still chilled her skin.

Releasing her hand, he crouched to swipe up her underclothes in his hands. After wringing the water from them, he spread them out in the sun to dry.

Eve watched his movements with a hungry gaze, loving the way he moved. His body, so large and powerful, contained so much grace and beauty. Observing his self-assurance and lack of shame, she felt free to shed her modesty as well. Closing her eyes, she tipped her face to the sky and breathed deeply and fully. When she opened her eyes again, it was to see Gabriel standing in front of her, watching her with a calm, heated focus.

An intimate thrill coursed through her.

Saying nothing, he stepped forward and offered his hand. As she slipped her palm against his, more lightning sparked through her, but it was less impatient now, more...certain.

He led her to where she'd laid out her dress and gestured for her to sit on the spread skirts.

The grass was lush and soft beneath her as she sat with

her legs bent in front of her chest and her arms loosely wrapped around them. Gabriel knelt behind her and diligently worked his fingers through the length of her hair.

With desire still dancing inside her, she allowed the moment to lengthen, soaking up his attentive care. She had declared herself and exposed herself to him. And he had accepted her, offering himself in return. It was unprecedented, and for now, at least, she was content to wait for what would come next.

Thirty-One

His body thrummed with life, deep within his core where the most base and natural needs originated.

He wanted this woman. He needed her like he needed the warmth of the sun on his back, the caress of fresh mountain air on his face, the feel of the earth beneath his feet. She had been created for him. And he for her.

But he could not rush this.

He'd noticed a layer of innocence in her kiss. Despite her obvious desire for him, she reacted more with instinct than experience. Her reactions to his kiss—to his touch—had been those of an awakening and discovery.

Anger coursed through him as he considered what that meant.

She had been married. To a man who had marred her beautiful skin and damaged her spirit. Had her husband never shown her tenderness in the marriage bed? Had he bothered to give her pleasure, or had she only experienced pain and punishment at his hands?

Gently working his fingers through her pale-gold hair, he could see the fading bruises and healing wounds that crisscrossed her narrow back beneath the silken tresses.

Given enough time, her skin would rejuvenate and the scars would fade. But the harm done to a woman's soul was more difficult to heal. She deserved to feel safe. She deserved to be loved in all the ways a woman could be.

And she'd chosen him.

"Gabriel?" His name was warm and languid on her lips. "Will you make love to me?"

Every muscle in his body tensed. His hands fisted involuntarily in her hair, likely tugging at her scalp before he forced his fingers to relax. His erection throbbed painfully, craving the encompassing heat of her body.

He could barely choke out a response, his throat raw in the fresh morning. "I would like to, if that is your desire as well."

"It is."

Lust and longing flowed thickly through his blood. His body thrummed with need. His hands shook as he resisted the urge to stake his claim.

She'd chosen him, but he had to be sure there was no uncertainty between them. He'd seen it flicker in her gaze so many times in the past. When he claimed her, he did not want anything holding her back from the pleasure he ached to give her. No fear, no hesitation.

Gabriel spread her hair over her back like a veil to dry better in the sun, then pressed his hands flat to the surface of his thighs. "It would destroy me to cause you any further pain or fear."

She sat quietly for a moment, then turned her head to look back over her shoulder at him. Her eyes were clear and deep, like a crystal lake. "You could never hurt me, Gabriel. I know that. I trust you with everything I am."

The resistance within him shattered and fell away as he

soaked in the truth of her words. His body warmed, and the stone-hard muscles of his thighs released beneath his hands. The certainty and strength in her eyes left no room for doubt. He would do everything in his power to ensure her trust was not misplaced.

Her voice dropped to a sultry sigh. "Kiss me."

With no hesitation, he leaned forward.

At the same time, she rolled to one hip and placed her hand on the ground to brace herself as she partially turned to face him. So easily, their mouths met, and Gabriel was unable to keep from touching her. Lifting one hand to the side of her face, he slid his fingers into her hair as he rested his thumb under her chin. He craved greater contact. His body strained against the desire to haul her fully into his arms, but he forced himself to be patient, allowing her to lead the way.

Her eyes had drifted closed at the first touch of his lips. Her mouth was soft and warm beneath his. Pliant and vulnerable. He took care with that kiss. Pressing his mouth sweetly to hers before lightening the pressure just enough to caress her lips with delicate friction.

Her sigh was a soothing balm to his swiftly rising need.

Then she leaned toward him, angling her chin in a way that requested deeper contact. He obliged. Pressing his fingertips to the base of her skull, he took her mouth in a more deliberate, passionate kiss. Parting her lips to sweep his tongue inside, letting her taste the lust in every languorous thrust of his tongue.

She melted. The sound that issued from the back of her throat was one of pure need.

Reaching around her, he pressed his hand to the small of

her back. With gentle but insistent pressure, he pulled her toward him. Her body reacted smoothly to his urging. She rolled up onto her knees to face him. With one hand still holding her head in position to accept the deeper thrust of his tongue, he splayed his hand and drew her forward. He sat back on his heels as her slim legs parted over his and her buttocks came to rest atop his thighs.

Suddenly realizing the new and intimate position as she sat straddling his thighs—her body open to him, her slight form vulnerable in his arms—she broke from the kiss with a heavy gasp, but she did not pull away. Her hands came up to rest on his shoulders, and her eyes widened. Their gazes met and held as their breath mingled hot and swift between them.

He did not hide the lust in his gaze. His erection stood proud and thick between them, and his hands were firm on her body. He wanted her to feel his greater size and superior strength. And he wanted her to understand that he would never use that against her. He needed her to know that his body was hers to find comfort in. Security. And pleasure.

In that moment, he wanted her to accept how much power she had over him.

Her eyes flickered as she dropped her gaze to where his cock throbbed only a few inches from her core. Her fingers curled into the muscles of his shoulders, and she drew a swift breath that lifted her breasts. A raw and involuntary sound escaped his throat and brought her gaze back to his.

Looking into her wide eyes, Gabriel withdrew his hand from her hair. He trailed his fingers down the side of her neck and across the delicate crest of her shoulder before he flattened his palm above the swell of her breast where her heart beat fiercely behind her ribs.

She held her breath. Waiting.

With infinite patience, he eased his hand lower, curving his palm over the soft mound of her breast before brushing the peak with the flat of his thumb. Her eyelids fluttered and fell over her gaze. A deep sigh slid from her lips.

Gabriel braced both hands against her back, urging her body into a deep arch that thrust her breasts forward and upward. With another heavy sigh, she dropped her head back, exposing the long line of her throat. The silken fall of her hair teased the tops of his thighs. The flush of desire colored her skin and darkened her hardened nipples to a deep rose.

Curving his spine, Gabriel bent forward to cover one pebbled peak with his mouth. He suckled deep on her sweet flesh before rolling the tip against his tongue. Her gasps and sighs blended with the sound of the wind through the trees. When he shifted his attention to the other breast, he lowered his hands to grip the lush curves of her buttocks. As he teased her breast with the play of lips and tongue, he drew her hips closer until his hard length pressed firmly to her hot, wet center.

His name was a whisper on her lips as she released her grip on his shoulders to wrap her arms around his head, holding him close. Gabriel devoured her softness and her warmth. He ached to be inside her, to feel her heat surrounding him, but he contented himself with the fervent press of her body. For now.

Releasing her breast, he trailed his open mouth along her collarbone, flicking his tongue against the pulse at the base of her throat before licking up the length of her neck to her ear. With a growl of need echoing in his chest, he closed his mouth over her earlobe, gently nipping it with his teeth.

Her body jolted at the sensation, and he worried he might have gone too far with the subtle expression of pain in pleasure. Her hands framed his jaw as she eased his head back until she could look into his eyes.

The brilliant blue of her gaze, so deep and soulful, went straight to the center of his chest.

"I choose to share myself with you. Only you," she murmured before pressing her mouth to his in an open, passionate kiss that touched the darkest recesses of his being, where he'd buried old hurts and longings.

The craving inside him broke past his last reserves.

His arms doubled around her hips, and he thrust his tongue deep into her mouth. At the same time, he rolled his hips beneath her in a way that caused his hardened flesh to glide hotly against her. He needed to give her just a taste of how fiercely his passion burned, how desperately he hungered for her. How completely he wanted to fill her and take all that she offered.

Her legs tightened around his hips, and her fingernails scored his scalp as her hands dove back through his hair. When he withdrew his tongue from her mouth, she followed it with hers, darting past his teeth with an urgent insistence for more. The edge of her teeth scraped his lips, and her body pressed tightly to his, as if she wished to crawl into his skin.

The need to grasp her hips in his hands and raise her over him so he could plunge into her practically had him shaking. His hands gripped hard on the flare of her hips. His entire body stiffened against the lust raging through him.

As though sensing the change in him, she ended the kiss

to draw a deep, unsteady breath, and her sultry gaze sought his. "Please, Gabriel, I need you," she gasped.

His body hardened even more at her words. He replied through a clenched jaw. "I need you, too, but not here. When we come together, it will not be in a hurry to avoid the eyes of anyone who might pass by."

At his words, she gave a quiet start and quickly scanned the area around them.

He smiled. "Be at ease. I would have heard someone approaching. But the morning grows late. It's time to go back."

Her focus returned to him, and she seemed to study him for a moment. Her arresting passion slowly became layered with a quiet, thoughtful expression. She nodded and used his shoulders as leverage to push herself to her feet before she turned away to fetch her underthings.

Gabriel let her go. But not before the rich female scent of her filled his nostrils. The undeniable evidence of her desire—her readiness—nearly had him jumping to his feet to grasp her around the waist and lower her to the ground where he could cover her and claim her right there, despite what he'd said.

But he wanted to take things slowly—savor every moment of their joining—for her and for himself.

Thirty-Two

There was a bright and beautiful buoyancy in Eve's heart as they walked together back to the meadow. It felt like hope and excitement. And deeper inside, where secrets were kept safe and private desires burned, there was a distinct sense of anticipation.

After the way he'd caressed her and cared for her at the river, the respect and consideration he'd shown her through every interaction they'd ever had… She had no fear of what being with him might be like.

Though imagining the actual act of physical intimacy between a man and a woman was daunting when she put it the context of her past experiences, Eve trusted Gabriel to guide her through it. She could not imagine it being anything but completely wonderful.

And she wanted it.

No. It was far more than that. She needed to finally complete the connection she'd felt from the very start when his eyes had met hers across the fire and she had experienced that stark and sudden sense of knowing.

He saw her as no one else ever had. When she had been desperate to keep anyone from ever discovering the dark trove of secrets she held inside, he'd looked past the barriers and seen it anyway. Her fear and uncertainty, her desperation and her determination to start anew. He held no judgment for her past. He knew the truth and wanted her anyway.

She recalled the sensation of being held in Gabriel's strong arms, knowing he'd never hurt her. She relived the feeling of his mouth moving over hers—the taste of the desire on his tongue—and knew that he'd never speak words intended to break her down.

Despite the work he'd done as part of Luke's gang, Gabriel was the most noble and honorable man she'd ever known. She wanted to know more of him. She wanted to know what he feared, what he dreamt of at night, what he yearned for.

She wanted to know his heart.

As they reached the cabin, Gabriel waited for her to step inside ahead of him. The interior was illuminated by a bright shaft of sunlight pouring down from above. Earthy, welcoming scents surrounded her. She took a deep breath, filling her lungs with a sense of comfort and security. And certainty.

She turned in place to see Gabriel standing in front of the door, much as he had the day he'd first showed her this place. His body was tense. His eyes were focused only on her. She looked into his eyes and saw herself as he saw her.

He'd called her beautiful and brave.

When in his presence, she felt it to be true. That and so much more.

Every doubt she'd ever been convinced to embrace—every self-conscious concern she'd been molded into believing about her appearance, her manner, and her ability to be what

Matthew—or any man—needed…was swept away the second she looked into Gabriel's eyes and recognized the yearning, the hunger, and the admiration banked in the dark depths.

His desire had not faded during the short walk back. If anything, it had intensified.

The wave of emotion she felt was more than relief. More than excitement.

She wanted him so fiercely in that moment, it nearly overwhelmed her. Her lips parted on a breath as liquid heat flowed to the juncture of her thighs.

His nostrils flared, and the muscles of his jaw bunched and released.

Determined to convince him that the time for holding back was over, she slowly approached him.

He followed her movements with his dark eyes. The heat smoldering there, barely banked, intensified the feelings coursing through her. Anticipation and exhilaration. Desire. A sense of inevitability.

Stopping in front of him, she lifted her hand to the side of his face. She reveled in the warmth of his skin, the strength of his hard jaw beneath her palm, and the fact that he remained so still, watching her and waiting.

Holding his gaze, she rose up onto her toes and placed her lips on his.

It was a gentle kiss.

She was tempted to close her eyes and press more firmly against his mouth in a quest for more, but she drew back instead and took a shallow breath. It was all she could manage with her chest so tight and her belly fluttering so wildly.

His head remained tilted down toward hers, his breath slid warmly across her lips, and his eyelids partially concealed his gaze. But he did not reach for her; he did not pull her close.

The next breath she took was deep and long.

Time to be brave.

With her hand resting over his heart, she said, "There is something...strange and powerful between us. I'm not sure what it is or what it means." Her voice faded into a whisper. "Perhaps it doesn't have a proper name. Maybe it's just... not meant to be defined."

She shook her head gently. "When I left Boston, I swore to myself that I would never again accept a life of fear. But right now, I am fearful in a way I've never been before."

His body tensed, and she could see—she could feel—that he wanted to reach out to her, to lend her his strength and comfort. She knew why he didn't, and the warmth that burst in her chest stole her breath. He understood that she needed this moment to stand on her own. To declare herself.

His restraint gave her the confidence to continue. She tipped her head back to meet his steady regard. "I am afraid my courage will fail me as I stand here struggling to find the words to explain what I am feeling."

A rich sound vibrated from his chest. "There is no need for words. I feel the same." He covered her hand with his, pressing her palm firmly to the steady thrum of his heartbeat. "Here."

His voice was deep and strong. It wound through her with a gentle, irrevocable force.

He was right. Words weren't needed.

Sliding her hand free from beneath his, she took a step back. Then another one.

As badly as she wanted to step into him, feel his arms

come around her as she melted against him, there was something that had to come first.

She would show him everything she felt through her actions. Her certainty, her desire, her trust. Her love.

Love.

The simple acknowledgment of her deepest feelings filled her heart with the light of pure happiness. Happiness she wanted only to share with the man in front of her in the most intimate way possible.

With hands that had started to tremble, she gathered her hair and let it fall down her back. She wanted no veil between them.

The heat of Gabriel's focus followed every movement of her fingers as she released the buttons of her dress. She slid the frock off her shoulders and pushed it past her hips to the floor. Her petticoat was the next to go, and then her boots and stockings. Lastly, with her heart beating in a furious rhythm, she removed her undergarments until she stood naked before him.

The breath she took was shallow because she could see the fire glowing deep in his eyes as he swept his attention down the length of her body. She could feel his desire like heated breath against her skin.

In silent communication, she waited, knowing he would understand what she wanted.

When his smoldering gaze returned to her, he lifted his hand over his shoulder, grasping a handful of the tunic he wore. He dragged it off over his head in a swift movement that revealed all the lovely, masculine ridges of his chest and abdomen, the solid width of his shoulders, and the defined muscles of his arms. He bent to quickly take off his boots before straightening to remove his pants.

Eve watched him undress with focused attention.

Every emotion she'd ever had swirled together inside her; confidence, anticipation, joy, desire, breathless excitement, and a wonderful sort of fear.

When he finally stood as naked as she was, they both stepped toward each other. His breath was long and even as he brought his hands to her hips. Her breath, on the other hand, seemed to shorten with the swift rise of her physical need. She ran her hands over the smooth surface of his chest, then lower over the ridges of his abdomen. He was a force of masculinity by the sheer nature of his size. But he was so much more in the calm tenderness he exuded despite his very obvious arousal.

His steadiness was the only thing keeping her grounded as she struggled to contain the trembling in her body.

Looking into Gabriel's beautiful face, she said the only words that came to mind, an echo of what he'd said to her in the river. "Please. Touch me."

Gabriel lifted his large hands to frame her jaw as he tilted her face up to meet his kiss. A step forward brought their bodies flush against each other. Skin to skin. Heat swirled as his lips moved over hers, rubbing in delicious play before he parted his lips to slip his tongue past her teeth.

On a sigh, Eve opened herself to him. Her head tipped back in his hands, her tongue twirled with his, and her hands grasped his sides where taut muscles wrapped a rib cage that expanded and contracted with his heavy breath.

There was an air of desperation in his kiss, as though after holding it back for so long, the wild desire inside him was clawing to break free.

She might have been frightened by the power she sensed

in him if she didn't have complete faith in him. It allowed her to revel in the subtle madness of his desperation as it fed her own.

She shifted her body against his. The slide of his warm skin across the peaks of her breasts made her gasp even as the thick, hard heat of his erection against her belly ignited a melting in her core and the thrust of his tongue into her mouth triggered a deep physical yearning for fulfillment.

As though sensing her rising agitation, Gabriel slowed his kiss, softening it as he smoothed his hands down the sides of her neck, then over her shoulders. She tensed at the first brush of his fingers over the scars on her back. But his touch was light and warm as he smoothed his palms down the slim length for her spine, leaving her sighing as goose-flesh rose in the wake of his caress.

Reaching the narrow span of her waist, he grasped her firmly in his hands. Lifting his head just enough to murmur against her lips, he said, "If you tell me to stop, I will. At any time."

"Nothing in my life has ever felt as right as this moment." She pressed a light kiss to his lips. "And this one." Tilting her head, she brushed her lips along his jaw as she eased her hands up the broad expanse of his back until her fingers curled over his shoulders. "And this moment." She kissed the side of his throat. "And the next," she whispered into his ear. "Every moment with you—even when I'm scared and unsure—feels right. Is it strange that I can feel terrified and elated at the same time?"

He replied gruffly. "I feel the same."

Thirty-Three

Eve looked into his face. "What terrifies you?"

His fingers flexed around her waist, making her belly swirl deliciously before he answered. "When our bodies join, our spirits will become linked." His voice roughened. "It will be difficult to let you go."

From anyone else, the words might have caused a flare of panic, but not from Gabriel. Because she knew without a doubt that no matter how desperately he might not want to, if it was her desire to leave, he *would* let her go.

"What if you didn't have to?" she whispered.

His eyes flashed with a possessive fire, fanning the flames inside her to greater heights, emboldening her to explore the full depths of her hunger for him.

Pulling back from his embrace, she pressed her hands against his chest, reveling in the rough texture of his ceremonial scars and the steady beat of his heart. Exerting more pressure, she urged him onto the bed, her eyes promising things she could not put into words.

As he lay back on the bed, his heavy-lidded gaze never left her face. Under his fixed and heated focus, she felt brave as she crawled onto the furs and knelt between his spread legs. She smoothed her palms along the hair-roughened surface of his thick-muscled thighs while her gaze fell eagerly on the hard length of his desire.

He was as large there as he was everywhere.

In all the times Matthew had come to their marriage bed, she had never seen him fully naked, and certainly had never caught a glimpse of the distinctly male part of him. She was grateful now for her limited experience as it freed her to look upon Gabriel with all the wonder he alone inspired.

She ached for him. Between her thighs, deep in her womb, and in the center of her chest where her heart beat heavy and strong.

Glancing up the muscled length of his body, she met his gaze and asked in a hoarse whisper, "Can I touch you?"

The sound that rumbled in his chest was so near a growl that it made her insides clench in a delightful way. "I am yours."

The surge of power his words inspired was a heady thing. She lowered her gaze to continue her exploration. Her touch was light at first, a gentle sweep of her fingertips along his hardened length. But as her fingers reached the ridged crest, his erection jumped beneath her hand, as though eager for greater contact.

She was just as eager.

Holding her bottom lip between her teeth, she took him more fully in her hands, wrapping her fingers tightly around him as she swept her thumb over the slit at the top. The heat of him—the silken strength so carefully contained—made her breathless.

Gabriel fisted his hands at his sides and lifted his hips slightly off the bed, but he said nothing. His focus remained intent upon her face as his jaw clenched in self-control. Sinking into his gaze, she slid her hands up and down his length, learning the feel of him. His absolute mastery of his own desires awed her as he allowed her to touch and tease him.

The more she caressed him, the needier she became, until she could resist no more. Holding him in both hands, she leaned forward and brought him to her mouth.

The moment her lips slid over the broad tip, she moaned softly in pleasure. The satiny texture against her tongue, the salty, male taste of him, the instant rush of power...and the love she felt nearly undid her. She looked up the hard length of his body to see his eyes clenched tightly closed and the cords of his neck standing out as he strained to maintain control. A pulse of warmth and wetness flooded her sex. She squeezed her thighs tightly together to contain the sensation, but the added pressure only increased the gentle throbbing.

Hungry now for more of him, she swirled her tongue over his tip as she eased her mouth up and down his length. Holding him tightly at the base, she followed her instinct as she indulged in her curiosity and explored and tasted every inch of him.

She would have gone on much longer if she hadn't felt Gabriel's hand sliding beneath her hair to gently grasp her nape.

"Eve." Her name on his lips was a raw and needy sound.

She eased her mouth up his length one last time, sucking and twirling her tongue as she went. The ragged groan that issued from his throat delighted and enflamed her. As soon as she released him, he sat up and pulled her mouth to his. Grasping her hips firmly in his hands, he lifted her to straddle his lap, then doubled his arms around her as his tongue tangled with hers in a drugging kiss that made her muscles weak and her insides tremble.

The length of his erection pressed hot between their bodies. She rocked her hips, seeking something more.

He answered immediately, rolling them both over until she lay on her back and his big body hovered over hers with his hips pressing heavily between her spread thighs.

She gasped at the delicious weight of him. This. This is what she craved—the undeniable evidence of his strength and power, the knowledge that regardless of how vulnerable she might be with him, he would only protect and support her.

She closed her eyes so as not to reveal the gentle wave of emotion rolling through her heart.

But she should have known better than to try to hide from him.

Propped up on his elbows, he framed her face with his hands. "Look at me," he murmured roughly and deeply.

She did and saw the concern in his furrowed brow.

"Is this all right?"

She sighed, smoothing her hands up and down his back. "No. It's more than that. It's wonderful and perfect. I ache for you...so deep inside..."

With a ragged groan, he closed his eyes and hung his head to rest his forehead against hers. His erection pulsed heavy and hot against her inner thigh. Lifting her chin, she fit her lips to his and slid her hands down to the hard curves of his buttocks.

The fiery hunger inside her was astonishing. She'd had no idea it was possible to feel so much lust and longing for a person. Her body was aflame, but the feeling went so much deeper than sexual craving. It was the intense need to meld herself with him, to become one, to join their hearts as well as their bodies.

As his tongue swept into her mouth, he shifted on top of her, aligning his sex with hers. The blunt, smooth head of his erection pressed against her opening, but he did not thrust forward. Instead, he gently rolled his hips, allowing his member to glide over her sensitive folds, teasing moisture from her body, making her insides clench with the need for deeper contact.

"Gabriel," she gasped.

He slid his mouth to the side of her neck, then up to her ear as he whispered, "Trust me."

"I do," she murmured as he closed his mouth over the curve where her neck met her shoulder and gently skimmed his teeth across her skin. "I need you. Gabriel."

"I'm here," he assured her, trailing his lips along her collarbone, then lower to press a kiss against her sternum.

When his large hand covered one breast, her head arched back and her low belly tightened with delicious sensations. He circled his palm and kneaded the soft mound before lightly pinching the pebbled peak between two fingers. A swift jolt of pleasure seared through her—and then another as he lowered his head and took the other breast in his mouth, suckling on the flesh and rolling his tongue around her nipple. He drew her into his mouth, devouring her and humming his pleasure deep in his throat.

Such a rich and heady feeling infused her body. She felt weighted and light at the same time. Her insides trembled with fire while the silken slide of his hair across her skin inspired tingling chills. When he slid his mouth lower to press a hot, open kiss to her low belly, her thighs tensed around his shoulders.

He lifted his head at her brief show of resistance. "Should I stop?"

Eve shook her head. "No. I just… My experience is… limited," she confessed.

His expression darkened as a hint of confusion crossed his brow. "Your husband never kissed you between your legs?"

A choked sound of shock escaped her lips as heat rolled through her. Was that what he intended to do? It took her a moment to retrieve her voice. "I did not please him," she confessed. "He struggled to feel desire for me and would become angry…"

She didn't want to say more. Her time with Matthew felt like something that had happened to someone else.

The sound Gabriel made rumbled thickly from his throat and made his chest vibrate where it pressed between her thighs. He slid his hands into the hollow of her back as he gazed intently up the length of her body. Despite his almost reverent position between her legs, he looked like the fiercest warrior just then, eager for battle.

"He did not deserve you."

Eve brought her hand to the side of Gabriel's face. "No, he didn't. And I'm sure I don't deserve you."

He made a low growl of denial. "You were made for me," he replied as he turned his head to press his full lips to the center of her palm. "And I was made for you."

"Yes," she whispered. It was all she could manage because he'd lowered his head again to dip his tongue into her navel. She moaned softly, and her eyes fell closed. Sensations swirled, wild and tender at the same time, as he awakened her to the beauty of what was to come.

She held her breath as he shifted lower between her legs. When he eased his hands beneath her buttocks and covered her sex with his mouth, she tensed from head to toe with a shock of pleasure so deep and wonderful it nearly stopped her heart.

Heat—velvety and lush—consumed her.

He guided his tongue in a long, soft caress over her swollen folds to the bud at the apex. Then he suckled gently, drawing on her flesh before soothing it again with another circling swipe of his tongue. He repeated the action, but firmer this time. Then again, but with lighter teasing flicks. Then again: another heated, velvety stroke.

What he did with his mouth was so much more than a kiss.

It was a reverent devouring. An intimate awakening. He was bringing her to life with sensations of pleasure so powerful and bright, she could do nothing but surrender. Thoughts completely disappeared, as did any feelings of uncertainty or nervousness.

Everything coalesced into the experience of being loved by Gabriel in such an unbelievably intimate way. And the pleasure continued to rise—to build and expand until the sensations started to tumble over themselves, and her body tightened in anticipation of something unidentifiable but infinitely lovely. She could sense it approaching. She needed it.

Her back arched on the bed, and her hands fisted so tightly in the furs that her fingers ached.

Gabriel's hands tensed on her buttocks. His breath was

hot against her sensitive flesh. His tongue demanding as it eased along her opening before he covered her tight, swollen bud and sucked her gently into the heat of his mouth.

A tense fluttering started deep inside her. She gasped and tipped her hips toward him, and he suckled harder.

She flew apart.

Pulsing pleasure swept through her in waves. Expanding from her core, spreading through her limbs to her fingertips and toes.

It was magic. It was life and love and everything beautiful.

He held his mouth over her until the intensity began to recede. Then he soothed her with slow, gentle licks as her body softened and her lungs filled back up with air.

Then his great body shifted, and he rose over her. Opening her eyes, she saw him braced on his elbows. His broad shoulders sheltered her and his long hair fell like a curtain, locking them in intimacy as he settled his hips between her thighs. Framing his face in her hands, she brought his mouth down to hers for a kiss. At the same time, she lifted her hips against him, gasping into his mouth when his hot length slid over her gently pulsing folds.

"Will you enter me?" she asked, arching to press her breasts to his chest.

"Is that your desire?"

"Yes," she answered readily, the word tense and impatient.

His lips played over hers as he pressed his hips forward. It was a languid penetration, erotic in how she felt the broad head of his erection pushing past her entrance. Slowly, wonderfully, her body stretched and burned to accommodate him. It was a lovely discomfort, eased by her own moisture and her pleasure-softened inner flesh. She had no idea of the effort it took for him to maintain the mindful pace until he issued a low, involuntary grunt.

He was going slow for her.

Even though she'd practically begged him for this. Even though he'd already given her the wildest pleasure. He was still thinking only of her comfort.

Her chest compressed so tightly with emotion that she momentarily lost her breath. Love infused her entire being. Sliding her arms around him, she tucked her face against his throat and held him close. "Gabriel," she gasped softly against his sweat-salty skin. "I need all of you. I want you to fill me."

His breath was heavy and shallow as he wrapped his arms around her, one arm braced beneath her shoulders while he reached his other hand down to palm her rear, lifting her hips as he slowly withdrew from her. The warm, wet glide sent shivers through her. Before she could fully catch her breath from the lovely friction, he gave a powerful thrust, going deep, claiming her completely.

Eve gasped at the shock of his full possession. Her legs squeezed hard about his hips, and her head pressed back into the furs.

Gabriel held her secure in his arms. He had completely stopped moving. All she felt were the subtle throb of his body inside hers and the warmth of his breath as he murmured soft words against her throat.

The slight burning sensation slowly receded as her body learned to accommodate him. Her limbs began to relax, and Gabriel lowered his head to her breast. Sucking her into the heat of his mouth, he rolled his tongue over the peak in soothing circles. After a bit, he shifted his attention to the other breast, lavishing it with languid stokes of his tongue and deep, pulling kisses. As his mouth drew on her breasts, wonderful sparks of pleasure angled down through her core to the flesh that stretched deliciously around his member.

As though sensing the softening within her, he gave a gentle rock of his hips. The deep, shifting movement sparked interesting, new sensations. Heat and fire and more.

He rocked again.

She gasped.

He slowly withdrew, inch by tantalizing inch, until just the tip of him remained inside her, dragging a soft moan from her throat.

Then he eased forward again with purposeful, delicious intent. Claiming her until he was fully sheathed. His thrusts were long and leisurely, sparking delicate sensations that tumbled through her. Her muscles tensed, and her insides tightened in anticipation of another free fall into that bright well of pleasure.

She turned her mouth to meet his and then kissed him. Moving her hips in a rhythm to match his, she thrust her tongue into his mouth to taste him. To feed on his desire and give him hers.

Their gazes met and held. The entire world existed in his eyes. Shadows and light. Hope and new beginnings. Love.

This time, the pleasure came on like a rolling wave. One moment, she still felt everything building. And the next, it crested and washed through her. Lovely, deep, pure.

Gabriel continued to move in long, even strokes as she pulsed around him. Then, after thrusting deep, he tightened his arms around her and stilled. His head lowered until he rested his forehead against hers. His breath caught on a guttural moan as he released his pleasure deep inside her.

Thirty-Four

As the delicate aftershocks left their bodies, he brought his mouth back to hers. The kiss was so languid and lovely that Eve only vaguely realized it when he shifted to lie beside her. Smoothing his hand down the center of her body, he rested it heavily on her low belly.

With a touch that inspired delicate tingling in its wake, he leaned forward to press a light kiss to her temple.

Then he propped himself on his elbow and gazed at her in silence. His expression was dark and serious when he shifted his gaze to hers, and his tone was heavy as he said, "You should have told me you'd never joined with a man."

Eve felt her cheeks warm. She wasn't sure if that was something he'd notice.

But she should have realized he would.

It was difficult to find the words, but she wanted him to fully understand. No secrets. No shadows. No shame.

She rolled onto her side to face him. "My mother did not explain anything to me about the intimate relations between a man and a woman. Her only advice before my marriage was that my…husband"—she didn't even like saying the word—"would tutor me on what I'd need to know. Unfortunately, one of my greatest failures as a wife, according to Matthew, was my inability to tempt him…sexually." Humiliation burned beneath her skin. Humiliation and regret for the naive and hopeful bride she'd been and the lost time she'd spent believing he was right.

Gabriel caressed her back in long, languid strokes as he stared intently at her face, listening with quiet consideration.

Feeling his compassion and lack of judgment made the rest come easier. "On our wedding night, I waited hours before he came to me. When he did, it was clear he'd been drinking." She paused, drawing a breath. She'd never spoken of that night. The idea of talking about it had never even occurred to her. But now, she couldn't seem to hold it back. "He joined me in bed, but I didn't know what to do. He became agitated and started cursing and accusing me of… horrible things. And then he struck me. Across the face. I was too shocked to do anything but stare after him as he rolled off me and staggered from the bedroom."

Gabriel's features hardened with barely concealed outrage. The outrage didn't frighten her. She knew it was on her behalf and was grateful for his attempt at restraining his reaction for her sake.

"I don't know why I'm telling you all of this," she muttered through her thick throat.

"Because I asked," he replied simply. "And because it is important for me to know."

She took a deep breath, anxious now to reach the end of her pitiful tale. "When he came to my bedroom the next morning and saw the mark he'd left, he said I couldn't leave the room until the redness was gone. It was more than a week before I saw him again, but the next time he came to my bedroom, it was essentially the same. He would shove himself against me, then grow angry and leave. I understand now…that he could not…grow hard," she explained hesitantly. "He didn't hit me again until sometime later, long after he gave up on trying to bed me."

Gabriel slid his hand up her spine and around the nape of her neck. The wide pad of his thumb brushed across the crest of her cheek, spreading moisture she didn't realize had escaped from her eyes.

"You did not deserve his cruelty," he said.

She heard the righteous anger in his tone and felt the truth of his words, all the way down to her marrow. "No," she replied with utter conviction. "I did not deserve it."

With a weighted sigh, she inched closer until her breasts pressed to his chest and her legs slid along his.

"It almost feels like it happened to a different woman," she whispered. "I wish my life with him had never existed, but I cannot change what was. I'm just glad it's over."

Despite the anger and turmoil rolling through him, Gabriel's touch was gentle as he slid his arm around her waist and pulled her even closer into the warmth of his body. All he could think to do for her in that moment was ensure that she felt safe and protected.

She snuggled into him, dipping her chin to tuck her face against his neck. Within only a few minutes, her breath evened out into a long, steady rhythm and her body became lax in his arms.

Knowing what Eve had endured with the man she'd married was like a sickening poison in Gabriel's blood.

The injustices in the world were great and widespread. He knew it as well as anyone. No matter how much he'd once wished it, he couldn't go back and erase his time with the missionaries. Nor could he erase what Eve had lived through.

But if she'd let him, he would do everything in his power to shield her from experiencing that kind of pain again.

He found it difficult to imagine parting ways. In all honesty, he didn't want to. His heart had recognized hers right from the start. But nothing had prepared him for the stirring experience of their physical joining. He had been stunned by the power and depth of what had occurred between them.

Without intending to, with no effort at all, she had claimed his heart.

But she might not wish to keep it.

The desperation he had sensed in her had calmed, but it was not gone. She was restless and unsettled. He knew that feeling—he had felt it himself in his youth. Now that she had escaped her painful past, he could not keep her from finding her own path.

Even if it took her away from him.

She napped for a short while as the sun continued its journey across the sky.

Gabriel did not sleep. He was content to hold her and listen to the calm rhythm of her breath, but as soon as she began to stir, he instantly hardened with need.

Her warm body shifted in his arms, her skin smooth and soft as it slid against his. A hum issued from her throat, and her eyes fluttered open just enough to meet his gaze.

The impact of her slow smile went straight to his gut before wrapping around his heart.

She was his.

He was hers.

The truth of it was as clear as a cloudless sky. As certain as the spring rain.

But he would let her go. He'd have to, if that was what she wanted.

Just not yet.

He slipped his hand up the narrow valley of her spine, sliding his fingers beneath the fall of her tangled hair until he palmed the base of her skull. Holding her gently, he lowered his head toward hers.

A sigh slid from her lips to lightly caress his face just before he covered her mouth with his. He absorbed the delicate shudder that ran through her body by pulling her closer. She slid her leg up to hook over his hip, and her warm hands smoothed over his skin.

Earlier had been about passion and desperation and need.

This time, it was about something deeper, something softer and quieter.

They made love slowly, their bodies awakening to each other. Discovering each other.

Unspoken promises were issued in sighs against heated skin. Hands soothed and roused sensations to fever pitch as tongues and lips tasted and teased delicate nerves.

By the time Gabriel rolled to his back, drawing Eve to lie atop him, they were both flushed and panting. Her eyes flashed bright and beautiful, and she pushed against his chest to sit astride his groin. He reached for her hips, brushing his thumbs over her belly as he urged her in a rocking rhythm against his hard length.

She gasped and bowed her head, but quickly took up the rhythm he initiated.

After a bit, he lifted her off him and grasped himself at the base of his erection. She held his gaze and shifted to take him into her body. The possession went both ways as he vowed to take all her past pain and replace it with pleasure. If she'd let him, he'd give her everything: his body, his spirit, the very heart from his chest.

It was already hers anyway.

THIRTY-FIVE

That evening, they returned to the bunkhouse.

Eve was a little concerned with what the others would think or say about the days—and nights—she'd spent with Gabriel. But aside from a curious glance or two, Johnny and George—who were both in the kitchen preparing the evening meal—seemed content to mind their own business. Of course, Gabriel's rather forbidding stare might have had something to do with how quickly they turned back to their tasks.

Luke, however, was a slightly different story.

He was sitting in a chair a little way back from the fire. One foot was planted firmly on the floor, while his other leg was extended in front of him. He looked up as soon as Eve and Gabriel entered the great room.

At first, he looked angry, possibly even furious. But then his eyes narrowed by a barely noticeable degree, and his lips twitched at one corner. A quick flicker of his gaze seemed to take in all he needed to know, and the anger slid into a more contemplative assessment.

He pushed himself to his feet. Directing his words first to Eve, he said, "I'm glad to see you didn't get lost on your walk the other day."

There was a slight hint of censure in his tone, and Eve responded with a proud tilt of her head. "You said I was free to roam the valley as long as it was not at night and I stayed out of the forest."

Luke frowned at her quick defense. "You should have made sure someone knew where you were."

Eve arched her brows. She had finally started to experience true freedom over the last couple of days. She wasn't about to let Luke or anyone curb that glorious feeling.

"Gabriel knew," she replied succinctly, declaring more than one thing with the short statement and inspiring a brief hum of appreciation from the man beside her.

There was a flicker of surprise in Luke's light-dark eyes as he glanced at Gabriel.

"I need you to ride into town tomorrow to fetch some supplies from the doc. It appears he won't be visiting the valley after all." He tipped his head toward Eve. "Maybe you'd like to go with."

Eve's eyes widened at the prospect of seeing the nearby town.

"It's just a few hours there and back," Luke explained.

Gabriel's expression was hard to read, but his gaze was steady as he said, "I'll keep you safe."

"I know," she replied without hesitation.

It was midafternoon when Eve and Gabriel rode into town. A few people could be seen going about their business, but for the most part, the narrow dirt roads through town were rather quiet. Some of the townsfolk glanced over Eve with mild curiosity before their gazes shifted to one of wary distress when they looked at Gabriel.

He had dressed in his usual denims with a light-colored shirt under an open leather vest. His hair was left unbraided down his back, and a wide-brimmed hat shadowed his strong features. He wore no gun on his hip, unlike some of the men they passed, but Gabriel did not need a weapon to appear intimidating. His size and unapproachable demeanor accomplished that well enough.

Eve tensed at the change in people as they noted Gabriel's appearance. One woman even grabbed her children and backed into a shop at the sight of him.

Yet he continued through town, his gaze proud and his bearing even more so. If he noticed the looks he was getting—and she had to believe he did—he gave no sign of it.

She couldn't fathom being the object of so much open belligerence and distrust. A lesser man might have reacted in kind to the harsh attitudes. That Gabriel managed to maintain a calm and self-assured demeanor despite it all just made her admire him more.

They were riding side by side and had turned down a street that took them away from the main part of town when she asked, "Does it bother you when people do that?"

He tilted his head in question.

"Look at you as though you might attack at any moment."

The corner of his mouth twitched. "No. It keeps me from having to make small talk."

He was making light of it, but she knew the issue went deeper than he would admit. She studied him as they rode. Everything in his posture declared he was unapproachable. But she knew now how much of a facade it was, and her heart ached with an intimate understanding of the loneliness inherent in always being at a distance from those around him.

"Do you ever let anyone know you?" she asked quietly.

Though his expression didn't change, his entire body tensed. He didn't turn to look at her when he replied. "You know me."

"I know you. But I still wonder what you shelter in the depths of your heart, what you yearn for."

The muscles of his arms flexed, and he finally turned his head. His gaze was deep as he replied. "You know that as well."

The words were a rough murmur, but they rushed through Eve with the force of a gale wind. Love and sadness and hope flowed along with them.

Then he looked away. "We're here."

Eve blinked to see that they had ridden up to the rear of a row of buildings that all faced the main street they'd just come from. Gabriel brought his horse to the hitching rail near the horse trough filled with water.

"Is this the doctor's office?" Eve asked, knowing they had come to town for medical supplies.

Gabriel dismounted and came to her side. Lifting her to the ground, he replied, "Out of respect for the doc, we keep our business with him quiet, if we can."

Eve nodded and followed him to the back door. He gave a short knock, and within a couple of minutes, a young woman—no more than seventeen perhaps—opened the door. She did not appear surprised by the sight of Gabriel, though she glanced at Eve curiously.

"He's finishing up with his last patient. You can wait in his office."

She turned and led them down the short hall to the first open door and gestured for them to enter.

The office was not at all what Eve would have expected of a doctor's office in a small western town. The walls were painted navy blue, and the room held a polished desk, neat bookshelves with wide medical tomes, sturdy chairs, and a distinct air of competence. In its style and tone, it was surprisingly similar to the studies in the mansions back east.

The familiarity made Eve suddenly rather nervous.

As though sensing her discomfort, Gabriel stepped up to her, bringing her focus to him. His chin was lowered and his voice assured as he said, "It's a quick stop."

She nodded, trying to calm her unexpected anxiety by wandering over to the corner of the room where a small window allowed her to see their horses enjoying a drink at the trough. Soon enough, they'd be on their way again.

Only a few moments later, footsteps could be heard coming toward them down the hall.

"I take it Luke couldn't wait for us to come to him," the doctor said with a hint of annoyance as he entered the small office.

Eve had turned toward the door at the sound of the doctor's approach, but she suddenly wished she hadn't. With everything in her, she wished she could be anywhere but in that office.

Gabriel stood near the door, but he hadn't bothered to turn at the doctor's entrance. He was looking at Eve instead.

In a desperate need for courage, Eve shifted her gaze to his face. He had been about to reply, but as his eyes met Eve's, his brows pulled together and his chin lowered in silent question.

Could he so easily detect her distress?

"Evelyn? What on earth are you doing here?"

Eve couldn't pull her gaze from Gabriel's. His dark stare held hers with a strength and steadiness she needed just then, as though he saw her sudden panic and uncertainty and wished only to assure her that she wasn't alone.

Once she looked away, the moment would instantly become real. She wasn't ready. She had gotten so far.

She couldn't go back.

She *wouldn't* go back.

Warren Reed passed Gabriel and crossed the room toward Eve in long strides. She couldn't avoid acknowledging her brother any longer.

It had been almost six years since she'd last seen him. He'd still been in medical school in Pennsylvania and had come home for Christmas. She'd been only fifteen—a child in many respects.

He looked nearly the same as he had then. Thick black hair—worn a bit longer now than it had been before—vivid, intelligent blue eyes, and that partially concerned, partially irritated expression big brothers always seemed to wear when addressing their little sisters.

Warren had never been unkind to her. He just hadn't been a very present or consistent figure in her life. So it came as a bit of a shock when he reached her and immediately drew her into a warm hug.

The open display of emotion was not something he had ever done in the past. They had both been brought up under strict rules of decorum that valued a reserved and undemonstrative nature above all else.

Eve took just a moment to soak up the comfort and

strength in her brother's embrace, before she recalled the threat he posed to her current situation. As she stiffened, he drew back, leaving his hands resting gently on her shoulders, almost as though he sensed her desire to flee.

When he met her gaze, his expression shifted again, confusion and exasperation warring for purchase. "What are you doing here? Do you have any idea how worried Mother is right now? She thinks you're on your deathbed in Boston. Why the hell aren't you in Boston? Why didn't you send word you were coming out to visit me?"

The rapid-fire questions made her want to shrink into the corner, but she held herself unmoving.

"Maybe you should let her answer one question before asking another," Gabriel suggested in a heavy tone.

Eve's stomach tightened in a deep and involuntary response to the low-voiced words. She glanced past her brother to see Gabriel standing with his feet in a wide stance, his arms crossed over his chest, and his features drawn in a firm representation of displeasure.

Warren turned toward him, his expression suggesting he'd forgotten the outlaw was there. "What the hell is my sister doing here, Gabe?"

Gabriel didn't answer. He just stood there, allowing Eve the space to respond to Warren, though she had no doubt he would step in if she needed him.

She appreciated his confidence in her and his fierce desire to protect her. Her heart expanded with courage. "Warren, I'd like to explain, but…"

Her brother must have misunderstood her reticence since he looked back to Gabriel. "Would you give us a few minutes, Gabe?"

Gabriel didn't acknowledge the request. His gaze remained focused on Eve until she gave him a subtle nod. Figuring out how to respond to her brother's questions would not be easy, but it was something she needed to do on her own.

Without a word, Gabriel left the room. As soon as he was gone, Warren turned back to her with a look of disapproval. "What are you doing out here, Evelyn? And how did you come to be in Gabe's company?"

Eve took a breath, unsure of just how much to tell him about the kidnapping. "There was a bit of a…misunderstanding on the train."

Warren frowned, apparently not satisfied with her answer. Then he stepped back and took a more thorough look at her appearance. "Wait a minute. That dress looks familiar. Is that Honey's dress?"

It suddenly occurred to her that Luke's sister was Warren's wife. The cabin had been the home of her brother's family. Did he know of the activities Luke and his men engaged in?

Warren's questioning gaze turned sharp. "Have you been to the valley?"

Of course, he knew. And he had been very careful not to let Eve or their mother know of his association with the outlaws. Apparently, she was not the only one adept at keeping secrets.

"Yes," she replied, choosing not to elaborate.

Warren shook his head in disbelief. "I'm trying really hard to understand what's going on here. I thought Mother's message was a bit dramatic, but it seems she was right to be worried."

Eve's muscles tensed painfully. "Mother? What do you mean?"

"She sent me a telegram a couple of weeks ago. She said she hadn't seen you in over a month, that you hadn't been out in society, and she was worried something had happened to you."

A stab of guilt momentarily overwhelmed Eve. Her mother had been worried about her absence. Worried enough to contact Warren.

"I assured her that if you were ill, the doctors in Boston were quite competent. I suggested she speak to your husband about her concerns."

No!

"Wait a minute..." Warren's black brows lowered sharply. "Does your husband know where you are?"

Eve met her brother's hard stare. "He does not."

Warren started shaking his head. "We'll have to get messages to Mother and your husband, letting them know you are safe."

Panic claimed her, nearly choking her. "No, Warren. You can't do that."

"I have to. They're likely worried sick about you. Why would you leave without telling anyone?"

She wanted to trust Warren and tell him everything she had been through since her marriage, but the idea of putting her experience into words was daunting. And she didn't know how he would respond.

Even if he sympathized with what she had endured at Matthew's hands, that did not mean he would agree with her breaking her marriage vows. Warren had been raised with the same guiding principle she had—that appearances were everything.

What if he still insisted on contacting Matthew?

She didn't know if she could take that risk.

When she didn't answer his last question, Warren lifted his brows. "Don't tell me you just ran away?"

Eve tensed at his tone. "It's complicated."

He tilted his head, and his gaze was not without compassion as he replied, "Marriage can be complicated, but that is no reason to run away. You have to face your problems and deal with them. From Mother's letters, I understand it was a rare love match. I am sure your husband will understand if you talk to him about why you left."

"You don't understand."

"I understand more than you know," he said firmly, his blue eyes darkening. "A misunderstanding kept Honey and me apart for far too long. I would give anything to have those years back. I won't let you make a childish mistake you will regret forever."

"No, Warren. I can't—"

He placed his hands on her shoulders. Eve felt like a block of ice beneath his touch, but he didn't seem to notice. "You have to go back, Evelyn, and face whatever it is. Trust me, it is the only way."

"I am not going back to Boston," she stated boldly. Firmly. Praying he would accept her declaration without requiring further explanation.

"Of course you are." His tone had shifted into one she recognized. Level-toned, commanding, in charge. It reminded her of their father's—at least what she remembered of their father before he had passed. "You are married. You belong home with your husband."

Eve didn't answer. Her chest was too tight to form words.

He wasn't going to listen to her. Disappointment, anger, and frustration warred for purchase inside her.

Seeming to sense her resistance, Warren sighed, then tilted his head. "We can talk about this more later, if you'd like. Nothing needs to be done today. If you'd just give me a few minutes to close things up here, I'd love it if you'd come back to the house with me. Meet Honey and the children."

Eve had no idea how she managed the smile, but it seemed to satisfy her brother as he gave a nod. "Great. I'll just be a few minutes."

THIRTY-SIX

GABRIEL STUDIED EVERY NUANCE THAT CROSSED HER face.

She was going to run.

Deep in her eyes—beneath the veils and the shields—shone the frantic fear and desperation of prey caught in a trap. They'd accompanied the doc back to his house, which was set a short way out of town, and Eve was introduced to his wife and their two kids. Warren had briefly explained to Honey that Eve would be staying with them until they could further discuss her current situation. Honey didn't press for more information as she welcomed Eve with a brief embrace.

Through the interaction, Gabriel witnessed a return of that perfect and polished facade Eve used to wear like a shield. But he could see through it now.

Though her pleasure at meeting the doc's kids was clearly genuine and her interactions with Honey were warm and friendly, there remained a gleam of panic in her eyes. It had flashed bright at the first sight of her brother before she banked it behind her unflappable poise.

She was not comforted by her reunion with her brother.

Just the opposite.

Despite her calm exterior, she seemed more skittish than ever. He lost track of how many times she glanced toward the door, only to force her gaze down to where her hands were clasped tightly in her lap.

She felt trapped.

Desperate creatures did extraordinary things when they felt trapped.

At one point, Honey and the doc were each occupied by one of their children, and Eve finally glanced his way. Until then, he'd sensed that she had been intentionally avoiding looking in his direction. He caught her gaze and held it.

He saw the panic and the fear she hid so well from everyone else. He also saw the strength and the determination in her stoic gaze. He tried to assure her that she was safe, that there was no need to run. That she could trust him.

Her lips parted softly in response, and her lashes lowered. When she opened her eyes again, her resolve was back in place, hard and unmovable.

Gabriel tilted his head in silent question, and the blue of her eyes darkened, almost sadly.

He frowned.

Holding his attention, she rose to her feet. Without a word, she left the parlor where they were all gathered and went outside to the front porch.

No one else seemed to notice she had left.

To him, it was as though a light had left the room.

He stayed where he was for only a moment more, standing against the wall across the room. He would follow her. There was never a question of that. The force of his entire being was already stretched across the space between them in an instinctual need to be near her.

But as he took a step forward, the doc was suddenly there in front of him.

Gabriel had not often had cause to engage in conversation with Luke's brother-in-law, but he had always believed the man to be noble and level-headed, which appeared to balance out Honey's more impassioned nature. Gabriel had long admired the doc's competence and loyalty.

But as Warren put himself between Gabriel and Eve, Gabriel felt a sudden stab of anger toward the man.

He lifted his brow in question, his arms tense across his chest.

"Let her have a moment."

So, he had noticed Eve's departure after all.

Though Gabriel could respect the doc's desire to protect his sister, he had seen the unspoken message Eve had given him. She expected him to follow her.

She needed him.

And he was going to go to her.

"You misunderstand," he replied.

The other man frowned. "No, Gabe. I believe you misunderstand. I don't know the details of how she came to be with you, but she is under my protection now, and—"

His words were cut off by a harsh and ragged scream.

Gabriel shoved Warren aside and bolted across the room and out the front door, just in time to see Eve's unconscious body being tossed into the arms of a man on horseback. The man still on the ground turned and drew his pistol.

A gunshot zoomed past Gabriel's head, splitting the wood on the house behind him with a loud crack. He dodged to the side and leapt from the porch, but he was too late.

Both men were on their horses and riding away.

"What the hell happened?" Warren shouted as he charged out of the house behind him.

Gabriel's chest had tightened so violently, his heart no longer seemed to be beating, but his steps never faltered. He swiftly changed direction to run toward the small barn beside the doc's house.

He needed his horse.

"Gabe! Answer me," Warren demanded as his steps sounded on the gravel in a running stride.

"He found her."

Warren caught up to him in the barn. "What are you talking about?" he shouted as he rushed to his own horse. "Who found her?"

Gabriel leapt onto Twig's bare back. "Her husband," he grunted as he turned the mustang and urged him into an instant gallop.

The sun was getting low in the sky, and the two horses were nearly out of sight. He had no time to lose.

He had *everything* to lose.

But while Twig was bred for endurance, high elevations, and rough terrain, the mustang was not exceptionally fast.

Warren caught up with him easily, and they rode together in silence. Eve and her abductors were long out of sight, so Gabriel kept every bit of his focus on following the trail they'd left behind.

The heavy, rapid beat of his mustang's hooves hitting the ground reverberated through him, taking the place of his heart, which had been torn from his chest the moment

Eve had been taken. The place where his heart should be was silent and still. His blood had stopped moving through his veins. Every bit of life inside him had simply ceased and would never start again if he didn't get Eve back.

She *was* his heart.

That first day on the trail, when it had been just the two of them, he had vowed to keep her safe.

He had failed.

His fists tightened in Twig's mane as a rough growl rose through his throat.

The sun was getting lower. Soon, night would come, and with it, only a sliver of moonlight.

Gabriel urged Twig to his limit, forcing the loyal animal to run his fastest. They were heading away from the mountains, so the landscape wasn't as treacherous as it could have been. But it was still a challenge to keep to Eve's trail as it wound its way through shallow hills and valleys and forests.

Just as they entered a wide copse of dense forest, two riders suddenly came up, one on each side of them, pressing in until Gabriel and Warren were forced to slow.

Gabriel nearly roared in frustration. Since this was just supposed to be a quick trip into town, he didn't have the hunting knife he usually tucked in his boot when out on the trail. He suspected the doc was not carrying a weapon at all, but he didn't bother to look.

It didn't matter. If these were more men sent by Eve's husband, he would kill them with his bare hands if he had to.

The two men came around to face them, each with a Colt trained sure and steady on Gabriel and Warren's chests.

Then one of them spoke in a woman's voice. "Holy shit! Is that you, Warren?"

The realization that one of them was female was instantly surpassed by the fact that she knew the doc. And that in knowing him, she immediately reholstered her gun. Her partner quickly followed suit.

"Alexandra?" Warren exclaimed. "What are you doing here? And why are you dressed like that?"

The woman, who Gabriel could now see had a long braid of black hair falling down her back, narrowed her gaze. "I received a telegram from Aunt Judith," she replied, ignoring the question about her masculine attire. "She hadn't seen Evie in a while and was worried."

"So you came here?" Warren asked.

"Not right away, but Malcolm is very good at what he does," she replied with a swift smile directed toward her partner, who had not taken his eyes off Gabriel. "Once we discovered she'd left Boston by choice, I figured there was only one reason she wouldn't have told anyone her plans—she didn't want to be found. There was also the fact that her husband seemed to be keeping his mouth shut about the whole thing..." she finished, as though the conclusion was obvious. "Then we found out about the abduction on the train down near Granger and figured it was Evie. But whoever took her knew how to hole up."

Warren sent a swift glance toward Gabriel, who ignored him. He was impatient with the conversation. Sensing Gabriel's growing agitation, Twig scuffed a hoof at the ground.

The woman continued. "Turns out, Matthew Preston very quietly left town shortly after Evie. A friend of

Malcolm's tailed him to Courtney's ranch in Montana, then to our place before he came down here. He left men behind at each location and has had men watching your house for days now."

Gabriel had had enough talk. "Where is she?"

The woman didn't answer right away, and the man she'd called Malcolm studied Gabriel with a wolfish gaze. He had an air of danger and violence about him that Gabriel knew better than to underestimate. After a moment, Malcolm gave a short tug on his reins, turning his horse as he replied, "This way."

Gabriel and Warren followed them to a spot where the trees started to thin. Dismounting, they left all their horses in thicker cover as they crept closer to where they could see a small ranch spread out before them.

The house was a grand two-story building with a wide front porch and shutters that were closed tight. A barn stood some distance apart from the house, but there was no indication of any cattle. Aside from a few chickens scattered about the yard out front, the entire place was still and quiet.

"Matthew moved in here several days ago. Apparently, the accommodations in town weren't up to his standards," the woman scoffed.

"How many?" Gabriel asked.

"In addition to the two who just rode in, he's got two more hired guns on the property," Malcolm answered. "They're well armed, but they don't appear to expect any opposition."

"Which will give us an advantage," the woman added before she started describing the various ways they could try to approach the house without being seen.

Gabriel didn't hear any more details, since he had gotten too far away. On silent feet, he crept through the trees to reposition himself so the sun would be at his back as he made his way in.

They could discuss the ranch's layout and how best to infiltrate the property if they wanted. He was going to get Eve.

Thirty-Seven

Eve came to full consciousness with a gasp and a moan. At first, the throbbing in her skull was the only thing she could concentrate on. But then her last clear memory returned with the force of a freight train.

The two men had come at her so fast outside Warren's home.

She remembered screaming before one of them raised his pistol and brought the butt of it down against her temple. Then everything went dark.

She pushed herself to a seated position, hoping with everything in her that she was at Warren's house with Gabriel nearby.

But the parlor she was in was unfamiliar.

The man seated across from her, however, was not.

Terror gripped her lungs like a vise. Her limbs went numb, and the pounding in her head grew louder. Her nightmare had reclaimed her.

"So good to see that you've decided to join me, darling," Matthew said smoothly as he tilted his head toward Eve with a smile.

He sat in an armchair, with one leg elegantly crossed

over the other and a snifter of brandy warming in his hand. As always, he was dressed impeccably. His smile was warm and charismatic. His blond hair was perfectly combed, and his shoes were polished to a reflective shine. He was flawless. The consummate gentleman.

On the outside, anyway.

Inside lived a monster.

The terror clutching at her tightened.

Her gaze darted about the room, but they were alone.

His soft chuckle brought her attention flying back to his face.

"Do not worry, my sweet and wayward wife. There is no one here. My men have been instructed not to interrupt our little reunion under any circumstances."

"Where am I?" Eve forced the words through a thick throat.

Matthew gave a graceful wave of his hand. "Just a little property I picked up. It's rather drab, but it was the best I could do." His eyes flickered with anger. "Do you see what your selfish little escapade has lowered me to? You will pay dearly for the discomfort I've endured as I traveled all over this dusty, primitive wilderness."

A shiver of pure terror slid down her spine.

"You were not easy to find," Matthew continued as he swirled his brandy. "I have to say, Evelyn, you have surprised me. Not only your current...wretched appearance"—he paused to slide his gaze over her plain cotton dress and dusty boots before his lips curled in disgust—"but your unexpected resourcefulness are not qualities I would have expected you to display. Once I discovered you'd left Boston on a train heading westward, I figured it was only a matter of time before you popped up at the home of your brother or one of your friends. Lucky for me, you happened to show up at your brother's. It saves me from having to wait any longer than necessary to see that you are taken back in hand." He lowered his voice threateningly. "You have caused a significant amount of trouble, my dear wife. I'm afraid your punishment will be quite severe this time."

Eve sat frozen in place, staring at the man she had married. Every ounce of fear, every moment of uncertainty and self-doubt, all the lies, the pain, the dreadful anxiety—everything he'd ever forced her to feel—crashed through her like a tidal wave. Fierce, breath-stealing, and utterly consuming. And then one word pushed up from her heart. "No."

Never again would she kneel in silence and stoic pride while she was abused. She had endured enough.

Matthew's mouth tightened with fury. His skin became flushed, and his hand shook as he set his brandy down on the table beside him. "No? You'd best remember your place, darling."

"I will not allow you to hurt me again."

"You have no say in the matter," he said in a menacing tone that sent chills across her skin. "You are my wife. You belong to me."

"I belong to me," Eve replied firmly despite the fear still coursing through her.

Matthew's eyes widened briefly before narrowing to dangerous slits. Then he smiled. It was a chilling sight. "This is going to be more fun than I thought."

Eve knew she couldn't stop him, but she would fight him

with every ounce of strength and courage she could gather from the deepest corners of her being.

As Matthew slowly set his glass aside and uncrossed his legs, Eve leapt to her feet.

He ignored her and casually walked over to a lacquered box set beside a crystal decanter of brandy.

Eve sped toward the room's closed door. Finding it locked, she turned to press her back to the door. Her fear continued to rise, but so did her fury.

"It's been far too long since you've felt the bite of my whip," Matthew said as he lifted something from the box. A black leather whip uncoiled from his hand to pool in elegant lines at his feet. "Your behavior leads me to believe you've missed your punishments. I know I have."

Eve scanned the room for something she could use to fight him off. The crystal brandy decanter, maybe. If she hit him in the head hard enough with it, she might be able to knock him out. But first, she'd have to get to the decanter, and afterward, she'd have to get past however many men he had outside.

A sudden crash sounded in another part of the house. Its force was strong enough to shake the walls of the parlor.

Gabriel!

She knew it was him by the swift rush of love and hope that swept through her. She should have known he would come for her.

Another crash—this one much closer—involved shattering glass and was swiftly followed by the crack of a gunshot.

Eve stumbled away from the door as the sounds of a struggle came closer. Glancing toward Matthew, she saw that he was following her movements intently with his light-brown gaze. Setting the whip aside, he reached into the pocket of his suit coat and pulled out a small handgun.

"You are not going to get away from me again," he said. But before he could raise the gun to point in her direction, the door to the parlor slammed open, the wooden frame splintering as Gabriel forged through.

He was covered in blood. His shirt was soaked in it. His face was splattered. A pistol was clenched tightly in his hand. It was the first time she'd ever seen him with a weapon, and she realized he must have taken it from one of Matthew's men. His gaze was hard and dead calm as it fell upon Eve's face.

She took a step toward him, lifting her hand.

"You're *my* wife. *Mine,*" Matthew shouted in blind fury.

Eve's attention darted back to see him shifting to aim his gun in Gabriel's direction.

She didn't think.

Twisting sharply, Eve lunged across the space separating her from Matthew, slamming her body against his. The force of her momentum had him stumbling back with a grunt as she wrapped her hands around his wrist, trying to force the barrel toward the floor. He regained his footing far too easily. He grabbed a fistful of her hair with his free hand, while he jerked the gun sharply upward to try to free it from her grip.

The pain in her scalp brought tears to her eyes, and she felt her hands slipping from around his wrist. She wasn't strong enough.

He gave another fierce tug of his arm just as her hands lost their grip. His arm jerked back sharply, and the gun slammed against his chest.

A shot rang out. Deafening. Jolting her with the impact.

The harsh, acrid smell of gunpowder filled her nostrils, followed swiftly by the scent of blood.

Matthew exhaled—a ragged, gargling sound.

The gun tumbled from his suddenly slack hand and dropped to the floor. Eve stumbled back.

Matthew's eyes, wide with shock, found hers as blood started to gush from the gaping wound at the base of his throat. He took a staggering step back, then another, until his back hit the wall. Then his legs just folded up and he slid to the floor, his eyes lifeless and flat.

Oh my God.

"Eve."

She spun around to see that Gabriel had dropped to his knees. The gun slipped from his hand as he looked at her with a glazed, faraway look in his eyes. Rushing to his side, she realized why there was even more blood soaking his shirt than before.

He'd been shot. The blood was his.

Pain exploded in her chest, seizing her heart in an icy grip.

"Gabriel," she whispered, dropping to her knees in front of him as she pressed her hand against his chest where the blood welled warmly beneath her palm. She forgot about Matthew. Forgot everything except her love for Gabriel. He'd fought to get to her. To save her.

He *had* saved her. In a thousand ways.

She couldn't lose him now.

He bowed his head to rest his forehead against hers as his eyes drifted closed.

"Hold on, Gabriel," she whispered fiercely. "Please."

"You...are my heart...always," he whispered before he dropped to the floor beside her.

"No!" Eve pressed both hands to the flow of blood as she leaned over him to whisper in his ear, tears tracking down her cheeks. "No, Gabriel. Stay with me. You are my heart too. My soul. My everything. Please."

And then suddenly Warren was there beside her. "He's still breathing," he said in a calm, confident tone. "Move back, Evelyn. Let me help him."

Though she hated taking her hand away from his chest, where she could still feel the faint beat of his heart, she backed away. But her eyes stayed fastened on Gabriel's face. His beautiful, strong, generous, kind, loving face.

Two more people charged into the room. Eve scarcely paid them any attention. For some reason, she felt that as long as she kept her eyes on Gabriel, he couldn't leave her. She didn't even glance away when a familiar presence crouched beside her to wrap her in a comforting embrace. But she did take her cousin's hand in a fierce grip, needing her strength and support in order to keep breathing. Alexandra held her tight and murmured gently, "Warren will save him, Evie."

He had to.

Eve could not fathom a world without Gabriel in it.

Thirty-Eight

Warren worked a miracle on that parlor floor.

While Eve watched in a helpless state of shock that was anything but numb, her brother removed the bullet that was lodged in Gabriel's chest with Alexandra's competent assistance. The bullet hadn't gone deep, but there was a great deal of blood loss and the wound had to be cauterized.

Eve had no idea how or why Alexandra happened to be there with her husband, but she was intensely grateful. While Alexandra and Warren knelt over Gabriel and Eve huddled not far away, Malcolm took the time to verify that Matthew—as well as the men he'd hired—were dead.

Eve had suspected as much.

So much death. Eve felt sick. Her head was cloudy, and her stomach rolled with the scent of blood. Alexandra suggested she step outside, but she wouldn't move an inch farther from Gabriel's side. She couldn't.

Once Warren was satisfied that the bleeding had stopped and he had done all he could at the moment, they loaded Gabriel, still unconscious, into the back of a wagon they found in the barn. Eve cradled his head in her lap on the drive back to town, where they got him settled in a room at Warren's home before Malcolm went to report the deaths to the local sheriff. He sent notice to the law up near his and Alexandra's place and Courtney's ranch so the men Matthew had stationed there could be located and either scared off or brought in, depending on their criminal history.

The sheriff of Chester Springs was a man nearing eighty who had no desire for more work than necessary. Malcolm Kincaid's reputation from his former life as a bounty hunter—along with Warren's well-respected position as the town doctor—were more than enough for the sheriff to take their word about the unfolding events at the ranch.

Eve could barely bring herself to care.

Matthew would never hurt her again. She was finally free.

But it seemed such an inconsequential thing when put alongside the possibility of losing Gabriel.

Warren tried to get her to retire to another of their guest rooms to sleep, but she couldn't even bother to acknowledge him. Eventually, Alexandra and Honey were both required to convince Warren to leave it alone and let Eve stay at Gabriel's side.

She sat in a chair pulled up to his bed, his hand clasped in both of hers, her gaze locked on his face. He was still so large and forbidding, even as he lay unconscious in the narrow bed. But there was no way to ignore the wide, white bandage wrapped around his chest.

She could hear the others moving about the house, their voices low and reserved—even the children. Eve realized she would have to give some sort of explanation, and she would, but right now all that mattered was seeing Gabriel open his eyes again.

Though she didn't intend to, she must have fallen asleep

because the next thing she knew, she was being pulled back to awareness by a strong squeeze of her fingers and Gabriel's low, murmured voice.

She lifted her head from where it had been resting on her folded arm.

He looked at her with tired, pain-filled eyes.

"Gabriel." She sighed as tears clogged her throat and slid down her cheeks.

With a tense grimace and a tightening of his mouth, he brought his hand to the side of her face and brushed a tear away with his thumb. "My heart."

Eve held back her sob as she turned to press her lips to his palm.

"Your husband...is he dead?" Gabriel asked.

She nodded.

Gabriel's eyes fell closed again. "Then you're free," he muttered just before his hand dropped to the bed and he slipped back into unconsciousness.

Throughout that day, Warren monitored him for signs of infection, and Alexandra showed Eve how to administer small and careful doses of medicinal tea. As the hours passed without the heat of infection entering Gabriel's body, Warren grew in confidence that Gabriel would make a good recovery. By the next night, Alexandra finally convinced Eve to get some real rest by promising to stay with Gabriel herself in Eve's absence. Eve only managed a couple of hours of sleep before she awoke with the need to return to Gabriel's side.

Alexandra—loyal, fierce, and wonderful Alexandra—looked up as Eve entered the room.

Eve went to her first and gave her cousin a heartfelt

embrace, realizing that as close as they had been as girls, they had never fully embraced. As Eve felt her cousin's love and support, her throat grew tight with regret.

Pulling back, she met Alexandra's bright-blue eyes and confessed, "I should have told you—and Courtney—what was happening with Matthew. I should have trusted your friendship. I'm so sorry. I should have—"

"Stop it, Evie," her cousin chastised gently. "You have nothing to apologize for. Come now. Let's leave him to rest and go talk."

Eve looked at Gabriel. "But..."

"He is doing well. Trust me. Your Gabriel will make it."

Eve felt a slight loosening of the binds around her chest as she went to his bedside and bent forward to place a kiss to his lips. They were warm and soft. "I'll be back soon," she whispered before straightening to follow Alexandra from the room.

They sat together in the dark of the front parlor, not bothering to light any lamps. When they were younger, after Alexandra had first come to live with her in Boston, they had often shared a bed, telling secrets in the dark until morning arrived.

"Warren is worried about you," Alexandra said. "He hates not having a concise explanation for the events that took place, but he can see that you have suffered."

"It's over now," Eve replied, wanting to assure her friend and herself. Sometimes, when she thought of it, it was hard to believe Matthew could never hurt her again. There was no need to run or hide any more. She supposed eventually she would feel relief for that, but not until Gabriel was well again.

"I'm so proud of you," Alexandra whispered. "It took so much courage to leave."

"To run away," Eve corrected.

"Yes," Alexandra insisted with a squeeze of Eve's hand. "To seek the freedom and happiness you deserve. And you do deserve it, Evie, so very much."

They lapsed into silence for a bit, then Alexandra, who never could contain her curiosity for long, asked, "Do you love him?"

Eve answered readily, "So much it hurts sometimes."

Alexandra gave a soft laugh. "I know how that feels."

"Oh, Alexandra, your Malcolm must think me so rude. I have barely acknowledged him."

"Oh goodness, don't worry about that. Malcolm isn't exactly a paragon of manners." She grinned. "But I adore him anyway."

"I am so unbelievably grateful the two of you are here. I owe you both so much."

"You owe us nothing," Alexandra insisted. "I'm just glad you're safe."

The next few days brought further improvement. Gabriel awoke more frequently and stayed awake longer each time. Long enough for him to manage some more fortifying foods. Eve continued to stay close, but so did Warren. After a while, Eve began to wonder if her brother's attentiveness was all part of his doctoring or if some of it had to do with not wanting to leave Eve alone with Gabriel.

She realized Warren had to know that Luke and the others

who lived the valley were outlaws. She wondered if that was the reason he felt a need to chaperone her interactions with Gabriel. His constant presence was frustrating, but she kept her mouth shut since Warren was Gabriel's doctor, and as long as he did his job in that regard, she would have all the time in the world to be alone with Gabriel in the future.

On their fourth day in town, two newcomers arrived in Chester Springs.

Apparently, Courtney and her husband, Dean Lawton, had left their ranch in Montana the day they received the telegram from Alexandra stating that Eve had been located.

Courtney swept into town with her usual exuberance and charm. Once a society princess in Boston, she had settled down as the wife of a cattle rancher just a year ago, and her life clearly suited her. Courtney's husband was nearly her opposite; socially reserved with an air of understated confidence, he balanced Courtney's impulsive, winsome nature perfectly.

Courtney and Dean rented a room in the hotel where Alexandra and Malcolm were staying and promised to stick around as long as Eve needed them. Eve couldn't believe how blessed she was to have her two dearest friends at her side once again.

Eventually, she managed to explain some of what she'd endured in her marriage—avoiding the harsher details—and her decision to run away. She was surprised by the fury she saw behind Warren's fierce scowl and was even more surprised when he wrapped her in his arms and held her tight for a long moment.

He had sent a telegram to their mother days ago, letting her know Eve was safe, and Eve followed it up with a long letter that told her mother everything, along with a request that she seek out a young maid in Matthew's household named Lettie and see to the girl's well-being. Finally being honest with her family and friends about something she'd hidden for so long was healing in a way she hadn't expected.

No one pressed Eve to tell them if she intended to return to Boston or stay in Wyoming, though she had seen the urge to pry in her brother's narrowed eyes on more than one occasion. She had her sister-in-law, Honey, to thank for the fact that he didn't push. Eve had caught Honey's forbidding expression directed toward Warren often through those days, and she was grateful for it.

It was hard to believe Honey and Luke were twins. They looked nearly nothing alike and had very little in common in terms of temperament.

It was equally hard to believe that Luke hadn't suspected Eve was Warren's sister right from the start. Especially considering her brother had a photograph of her as a schoolgirl on his mantel beside an old image of their parents. Assuming Luke had been to his sister's home a time or two, he would have seen Eve's image and likely wouldn't have missed the resemblance when she showed up in the valley.

The fact that Luke had suggested she accompany Gabriel to town made it clear that he had intended the reunion all along.

After those first couple of days, Gabriel began to improve quickly. He was soon on his feet and moving around. Eve worried that he was doing too much too soon, but Warren assured her it was good for him to walk around if he felt up to it.

Each day that passed, Gabriel continued to get stronger.

He joined them in the parlor when everyone gathered in the evenings, though he kept to the edge of the room and observed more than participated in the socializing. Whenever he was present, Eve was at his side, ignoring the furrowed-brow looks from her brother. Warren would have to learn to accept that her loyalty to Gabriel was not a fleeting thing.

When Gabriel needed rest, Eve spent as much time as she could with her friends, knowing that once they left Chester Springs, it might be a long time before she saw them again. She got to know Honey and truly came to adore her niece, Stella, and nephew, Thomas.

With so much constant activity in the household between the guests and the children and Warren's frequent checks, it was difficult for Eve to find time to talk to Gabriel as she wanted to. There was so much she wanted to say, but she had to content herself with brief conversations and long looks that made her chest tighten with emotion.

Though no words were spoken about their future, everything she yearned for was still there in his eyes.

But then one morning just over a week after he'd been shot, she woke up to find that he had gone.

THIRTY-NINE

"HE TRULY DIDN'T SAY A WORD?" COURTNEY ASKED IN astonishment. "He just left?"

Warren was at his office for the day, and the children were occupied with a baking project in the kitchen. Malcolm and Dean had remained back at the hotel so it was just Eve, her two best friends, and her sister-in-law in the parlor. Honey had made some tea, and upon learning of Gabriel's sudden departure from town, Alexandra promptly added a good dose of whiskey to their cups.

"I've noticed he isn't one to say much," Alexandra stated in an indignant tone, "but the man at least could have said goodbye."

Eve shook her head. "That's not his way."

"Is it his way to be heartless?" Courtney asked in a smart tone, clearly irritated on Eve's behalf.

"No, he could never be heartless," Eve assured her. "He's the most compassionate, utterly selfless man I've ever met."

"It's a good thing you think so," Honey said thoughtfully, "because I believe it's safe to say that man is madly in love with you."

Eve's cheeks warmed, but she didn't deny it.

"Whenever he's in the same room with you, his gaze follows you like a hawk watching his dinner," Alexandra added with a knowing smirk.

Courtney lifted a haughty brow. "Then he should have stayed."

Eve's heart welled with gratitude for her friends' staunch loyalty, but it was important to her that they fully understand.

She took a long breath. "I think he wanted to allow me the freedom to decide my own path," she explained, her throat thickening with a swell of emotions she wasn't quite sure she'd be able to put into words. "He's showing me that he understands how important it is for me to have my family and friends again. By leaving, he's honoring the possibility that I might choose not to return to the valley. When I join him, it will be because it's solely my desire to do so."

Alexandra's eyes were wide and glistening. "For a man who rarely speaks, he sure says an awful lot in a single act, doesn't he?"

Eve's laugh sounded awfully similar to a sob. "He does. I love him so much."

"Then go to him," Courtney urged.

Eve looked back and forth between her two closest friends. Alexandra with her bright-blue eyes and competent manner and generous compassion. Courtney, all fiery hair and flashing eyes, possessing a wealth of optimism and love.

"You won't think I'm being foolish for rushing into something so soon after..."

"Goodness no!" Alexandra nearly shouted. "When a man loves you like that and you love him just as fiercely, the foolish thing would be to waste even a moment apart."

"I wholeheartedly agree. You really should just leave right now," Courtney insisted with a grin.

Love and gratitude filled Eve's chest. "I'll miss you both so much when you return to Montana."

"We're not so far away as Boston. We'll visit each other all the time," Courtney declared. "I'm just glad you'll be safe and happy."

"I still have to convince Warren to take me back to the valley," Eve said with a glance toward Honey.

"Your brother just wants to know that you'll be well protected," her sister-in-law replied, a gleam of determination in her eye as she smiled her assurance. "He'll take you."

The midday summer sun bathed the valley in warmth and optimism as Warren and Eve approached the bunkhouse.

Luke came out onto the porch as they rode up. His hazel eyes were hard but held a glint of mischief as they settled on Warren. Any doubts Eve might have had that Luke had known or at least highly suspected she was Warren's sister were put to rest by his utter lack of surprise at seeing the two of them together.

"What the hell were you thinking, Luke? You should have let me know the second my sister showed up here," Warren accused him without bothering to offer a polite greeting.

Luke shrugged. There was an anticipatory air about him, almost as though he was hoping for a fight. "She didn't want anyone to know who she was or where she was. I couldn't be sure if that included you." His tone held a distinct lack of concern, even though Warren's eyes were shooting sparks.

"If you had just told her you recognized her," Warren countered sharply, "you could have *asked* her if she wanted to see me."

Luke lifted his brows. "Would she have said yes?"

Eve had been patient long enough. Whatever issue the two men had with each other, it clearly had nothing to do with her. "If you two wish to squabble over details that no longer matter, that's entirely up to you, but it's not why I'm here."

Luke gave a soft chuckle. "You know where to find him."

Eve smiled. "Thank you." Then to Warren, she said, "And thank you for everything you've done. I promise, I'll see you again soon."

Warren nodded. "I hope so. Mother will be anxious for more news. You know she's probably still hoping you'll return to Boston."

"I'm not going back," Eve replied.

Her brother smiled. "I know."

Eve turned her horse and rode around the bunkhouse, urging him into a trot and then a lope as she passed the barn and continued along the river to the meadow. She slowed enough to cross the shallow part of the river before leaping from her horse's back. Leaving the animal to graze beside Twig on the grassy bank, she walked up the slope toward the cabin.

Exhilaration mounted with every step. It felt as though she'd been waiting a lifetime to claim something that had been hers all along.

She was still several paces away when Gabriel stepped outside.

Dark eyes met blue. The warmth of the sun bathed the

meadow around them, summer insects buzzed, and the grass waved gently in the breeze as they stood for a breathless moment, staring at each other.

The love, the trust, the peace, the dark quiet of his gaze, and the confidence in her heart all came together in perfect harmony. No matter where she went in life or how long it took to get there, her path would always lead to him.

Eve was finally exactly where she needed to be.

Unable to contain the beautiful feelings inside her, Eve curved her lips in an easy smile.

Gabriel lowered his chin. His answering smile inspired a wave of love so deep it stole her breath.

She walked toward him, not stopping until his arms came up around her and his head bowed beside hers. She pressed a palm to his chest, anxious for the feel of his heartbeat, strong and steady. Then she tipped her head back to meet his lovely gaze.

"I choose you, Gabriel," she whispered. "Always."

His arms tightened for a moment before releasing her. Turning, he held the door open for her to pass through. The familiar earthy scents embraced her, welcomed her.

She turned back to face Gabriel as the door closed behind him.

Unwilling to waste another moment, she stepped up to him and took his face in her hands to draw him down for a kiss.

Her calm confidence shifted into quiet desperation as the smell of his skin filled her nostrils and the heady taste of him intoxicated her.

His arms came around her waist, and he lifted her high against him as he slowly turned her toward the bed. Laying her down, he followed until his body settled heavily atop hers. The kiss grew more urgent as desire claimed her, heating her blood and infusing her brain with the need to get closer, to feel him inside her.

With a low growl of hunger, Gabriel grasped her skirts in one hand, dragging the length up to her hip before he reached beneath to cup her buttocks in his hand. She lifted her leg over his hip, urging him to press harder to the place that ached for him.

He pulled back instead.

The weight of his gaze—the heat and ferocity—was a stark contrast to his sudden physical restraint.

She touched her fingers to his mouth. She could afford to be patient. All would come. Everything she needed was there in that moment. Her future was now.

Lowering his head to rest his forehead to hers, he looked deep into her eyes. In a low voice, rich with emotion, he said, "Today and all the days I am blessed with in this life, I will love you. I share myself with you," he vowed, saying the words she'd once said to him.

Love filled her heart, grounding her and giving her wings. She lifted her chin and murmured against his lips. "I love you, now and always. And I share myself with you."

The kiss started as a seal to their vows, but quickly slid into a promise of passion.

His tongue licked and teased, delving past her teeth to taste her hidden desires. There were no secrets between them, no walls, no resistance.

They shed their clothes as they shed their pasts, leaving them naked and trusting in each other's arms. Needing only each other. Needing only love.